Remaking Meredith by Carol Cox
Meredith Blackwell is sick of watching life pass her by. She's equally tired of being overweight and uninteresting. A motivational speaker inspires her to write a list of New Year's resolutions to remodel herself into an confident, attractive woman. But how will she feel when she learns a work acquaintance has made remaking Meredith his ministry project?

Beginnings by Peggy Darty
A hospital bed is no place to spend the holidays. Far from home and family, a frightening car crash left Erin McKinley, a university student bruised and battered. But just when she is becoming overwhelmed by self-pity, she gets interested in the numerous visitors next door and the handsome police investigator confined in a leg brace.

Never Say Never by Yvonne Lehman
Every year Amy Treadwell's singles' Sunday school teacher has each member write New Year's resolutions, then she pairs those who have similar goals. Amy is awkwardly paired with new-comer Jason Barlow. She is to teach him to swim, while as an editor, he is to help her write a novel. But Amy doesn't like Jason's attitude and they are off to a rocky start.

Letters to Timothy by Pamela Kaye Tracy
Rita Sanderson has assigned elderly pen pals to her class of third graders. But little Timothy struggles to complete a letter until Rita helps him set a New Year's resolution. David Reeves aides his arthritic grandfather in responding to Timothy's letters, but he refuses to allow his grandfather to participate in any of Rita's field trips. How can Rita unite the pen pals when David is acting so protective?

Heart's
PROMISE

Published by Barbour Publishing, Inc., P.O. Box 719, Uhrichsville, Ohio 44683, www.barbourbooks.com

Our mission is to publish and distribute inspirational products offering exceptional value and biblical encouragement to the masses.

ecpa Member of the
Evangelical Christian
Publishers Association

Printed in the United States of America.

Heart's PROMISE

four decisions to make
a change inspire romance

carol cox

peggy darty

yvonne lehman

pamela kaye tracy

BARBOUR
PUBLISHING

Remaking Meredith

by Carol Cox

With grateful thanks to the Lord Jesus,
who looks beyond the surface and sees the heart.

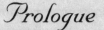

Meredith Blackwell checked her image in the full-length mirror. Her navy skirt hung in businesslike lines below the matching jacket, every seam and pleat in place. With the crisp white blouse and red-print scarf, the effect was professional, if not attractive. "Attractive" was not a word Meredith applied to herself. Not with her nondescript face and mousy brown hair—never mind those extra pounds.

Turning away without a second glance, she left the ladies' lounge and crossed the thick beige carpet, pausing outside the open auditorium doors at a table holding a stack of fliers.

"What's the topic this time?" a disgruntled female voice behind her grumbled. Meredith permitted herself a slight smile. Lyman Associates was a wonderful, innovative place to work, but Mr. Lyman did lean a bit heavily on required attendance at his company-sponsored motivational seminars.

"Self-improvement," a second woman answered. "Old Lyman thinks if we feel better about ourselves, our productivity will improve."

The two snickered and moved past Meredith to enter the auditorium. Meredith stepped back out of their way, her right heel landing on a yielding surface. She spun around in time to see the grimace of pain on Gordon Winslow's face.

"I'm sorry! I didn't mean to step on your foot." Meredith felt the hot rush of blood stain her cheeks.

"I'll live," Gordon answered shortly, forcing a tight smile before he walked away. Meredith watched his retreating figure with a sinking feeling. For months she'd daydreamed about having a conversation with her handsome department head, one having nothing to do with work. This was hardly the kind of dialogue she'd envisioned.

Gordon stopped a few feet inside the auditorium doors to talk to the two women who had entered the room just ahead of him. He threw back his head and laughed at one of their remarks, his white teeth flashing against his tanned face.

Hot tears stung Meredith's eyes, and she blinked rapidly to keep them from spilling over. She had just as much to offer as either of the women who were charming him so effortlessly.

How she'd love to be the one to receive Gordon's smile, to be involved in that lively conversation! Meredith knew it could happen, if he'd pull his gaze away from those size-six bodies long enough to give her a chance— long enough to find out she wasn't just an overweight woman with a bland personality and a life to match. There had to be a way to catch his attention.

The lobby began to fill with employees heading for the seminar. Meredith sighed and reached for one of the fliers on the table. She didn't know if she could take another upbeat, "go get 'em!" presentation. Glancing at the colorful paper in her hand, Meredith focused on the first line of print and froze.

"Finding the Real You." The words were emblazoned across the top of the page in inch-tall letters. Underneath the speaker's picture was a paragraph with the heading: "One of America's foremost experts shows you the steps to becoming the person you were meant to be."

Meredith's heart raced and her eyes flashed with hope. Determinedly, she strode into the auditorium, took a seat at the center of the front row, and prepared to take notes.

❧

Todd Andrews shifted in his chair and stretched out his long, jeans-clad legs. The final session of his church's fall singles' retreat was running overtime, but Todd's attention was riveted on the speaker at the front of the room.

"In summary," the session leader said, "remember, Jesus told the parable of the Good Samaritan in response to the question, 'Who is my neighbor?' Missions in foreign lands are vital, but don't miss opportunities right under your nose. Find someone within your circle of acquaintances who needs a healing touch from the Lord, and see what God would have you do."

Todd joined in the outburst of applause, his heart responding to the challenge. Before the closing prayer had ended, he knew just who God wanted him to help—Meredith Blackwell.

Todd knew Meredith's reputation at Lyman Associates, where they were both employed, for efficiency and top-notch work. He also knew she hadn't made a single friend in the year she'd worked there. How anyone so capable could have such an amazing lack of self-assurance was more than Todd could understand, but he was determined to give Meredith's confidence a much-needed boost. It would be easy.

Chapter 1

Meredith rolled the pen between her thumb and fingers and stared at the blank sheet of paper on her kitchen table. She was ready to make the list that would change her life. Following her meticulous seminar notes to the letter, she had determined the major areas she wanted to change. That was easy—*Looks* and *Personality* headed two columns on the paper. After consideration, Meredith added a third area, *Spiritual,* reasoning that the inner woman probably needed a boost as well.

For a week she'd brainstormed in the evenings, jotting down all the ideas that came to mind, no matter how ridiculous they seemed. To Meredith's surprise, it actually became fun. Anything that popped into her mind was fair game, and she found herself giggling when she wrote "skydiving" in the *Personality* column and "glamour makeover" under *Looks.*

Then came the task of culling out the most farfetched items and looking at the rest to find the common denominators among them. "For instance," the seminar speaker had said, "if 'Financial' is one of your main headings, you may decide you want to buy a

Lexus, take an extended vacation, get a bigger house. The common denominator there is that you need more money. How much will it take to do what you want? What can you do to bring in that amount?

"Whatever it is, that's the entry that goes on your final list. Focus on specific points that will help you achieve your overall goals, rather than getting bogged down trying to chase each individual desire."

Meredith started with the list of spiritual items, since it had the fewest entries. She hadn't been to church since she relocated. Getting back into the habit wouldn't be a bad idea. She jotted "Find church" on her short list. What about Bible study? Personal devotions had gone by the wayside as well. She made another note.

Meredith whittled down the long *Looks* list of notations about smaller clothes, correcting figure flaws, and doing something with her hair to: "Lose weight" and "Exercise," deciding to add "Makeover," after some deliberation. Desperate situations called for desperate measures.

And what about becoming more interesting and adding zest to her personality? That one was trickier. Meredith had her own likes, but they didn't seem to coincide with the interests of anyone else she knew. It was time to break new ground.

Meredith scanned her notes, looking for specific entries. *One good thing about being unnoticed,* she thought grimly, *is that people talk freely around you without being aware of your presence.* During the past week she had gleaned an amazing amount of information on activities Gordon Winslow enjoyed. She would focus on those.

Once she looked attractive enough to draw his notice, they would have common interests to discuss. Interests far more engaging than his squashed toes.

Meredith crossed skydiving off the list with a sigh of relief. Thank goodness it hadn't turned out to be one of Gordon's favorite pastimes!

She eyed the remaining items with a rising sense of hope. This looked like something she could work with.

❧

Meredith looked down at a heading on the page: *RESOLVED*. The word itself was crisp and matter of fact, an ideal reflection of her frame of mind. The small leather-bound notebook she had just purchased on her way to work reflected her attitude, too. Slim and elegant, its ultra-efficient lines, and even its new smell, raised images in Meredith's mind of a fresh start, a new image.

According to her seminar notes, a one-year commitment to building a new image would work well, allowing time to concentrate on the various items listed and for new habits to become firmly ingrained.

Knowing how the best laid plans often go awry around the holidays, Meredith decided to put her strategies into action on January 1. These would be her best New Year's resolutions ever. By this time next year, she would be an attractive, confident woman—just the type to catch Gordon Winslow's interest.

Meredith looked around guiltily, hoping no one noticed her doing personal work on company time. *Like anyone notices me anyway,* she thought mockingly. No one would suspect the efficient Meredith Blackwell of being anything other than her usual businesslike self.

A few minutes later, Meredith sat back with a pleased smile. There they were—the goals that would make her a new woman. Maybe they weren't graven in stone, but they were set down in black and white in their own special notebook. She allowed herself a moment of complacency. How many other people had their New Year's resolutions made this far in advance? And how many would keep theirs past the first week in January, much less all year? She read the list again.

RESOLVED

1. Lose 30 pounds.
2. Exercise regularly.
3. Get a complete beauty makeover.
4. Read through the Bible in a year.
5. Find a church.
6. Attend symphony performances.
7. Visit one museum a month.
8. Read a new book every month.

The simplicity of the plan took her breath away. By following the process and paring down her goals to their basic components, here was a plan she was sure she could keep.

Losing thirty pounds sounded like the impossible dream, but if she broke that down into smaller increments, it came out to less than three pounds per month. She could do that. Regular exercise would take care of any trouble spots left when the pounds melted away, and the makeover would put the glamorous finishing touches on the slim new Meredith.

Finding a church would ease the nagging sense of guilt she felt whenever her grandmother called and asked where she was worshiping. It would be good, too, to be able to tell her she was reading her Bible regularly.

The last three entries on the list were inspired by Gordon. Meredith knew he had a season ticket to the symphony, talked about current museum exhibits, and enjoyed discussing the latest best-sellers.

It was an easy list, a doable list. She patted the notebook before she slid it to one side of her desk and got back to work. Setting up her New Year's notebook hadn't taken much time, but she didn't like the idea of shortchanging her job; she would take work home tonight to make up for it.

❧

Todd Andrews placed a stack of folders neatly in his briefcase and glanced at his watch. Almost time to go. *The Hansen project is progressing well,* he thought with satisfaction. He only wished he could say the same for his ministry project.

Getting close enough to Meredith Blackwell to boost her self-confidence and rattle her out of her shyness had seemed simple enough. He would find some common interest and use that as a springboard to launch his plan. People—even shy people—enjoyed talking about things that interested them.

Todd soon discovered a problem with his plan: Meredith didn't let anyone get close enough to her to find out what those interests might be. As far as he'd been able to learn, she was a model of efficiency who did exemplary work, but no one at Lyman Associates seemed to think of her in personal terms.

He'd tried to play detective, thinking the other women in Meredith's department might have overheard her say something about her personal life.

"Personal life? I don't think she has one," Lydia Myers snickered. "She comes in, she works, she goes home. I tried talking to her when she first got here, but she didn't say much, so I quit trying. Who needs to deal with someone else's problems?"

Todd looked down at Lydia's pencil-thin figure and sharp features, which now registered impatience. Lydia's whole focus was Lydia—first, last, and always. He'd been wrong to think she could help him. But how could he proceed without some inside information?

Todd's gaze swept over the employees heading toward the elevators. *Lord, I really believe You are in this, but I need help. Could you show me someone here who knows anything at all about Meredith besides the fact that she's a marvel of efficiency? I want to help, but I can't begin until I know how to reach her.*

No one made eye contact with him. No one stood out as a source of information. Within the group now entering the elevator Todd could see the subject of his prayer, her arms piled high with a mountain of work. He watched and waited until the last person had gone home, then turned away dejectedly. His foot struck something, and he bent to pick it up.

Todd looked around, but no one was coming back to reclaim the small notebook he held in his hand. Surprising, he thought, since it looked brand new. Hating the thought of invading someone's privacy, Todd flipped open the cover to see if he could find some clue to its ownership. The name, written in small, neat script, jumped out at him: Meredith Blackwell.

All thoughts of invasion of privacy cast aside, Todd thumbed through the pages. Maybe here he could learn more about the reclusive Miss Blackwell. Only one page seemed to have any writing on it, and he turned back to it.

A broad grin spread over Todd's face as he realized what the notebook contained. It was a list of things Meredith planned to do. Things she was interested in. Things he could use to make contact.

Thank You. That was fast. Todd made a few notes in his daily planner, returned the notebook to Meredith's desk, and began mapping out his strategy.

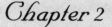

Chapter 2

Meredith glared at the lighted numerals above the elevator door, wishing she could make the car rise faster by sheer force of will. "Come on. Come on," she muttered under her breath, earning a curious glance from a pair of secretaries. They burst into giggles when the door opened and they stepped out onto the third floor.

"You'll never catch me being that eager to get to work!" Meredith heard the words just before the door slid shut and the elevator began to ascend once more, this time to her floor.

Meredith hurried to her desk, struggling to balance the stack of work she had taken home the night before. *Half-finished work,* she reminded herself. The discovery that her resolutions notebook was missing had sent Meredith into a panic, and for the first time she could remember, she found herself unable to concentrate fully on her work.

She scanned the floor as she hastened along the corridor, even though she knew the cleaning crew would have picked up the notebook if it had fallen there. *What would they have done with it then?* she wondered. Having her secret goals in strange hands made her feel vulnerable, exposed.

Did the notebook have her name in it? Meredith tried to remember, then didn't know whether to be elated or afraid when she recalled it did. All she could do was hope it hadn't been passed around her department, where everyone could learn of her plans before she even had the chance to set them in motion.

Turning the corner, Meredith stopped dead in her tracks and stared at her desk. There was the notebook, centered precisely on her meticulously organized workspace.

Meredith set down her armload of work, not caring that it slid across the desk in an untidy heap. Sinking into her burgundy leather chair, she reached for the notebook with shaking hands. How could she have lost it? It was totally unlike her, especially with something so intensely personal.

Another question came to mind: How did the person who found the notebook know where to return it? The answer to that made her weak-kneed, realizing the finder must have found her name written inside the front cover. Had they read more than just her name? Meredith thumbed through the pages to her neatly written list, hoping against hope that the notebook's finder hadn't read its contents.

There was no way of telling, she decided wearily. Meredith glanced around, studying her coworkers covertly while she took her time hanging up her coat. No one seemed to be paying any attention to her.

Meredith drew a shaky sigh of relief and tried to laugh at her concerns. Why would anyone want to read her notebook, anyway? It was silly to worry about such a thing.

❧

Todd stared past the partitions dividing the departments on the fourth floor, grateful for once that Mr. Lyman had insisted on open work spaces, with private offices reserved for department heads.

Todd watched Meredith make short work of sorting through the papers on her desk. A small crease formed on his forehead as he drew his eyebrows together, remembering the items on her list.

Lose weight. For the life of him, Todd couldn't figure out why. He also couldn't see any way to help her with that. *Get a beauty makeover.* That was another puzzler. His gaze rested on Meredith's soft brown hair, the same color as the robin's nests he used to find in his grandfather's apple trees when he was a small boy. Those dark brown eyes, the color of molasses, didn't need help, either, in Todd's opinion. Didn't the woman ever look in a mirror?

Some of the other items—*exercise, Bible reading, and church attendance*—held out more promise. He could work with those, if he ever got close enough to her.

In the meantime. . .Todd eased the copy of the list from his desk drawer and studied it. "The symphony, museums, and new books," he murmured, and a smile crept across his face. Maybe, just maybe, he had found a starting point.

❧

"Meredith Blackwell?"

Meredith looked up to see a uniformed delivery man standing next to her desk. "Yes?"

"Sign here, please." Meredith scribbled her name on

the form and took the envelope he handed her. She examined both sides of the envelope, but there was no name or address to be found.

Shifting her position slightly to block her actions from her coworkers, she slit the envelope and tipped out its contents. A stiff piece of pasteboard fluttered to her desk.

Meredith studied it a moment before realizing it was a ticket to a symphony performance on Friday, two days away. Blinking rapidly, she stared at the ticket, then looked over her shoulder, expecting to see one of her fellow workers coming to claim his or her property. No one was doing anything out of the ordinary.

Turning back to her desk, Meredith slid her fingers inside the envelope, looking for an explanatory note. When her fingers encountered nothing, she held the envelope wide open and peered inside to satisfy herself it was empty.

She held the ticket by one corner, tapping the opposite corner on her desk. Surely this belonged to someone else! But the man who delivered it had asked for her by name. Thoroughly confused, Meredith picked up her phone and dialed the number of the delivery service.

"All I can tell you is that we were asked to deliver an envelope to Meredith Blackwell, on the fourth floor of the Lyman Building." Meredith sighed. After talking to three people at Mercury Delivery, it appeared that no one had the slightest interest in helping her solve this mystery.

"What about a billing address?" she asked.

"The fee was paid in full. . .in cash," the voice replied with a trace of impatience. "Was there something offensive in the envelope, ma'am?"

24

"No," Meredith said slowly. "I just wanted to find out who—"

"Then I'm afraid I can't help you any further. Have a nice day."

Meredith stared at the now silent receiver, then at the symphony ticket. Slowly she replaced the receiver, then picked up the ticket, turning it over in her hands. This had to be a mistake of some kind. But with no way to trace the sender. . .

Her lips curved into a smile. After all, attending the symphony was on her list. She would look at this as a happy coincidence and enjoy her unexpected opportunity.

❧

Two days later, Meredith stood in front of her closet, hating every dress she owned. By this time next year, with most of her goals accomplished, she would have any number of attractive options to choose from, all of them complementing her alluring new look.

Tonight, though, the clothes she had so carefully selected for her professional wardrobe all made the same fashion statement—boring and fat. Meredith sighed and began sorting through her closet for the fourth time.

Her hand stopped at one dress. She lifted its hanger from the rod and held it out at arm's length. The sophisticated black sheath would be perfect to wear to the symphony, if only it were the right size. Rather, if Meredith were the right size. That's what she got for buying a dress three sizes too small in a fit of optimism.

If—no, when—she lost those thirty pounds, she would be able to slip into that gorgeous sheath without a single bulge marring its sleek lines. Now, though, she knew better than to even try it on. The last time she did, the dress had looked like an overstuffed sausage, and that had been five pounds ago. Meredith sighed and continued her search.

She finally settled on a simple navy dress—boring but adequate. A pair of gold hoop earrings would add a nice touch, she decided. And her makeup. . .left a lot to be desired, she admitted, her gaze falling on the fashion magazine lying open on her dressing table.

The model featured on the exposed page wore a swirly gauze skirt and top that hung beautifully on her svelte figure. Eyes the exact shade of the skirt were skillfully shaded in smoky hues, and her smooth complexion glowed. In comparison, Meredith looked. . . "Dowdy," she said aloud. "Positively dowdy." Try as she might, she didn't look a thing like the magazine model.

Meredith squared her shoulders and resolved not to give in to defeat. By this time next year she would be able to give any model in that magazine a run for her money. Patience and persistence were what she needed.

She paused at the table near the front door and tucked her ticket into her bag, averting her eyes so she wouldn't have to look at her reflection in the large mirror that hung above the table. Meredith liked the decorative effect of the mirror and loved the way it increased the apparent size of her entryway. But she hated the way it showed every one of her facial and figure flaws.

Another magazine lay open on the table. Meredith looked at the rail-thin models enviously, thinking they were just Gordon's type. For a moment, Meredith imagined what it would be like to have Gordon ask her to accompany him to the symphony. She would be standing where she was now, ready to open the door and greet him. His gorgeous blue eyes would take in every detail of her appearance with approval while he helped her into his midnight-blue BMW. Meredith sighed, envisioning their evening together. She would make lighthearted, witty comments with ease, while Gordon's face glowed with admiration and pride.

An involuntary glance at the mirror showed her that she looked the same as she had five minutes before— hardly Gordon material. Her momentary confidence sank like a stone.

"Next year," she promised herself.

❧

Meredith closed her eyes, the better to concentrate on the final item on the program. The evening had surpassed her highest expectations. She could see why Gordon enjoyed this. Being only yards away from the source of the music in an acoustically perfect performance hall made the experience more personal and powerful than she could have imagined. Only having Gordon seated next to her would have made the evening any more perfect.

The final notes hung in the air a moment before the applause began—a deep, swelling wave that swept through the audience. Meredith joined in with fervor.

❧

Seated across the aisle and three rows farther back, Todd added his own applause. He had watched Meredith throughout the program, noting the tilt of her head and the way her lips parted in wonder. When she leaned forward, completely caught up in the performance, Todd wanted to cheer. He had never made a better purchase than those two tickets.

Todd watched Meredith rise from her seat and wait to file out into the aisle. Her face glowed with a look of pure joy, transforming her from the solemn Meredith Blackwell he saw at work into a radiant stranger.

He rose and joined the shuffling procession, intent on reaching the aisle at the same time Meredith did. The shuttered look she usually wore was gone; he was sure she would respond to the friendly greeting he was rehearsing.

The couple in front of Todd stopped just as they reached the aisle, waving to another couple who were approaching. To Todd's irritation, the foursome began an animated discussion right where they stood, completely blocking his exit and apparently oblivious to his attempts to get past. He stood poised for action, ready to flag Meredith down when she passed his row.

She was just now reaching the aisle and turning his way. Todd shot a caustic glance at the two talkative couples, wishing he could reach out and move them bodily. A glance over his shoulder told him the others in his row had given up on getting past the bottleneck and were filing back in the other direction.

His head swiveled back to look at Meredith again, and he decided he didn't have time to circle around and still intercept her. She was only two rows in front of him now. Todd breathed an irritated sigh and prepared to smile and wave.

A man in the row ahead stopped directly in front of Todd, blocking his view. Todd bent and twisted, trying to see past him. He caught a glimpse of Meredith, who had stopped and was talking to someone.

Todd frowned. What was going on? He was the one who was supposed to be talking to Meredith. She never got out, didn't have a social life. Who could she possibly know here?

❧

Making her way through the crush of people in a dreamy haze, Meredith was startled when she bumped squarely into the front of an impeccably tailored charcoal pinstripe suit. She raised her face to apologize and realized she stood only inches from Gordon Winslow.

Gordon frowned his annoyance at their collision and opened his mouth as if to make a brusque retort. Then his eyes widened, narrowed, and widened again.

"Meredith?" he said hesitantly. "Meredith Blackwell?"

Meredith struggled to close her mouth and keep her lower lip from trembling. Here she stood, face to face with Gordon. It was almost a scene from her daydreams! "Yes, it's me," she said, trying to control the smile that threatened to cover the lower half of her face. "It's nice to see you . . .Gordon." His name came out in a shy whisper.

"You look. . .different. Nice." Gordon seemed to be as much at a loss for words as she was. Then someone standing behind Gordon coughed impatiently and he turned to leave, nodding at Meredith as he walked away.

Meredith followed in a happy daze, not noticing the people who jostled against her. Gordon had spoken to her!

Granted, it hadn't been a long conversation, but he had noticed her. He thought she looked nice!

❧

Todd stretched and strained, trying to see past the person blocking his view. The man she was talking to turned, giving Todd a view of his face. Gordon Winslow? Why would Meredith be talking to him?

Todd knew Gordon slightly from work and didn't want to know him better. The man's work was adequate, but what Todd had seen of the way he treated women made Gordon a snake, in Todd's book.

Todd looked back at Meredith. Her face was glowing even more than it had just after the program ended, and she walked with slow, dreamy steps. A few more steps would carry her past Todd. He tried to stifle his impatience, then wanted to whoop with joy when the garrulous quartet in front of him finally decided to move off.

The timing was perfect. Todd stepped easily into the aisle just as Meredith reached his row. He stuck out his hand and beamed. "Meredith!" he exclaimed. "How nice to see you here."

Meredith continued on, dreamy-eyed, without a glance in his direction.

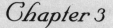

Chapter 3

T odd stood outside the columned entrance to the Museum of Art, shuffling to keep warm. He turned up his collar in an effort to keep the chill November wind from blowing down his neck. Meredith should have shown up by now.

If she's going to show up, he thought glumly. Todd had been excited when he came across a notice in the Culture section of the newspaper about the museum's new temporary exhibit, seeing it as a golden opportunity to move ahead with Project Meredith.

Circling the notice, then leaving it in a conspicuous spot near Meredith's customary seat in the loneliest corner of the employee dining room seemed like a stroke of genius at the time. Right now, it only seemed like a good way to get frostbite.

He could wait inside where conditions were sure to be less frigid, but museums had never been on Todd's list of all-time favorite places to visit, and he knew he'd feel conspicuous loitering near the entry.

He'd loiter outside instead, where he would be less noticeable. And colder.

Todd ducked behind a column, trying to use it as a

windbreak. He'd give it five more minutes, he decided, then admit defeat. This project was turning out to be more complicated than he'd expected. If he didn't believe God had led him to do this. . .

A figure in a dark blue coat, with matching cap, scarf, and gloves, turned toward the entrance, and Todd realized with relief it was Meredith. Now he could go inside and thaw out. And figure out how to look like he belonged there.

Todd watched from just inside the door while Meredith paid her admission and passed through the large central gallery, apparently following the colorful signs pointing the way to the temporary exhibit of French Impressionists.

Good. He wouldn't have to traipse around trying to locate her. Todd counted out the price of admission with cold-stiffened fingers and set off in pursuit.

He spotted Meredith's navy coat in the crowd and eased his way through until he was only a few feet from where she stood admiring a painting of two women. Squinting, Todd could see the information card underneath the painting. The artist's name was Morisot.

Unaware she was being observed, Meredith's expression lost its customary wariness. Todd watched a combination of awe and delight play over her face. If he could just get past that reserved exterior, he was sure he would be able to help her break out of her shell.

Without taking her gaze off the paintings lining the wall, Meredith drifted around a center partition. Todd, seeing the opportunity to set the scene for an "accidental" meeting, moved to intercept her at the other end.

He was waiting, apparently paying rapt attention to a view of the Seine by Monet, when Meredith rounded the corner. Todd shifted his weight just enough to be sure she bumped into him.

He heard her startled gasp, then turned and saw the bright pink flush that stained her cheeks. "I. . .I'm sorry," she stammered. "I guess I wasn't paying attention to anything but the paintings."

"That's all right—no harm done," Todd answered, then did a double-take that he hoped wasn't too overdone to be believable. "Meredith?" When she didn't respond, he added hopefully, "It is Meredith, isn't it?" *Don't blow it,* he cautioned himself. *If you scare her off now, you may not get another chance.*

Meredith's face had taken on the shuttered look Todd remembered from the office. He tried again. "I'm Todd Andrews. I work at Lyman Associates, too. In the marketing department," he prompted.

A flicker of interest sparked in Meredith's eyes, then disappeared just as quickly. Memories of boyhood visits to his grandfather's farm flashed into Todd's mind. He had spent hours crawling across the grass with a salt shaker in his hand, trying to creep within an arm's reach of whatever hapless bird he could find.

At that age, he was convinced he could catch the bird and hold it in his hand if only he could shake salt on its tail before it flew away. Over and over he tried, but no matter how carefully he moved, the bird always took fright and flew away before it was in his grasp.

Todd felt the same sensation of imminent loss now. Meredith's eyes darted left and right, as if seeking an escape route. Breathing a quick prayer, Todd made one more try. "Could you answer a question for me?"

Meredith, already turning to move away, paused. "What is it?" she asked in a soft, hesitant voice.

Caught totally unprepared, Todd cast about for a credible question to ask. "Umm, how come all these guys start with an 'M'?"

Meredith blinked. "Excuse me?"

Boy, that was brilliant. "Well, look at the names—Manet, Monet, Morisot. Do they display them alphabetically, or what?"

A gurgle of laughter escaped Meredith's lips, and Todd sighed with relief. He hadn't lost her yet. "First of all," she said, "Morisot was a woman, so she doesn't quite fall into the category of 'these guys.' And I saw a Degas and a Renoir back there." She pointed to the other side of the partition. "I'm afraid that ruins the rest of your theory.

"Of course," she added, "there's always another possible reason so many of their names start with 'M.' "

It was Todd's turn to blink. "What is it?"

"They're all *Im*pressionists," Meredith said. Her nearly perfect deadpan expression was betrayed by the tiny curve of her lips.

Todd gaped in wonder. Painfully shy Meredith Blackwell had a sense of humor? His stunned expression gave way to a broad grin. It was nice to know he had such promising raw material to work with. He decided to push his luck a little.

"Would you mind if I walk around with you? I may come up with some more questions that need a serious answer." Todd held his breath while Meredith considered the request, the watchful look back on her face. To his surprise, she nodded.

"I guess it would be all right, but I have to warn you—this is my first time here, so we'll both be learning."

"Not a problem," Todd said. "Ready to explore?" At Meredith's cautious nod, he led the way out to the central gallery. As they passed a door labeled CONFERENCE ROOM, it swung open and half a dozen well-dressed men emerged.

Meredith stopped abruptly, her face taking on the same glow Todd had observed at the symphony. And for the same reason, he discovered, when he followed the direction of her gaze and saw Gordon Winslow chatting with two gray-haired men.

Todd took a step away and waited for Meredith to follow, but she seemed to be rooted to the spot. The pink flush was back in her cheeks, but this time it wasn't from embarrassment. What was it about this guy, anyway? Todd had seen women at work practically throw themselves into Gordon's arms.

Gordon clapped one of the older men on the shoulder, then walked toward the exit, his route taking him within three feet of Todd and Meredith. He glanced at them briefly, glanced again, and stopped.

"I seem to be seeing you a lot lately," he said, addressing Meredith. He nodded and left, not waiting for an answer. Meredith was still standing silently, watching

Gordon exit into the chill night.

❧

Saturday morning brought lowering gray clouds and a drop in the temperature, but Todd's spirits were as bright as if it had been a sunny day. In his view the museum gambit had been an unqualified success, matched only by yesterday's progress.

Knowing Meredith often stayed after the normal quitting time, Todd had waited near the elevators, feigning a problem with the latch of his briefcase until he saw Meredith crossing the carpet to push the "Down" button. His simple ploy enabled him to reach the elevator at the same time she did.

Meredith offered a shy smile, and Todd felt like he'd been awarded a prize. He shifted his briefcase to his left hand, dropping a book to the floor as he did so. When he bent to pick it up, the toe of his shoe nudged the book toward Meredith, who scooped it up and started to hand it back to him.

She glanced at the cover, then flipped the book over to read the back cover copy. With a start, she realized what she was doing and held the book out to Todd; she was the picture of embarrassment.

Todd didn't reach for the book. "I'm finished," he told her. "Would you like to borrow it?" He could almost feel her struggle before she timidly nodded her head.

"I've always enjoyed C. S. Lewis," she said. "Thank you."

Todd tried to conceal his elation. *Yes! Thanks for leading me to that book, Lord.* Aloud he said, "He's one of my favorites, too. I think you'll enjoy this." Casually, he added, "Do you have big plans for the weekend?"

"Nothing much," she answered. "I thought I might go over to Whittier Park tomorrow morning and get a little exercise."

Todd beamed. Exercising regularly was another item on Meredith's list. He could run at Whittier Park as easily as anywhere else and get to know her better at the same time. *Project Meredith is coming along quite nicely,* he told himself smugly.

❧

When Meredith caught sight of Todd waiting near the tennis courts, his sandy hair ruffled by the breeze, she thought his smile more than made up for the gloomy Saturday sky. Her loafers tapped along the sidewalk at a brisk pace. Todd's suggestion to meet him here today had come as a total surprise, but it hadn't startled her nearly as much as her acceptance of the plan.

Even more surprising was her frame of mind as she hurried to meet him. She was looking forward to being with someone, something she hadn't done in a long time.

Todd smiled and waved when she drew nearer, then looked down at her feet and frowned. Meredith's smile froze on her face. "Did you bring some other shoes along?" Todd asked.

Meredith cringed inwardly, realizing her casual mention of "getting some exercise" might have a whole different meaning to Todd than her own thoughts of a casual stroll around the park.

"I. . .only planned to walk a little," she admitted.

"These are my walking shoes."

Todd lifted an eyebrow. "You'll ruin your feet if you do any serious walking in those. Come on," he said, grabbing her elbow and propelling her across the street to a small shopping center. "I know just what you need."

Meredith pulled back when he started into The Athlete's Outlet. "I don't think so," she said, her stomach in a knot. In answer to Todd's questioning look, she added, "I've never felt very athletic." Places like this were for lean, muscular types who had about 10 percent body fat and didn't bulge in all the wrong places.

An understanding smile crossed Todd's face. "Not to worry. They let normal people like us in there, too."

Meredith allowed him to hold the door open for her and entered, appreciating the fact that Todd had lumped them together as normal types. She actually enjoyed purchasing the pale blue walking shoes and cushioned socks from the friendly sales clerk, who encouraged her in her new endeavor and didn't seem to regard it as the least bit comical.

She crossed the street, bouncing a bit with every step in her springy new shoes. Todd chuckled at her enthusiasm. "They do make a difference, don't they?"

Meredith nodded happily. Who cared if the sun wasn't shining? For today, it was enough to bask in the glow of feeling comfortable with another person for the first time since she'd relocated. Todd seemed content to walk with her around the figure-eight track, although she felt certain he was more accustomed to a much faster pace.

When they had made one complete lap, Meredith

congratulated herself on her endurance and was ready to collapse on a nearby bench. Todd, however, never seemed to notice the milestone they'd accomplished and started around again.

Meredith gulped, swung her arms determinedly, and doggedly set out after him. Halfway around the second lap, she became acquainted with muscles she'd never suspected she had. By the time they had completed the third, Meredith knew she was going to die.

Puffing, she staggered to a bench, ready to sprawl across it. Todd caught up with her and tugged at her arm. "You need to cool down first before you stop moving. We can walk through the trees over there if you're tired of the track."

Meredith didn't care if she never saw the track again. Stifling a moan, she forced one leg in front of the other and strolled through the trees at Todd's side, trying to breathe normally again.

If she'd known exercise was this much work, she wouldn't have been so enthusiastic about doing it. But as her heart rate and breathing returned to normal, she had to admit she felt surprisingly invigorated.

When Todd led the way back to the bench, Meredith was able to sit down without feeling like she was about to collapse. She was even able to summon up a smile in response to his.

Todd looked at her eyes, sparkling now after her recent exertion, and marveled at the difference between the Meredith of today and the Meredith of two weeks ago. Somewhere in there, he was convinced, was a friendly, enjoyable person. Once he brought out those facets of her personality, he knew she'd be happier.

Maybe this was the time to ask his question. She seemed relaxed and at ease, no longer the startled bird about to fly away. And in her present condition, he remembered, stifling a grin, she was in no shape to run away from him. He cleared his throat a little nervously.

"I've been wanting to ask you something," he began. "I've really enjoyed spending time with you here and at the museum. . . ."

Meredith tensed. If she didn't know better, it sounded like Todd was about to ask her for a date. But that was impossible. Men didn't date girls with no personality and who had a figure like hers.

"I was wondering if you'd be interested in. . ." Meredith held her breath. He *was* going to ask her out. What should she say? Would it be fair to Todd to date him when she had her sights set on Gordon? ". . .coming to the singles' group at my church?"

Meredith's breath gushed out with a whoosh. Where had she gotten the idea Todd might be attracted to her? She should have known better! All he had ever shown her was friendly interest.

"We're having a get-together tomorrow evening. It's nothing fancy, but it would give you a chance to get acquainted with everybody."

Meredith looked at Todd's eager face. This seemed to mean a lot to him, and he had spent time with her today. It was only fair to reciprocate.

Chapter 4

Two large, galvanized tubs, each filled with water, sat on a plastic sheet spread on the floor of the fellowship hall. Two men, each with his hands behind him, knelt before the tubs. Guffaws and shrieks of delight from the onlookers greeted their efforts to catch a bobbing apple in their teeth.

"Go, Todd!" called a stocky man—was his name Bob?—who sat next to Meredith.

More good-natured bantering came from across the room. "Come on, guys. You're not supposed to drink all the water first!"

"You can do it, Michael!" shouted a blond woman—Meredith thought she had heard her called Sheila. Meredith doubted Michael could hear his cheering section with his head submerged under the water, but she had to admit the game was fun.

The whole evening had been fun. The singles' get-together, which she had assumed would be a Bible study of some kind, turned out to be the group's annual fall festival, complete with tons of food and more games than Meredith could count.

Todd had made sure she got involved right from the

beginning, urging her to participate in the games as though she were a longtime member of the group. Meredith found herself joining in with gusto during the opening ice breaker. She opted out of the doughnut-eating contest, but agreed to take part in the race to see who could finish eating a bowl of gelatin first without using hands.

She didn't back out when she learned she'd have to do it while wearing a blindfold. And even when she heard the hiss of an aerosol container and realized the gelatin was being piled high with whipped topping, Meredith bravely buried her face in the gooey concoction and slurped as fast as she could. She was proclaimed the winner by a round of applause that warmed her heart.

What was it about these people that made it so easy for her to feel a part of them? After the flurry of introductions when she and Todd first arrived, she knew she'd never keep all the names straight. Not everyone remembered hers, either, but it hadn't taken away one bit from her enjoyment of the evening.

Todd's head, water streaming from his plastered hair, emerged victorious from the tub with an apple firmly clenched in his teeth. He bowed, then straightened quickly, flipping water on most of the bystanders. Meredith, thoroughly splashed, laughed and clapped along with the others.

The party was over before she knew it. Meredith relaxed in the passenger seat of Todd's Saturn while he drove her back to her duplex. "Did you have a good time?" Todd asked.

"I did," Meredith replied, realizing with a start it was

true. When was the last time she'd been able to say that? In fact, she'd enjoyed herself immensely over the past couple of weeks.

Reflecting on the things she'd done lately, Meredith understood she had broken out of her self-imposed se-clusion and found life good. The trips to the symphony and the art museum, reading C. S. Lewis, and walking in the park—all these things had contributed to her realiza-tion that she was having more fun than she'd had in years.

"Would you like to join us on Sunday for Bible study?"

Meredith's newfound exuberance took over. "Sure, why not?" she heard herself reply.

Preparing for her first visit to church in well over a year, Meredith spent extra time in front of the mirror. For once, her hair responded properly to the curling iron, not falling in limp strands as soon as she released it.

When she was finished, soft curls framed her face. Her dark brown eyes sparkled with a new glow, and she didn't look so tired and discouraged. What had happened in those two short weeks to make such a change? *I found a friend,* she thought happily. Todd's easy acceptance and enjoyment of her company had awakened in her a zest for living that Meredith had thought was gone for good.

The inner Meredith was shaping up pretty well, she thought. Now if she could only do something about the outside. . . . Sparkling eyes and cooperative hair didn't make up for all those extra pounds. Her spirits dropped a few notches as she compared her figure to those of the women in the new magazines she'd scattered around the duplex as incentive.

But all she needed was the determination to lose that weight, starting promptly on New Year's Day. A year of deprivation wouldn't begin to compare with the joy she would feel when she looked the way she wanted to. . . when Gordon would look at her and see a person worth knowing.

Speaking of Gordon, bumping into him after working hours was paying off. Just in the last week there had been several times he'd greeted her with a polite hello instead of looking right through her.

Once, he'd even looked away from Lydia Myers to greet her—plain, uninteresting Meredith Blackwell. She could hardly wait to see his reaction when she had a gorgeous new figure. Things were certainly more promising than they had been a month ago.

Meredith added a dash of lipstick just as the doorbell rang. Scooping up her purse, she hurried off to meet Todd. "Your duplex is halfway between my place and the church," he'd told her. "I'll be going right past anyway, so why don't I pick you up?"

The offer had sounded good last week, and she was especially pleased she'd accepted a ride today, when they reached the church and Meredith saw the crowded parking lot. If she'd driven here on her own, she might very well have wheeled around and headed home again.

A sense of panic threatened to overcome her as soon as she entered the packed foyer, and she would have fled back to her safe, familiar living room if it hadn't been for Todd's comforting presence. He took her elbow and guided her confidently along the corridor until they reached the singles' room. "Are you all right?" he asked, just before they entered.

Meredith nodded her head and gave him a shaky smile. "I forgot there would be so many more people here than at the fall festival. It's a little overwhelming."

Todd smiled kindly. "You'll feel better when you see some familiar faces," he assured her.

Sure, thought Meredith. *I've only been here once. I'm still an outsider.* To her amazement, she found that Todd was right. As soon as she stepped through the door, friendly faces appeared; people shook her hand and warmly welcomed her to the class. She remembered many of them from the other night, although she still needed to put names and faces together.

"Meredith! Good to have you back." It was the husky man she'd sat next to while Todd bobbed for apples. He pumped her hand as though he were genuinely glad to see her. "I'm Bob Millbeck. And these. . . ," he said, gesturing to the couple next to him, "are Sheila Powers and Michael Emerson."

Meredith nodded a shy hello. Sheila, a tall, willowy blond, draped an arm over Meredith's shoulders and gave her a gentle squeeze. "There's coffee and goodies over here."

Sheila guided Meredith to a table set up with trays of pastries and a gurgling coffee urn. "Help yourself." Sheila used a napkin to pick up an eclair slathered with chocolate icing, then turned when she heard her name called.

"Excuse me," she mumbled around a bite of the gooey

confection. "I have to help Michael find some more chairs." Meredith watched her graceful, swaying walk and grimaced. Sheila was probably one of those people who could stuff herself full of any kind of food and still maintain her slender figure. Meredith, on the other hand, could look at a plate of doughnuts and feel five pounds attach themselves to her.

She eyed the calorie-laden goodies regretfully and settled for a cup of steaming coffee, feeling extra virtuous when she stirred in a packet of sugar substitute. Todd caught her attention from across the room and waved at her to join him. "It's almost time to start," he said. "We'd better grab these seats while they're available."

The teacher was just taking his place at the lectern in the front of the room. Meredith slid onto the folding chair beside Todd and sipped her coffee while she listened to the lesson.

By the time the morning worship service had ended, Meredith knew she had made a mistake in not finding a church sooner. Only two hours of worship and study brought back a joy in the Lord she'd almost forgotten. Thank goodness for her new friendship with Todd! Without his encouragement, how long would it have taken her to reach this point?

Todd stepped out of their row into the main aisle. He had watched Meredith during both the class and the sermon, noting her obvious enjoyment with pleasure. He might have gotten off to a slow start, but this project was turning out to be a lot more fun than he'd thought.

"Would you like to come back tonight? It's a little less

formal—lots of singing and praying. I'll pick you up if you like."

Meredith moved to join him, smiling and nodding her head in agreement. At the same moment, a hand clapped Todd on the shoulder, and he turned to see Clay Evans, the associate pastor.

Nodding a greeting to Meredith, Clay turned back to Todd, a worried frown creasing his forehead. "Do you have a minute? I need a favor from you, a big one."

"Sure." Todd motioned toward the row he and Meredith had just vacated, and the three of them slipped out of the stream of people heading for the rear doors.

Clay spoke rapidly. "Remember how you helped Marla Potter with the children's Easter program last spring?"

Todd nodded slowly, and Clay continued. "Remember how much fun it was and what a great time you had?"

"Hold it." Todd held up his hand. "How about dropping the sales pitch and cutting to the chase?"

Clay sighed. "Okay, the bottom line is this—Marla was supposed to direct the children's Christmas program."

Todd raised an eyebrow. "Was?"

"Two of her kids broke out in chicken pox yesterday. By the time they're over it, the other two will probably come down with it. Marla will have her hands full for weeks and can't possibly direct the program. We're really in a bind."

"What about Cathy Avery? Or Matt Rickard? Or someone else who actually has kids? Wouldn't that be more appropriate?"

Clay rubbed his hand across his forehead. "I've tried,

Todd. Believe me, I've tried. Every one of them has a legitimate reason why they can't do it. That brings it down to you, buddy. If you don't step in, we won't have a kids' program this year. Uh. . .can I tell them there's still a rehearsal tonight?"

Todd shrugged, then grinned. "Okay, I'll bail you out." He glanced at Meredith and saw her smile disappear. *Great move, Andrews.* If he agreed to direct the program, being at rehearsals would mean he'd miss the singles' activities on Sunday evenings. He'd be abandoning Meredith just when she was beginning to build up some self-confidence. How could he have forgotten? She was his ministry project, with a higher priority than rescuing Clay. This just wasn't going to work. Unless. . .

"On one condition." He put his hand on Meredith's shoulder. "I'll need Meredith's help. Do we have a deal?"

Clay's face registered profound relief. "We do, indeed. And I want you to know I really appreciate this!" He hurried off, his grateful smile including them both.

In the parking lot Todd wondered if his behavior had been too abrupt. "Did you mind me volunteering you like that?" he asked.

Meredith's eyes glowed with anticipation. "Not a bit. I haven't been around kids since I left home, and I've really missed my niece and nephews." She laughed self-consciously. "I don't have a clue about what I'm getting into, but I'm looking forward to it."

"It'll be fun," Todd promised. "How hard can it be?"

❧

Seven hours later, Todd sat in one corner of the fellowship

hall with his face buried in his hands. How had anyone ever imagined he was capable of something as complicated as directing a children's program? He had assumed Marla had already started rehearsals, that the kids knew what they were doing, that he was merely coming in to oversee a smooth-running operation already set in motion.

Clay hadn't mentioned that Marla hadn't gotten any further than assigning parts. Clay also had conveniently omitted the fact that these weren't the same kids Todd had worked with at Easter. He had thoroughly enjoyed the fifth- and sixth-graders, who had done programs like that often enough to know how to listen and cooperate.

This time, though, he was dealing with little guys, kindergarten through fourth grade, and Todd was at a total loss. They shrieked and squealed and wiggled until Todd was ready to pull his hair out. When he asked them to sit down and listen, they giggled and ran around the room, paying no attention to him. When he raised his voice and told them to sit down, three little girls burst into tears.

The Christmas program would be the flop of the century, and Meredith would never want to come back. What had he gotten himself into?

A small hand patted him on the arm. "Mr. Andrews?" Todd raised his head to see a small, freckled face regarding him solemnly. "You can come back now."

Todd looked past the freckled face and blinked in disbelief. At the front of the fellowship hall, the fourth-graders playing Mary, Joseph, and the innkeeper were having a spirited discussion over the availability of a place to stay. Scattered around the room, small groups of children were bunched together, practicing their lines.

Order reigned where chaos ruled before. And in the midst of it all, Meredith moved from group to group, showing one child where to stand, encouraging another with a smile and a touch on the shoulder. Todd shook his head. If a fairy godmother had appeared and waved her wand, the effect could not have been more dramatic.

He walked through the groups, intercepting Meredith. Her face shone as she looked up at him. "Aren't they doing well? You were right, this is a lot of fun!" Seeing his dazed expression, she frowned and added, "Are you all right?"

Todd nodded, shook his head, then nodded again. "What did you do?" His voice came out in a hoarse croak.

"Nothing much, just got them organized. I put one of the older children in charge of each group so they could help the ones who can't read very well learn their lines. It seemed like it would be more efficient to have them work on small sections at a time, then we can put the whole thing together later. That way we don't have the majority of them waiting around while just a few are rehearsing." When Todd didn't answer, she added timidly, "I hope that's okay."

Okay? It was more than okay. It was incredible, just short of miraculous. Todd stared at the smooth-running operation he'd envisioned but had no idea how to put in place. A broad grin spread across his face. "You are one amazing woman, do you know that, Meredith Blackwell?"

At the look of stunned pleasure on her face, his grin broadened even more.

Chapter 5

After dropping Meredith off, Todd drove home slowly, still marveling at the way Meredith had orchestrated the rehearsal. Each child went home knowing what lines to study. Each met his or her parents at the door with a smile, chattering excitedly about the program. Most of them had given Meredith a hug on the way out.

What had happened? He'd been a member of that church for three years, and most of those kids didn't even know his name. Meredith—shy, quiet Meredith Blackwell, the woman he had taken on as a ministry project—had been in that church a grand total of three times, and every one of those kids already loved her.

Todd had to admit her reputation for efficiency was well deserved. She had organized tonight's rehearsal on the spur of the moment. When Todd bemoaned his belief that with only four weeks to practice, they'd never be ready in time, she calmly outlined what needed to be done at each rehearsal. She'd already scheduled a dress rehearsal for December twenty-second, two days before the performance.

It would work, she assured him. And after seeing her

in action tonight, Todd believed her.

The strange thing was, he was so used to thinking of Meredith as needy, he had forgotten that she might have skills that could help him. Tonight had been a real eye-opener.

He remembered the joyful glow on Meredith's face while she coached the kids on their parts and the confidence she showed in making it all run smoothly. In his mind's eye, he could still see the tender smile on her face when she returned a hug from a shy little boy with a face full of freckles and no front teeth. Todd almost envied the kid being on the receiving end of that hug.

Whoa there, buddy. Hold everything! Meredith was his ministry project, not a romantic interest. It wouldn't do a bit of good if he sent her mixed signals. He was her mentor, her encourager, her friend.

Sure, she was fun to be around and he was enjoying this undertaking more than he'd expected. But he'd better keep in mind that his interest in her was that of an encourager, nothing more.

❧

It was Friday, and Meredith caught herself humming Christmas carols at her desk. She stopped, startled by this uncharacteristic behavior, then shrugged and went back to humming, a faint smile on her face. Why not hum when life was good and there was plenty to be joyful about?

And life *was* good. Who would have thought following a plan for self-improvement could be so much fun? Outside interests had added a new dimension to her existence. No longer did her path go straight from home to work and back home again, with only a few stops along the way to deal with groceries and other necessities.

Her evenings and weekends were filled with new pursuits, and in all these varied activities, the constant factor was Todd. His friendship brightened Meredith's life more than she would have dreamed possible. His quick smile and ready laugh had become essential parts of her days, and she wouldn't know what to do without them.

Meredith checked her copy for the new stock prospectus one last time, stacked the pages neatly in a manila folder, and headed for Gordon's office. She found him standing just outside his door and handed him the folder with a smile, ready to respond to his greeting with a bright remark.

Gordon reached for the folder and opened his mouth as if to speak. Then his eyes focused on a point beyond Meredith and stayed there. Disconcerted, Meredith turned to see what was distracting him. Two pencil-thin women, each wearing a skirt far shorter than decency allowed, were walking toward the elevators. Gordon's gaze never shifted. His fingers tightened around Meredith's folder and he gave her a brief nod. Swallowing her disappointment, Meredith went back to her desk, no longer humming.

The one thing marring her existence was the fact that while Gordon spoke to her now more than before, he still didn't seem to see her as a woman. His gaze never followed Meredith the way it followed those two women. His eyes never lit up when she approached.

Meredith slumped in her chair. *Next year,* she thought,

I'll be able to hold his attention like that.

She stopped at a newsstand on her way home to pick up a few new fashion magazines. The clerk counted out her change with a smirk. Meredith was sure he questioned why anyone who looked like her would buy magazines full of glamour advice. She thanked him through clenched teeth, then fumed all the way home.

Whap! One magazine landed on the table near her front door. *Whap!* Meredith threw another one onto her dressing table. The models on the covers seemed to sneer at her. "Just wait," she told them. "Someday I'll look as good as you do."

The joy Meredith felt earlier had faded like a puff of smoke. Why couldn't she be appreciated for who she was? Why wasn't just being herself good enough? Tears of frustration stung her eyes. She was thoroughly tired of being frumpy and dumpy, of being passed over and ignored.

❧

"Do not be afraid," the angel said to the quaking shepherds. "I bring you good news of great joy that will be for all the people."

So far, so good, Todd thought, although the two shepherds on the left might be quaking just a bit too much. They looked to him like they were experiencing a 6.2 tremor. Not a problem; he'd speak to them later. This was not a major glitch.

"This will be a sign to you; You will find a baby wrapped in cloths and lying in a manger."

Ten more angels entered precisely on cue, joining the first group in singing about peace on earth and good will toward men. *If those shepherds shake any harder,* Todd thought, *they'll jiggle right out of their costumes.* He jotted down a reminder: *Tell shepherds to tone it down.*

"Let's go to Bethlehem and see this thing that has happened, which the Lord has told us about." The lead shepherd picked up his staff and started toward Bethlehem. Todd nodded, pleased.

"Where is the one who has been born king of the Jews?" The strident voice rang clearly through the auditorium. "We saw his star in the east and have come to worship him."

Three boys marched on stage, making a determined beeline for the stable. Todd clutched his hair and winced. He'd have to start clutching new areas; the places his hands usually grasped were getting tender.

"No!" he roared, and the rehearsal ground to an abrupt halt.

"He did it again, Mr. Andrews." The young actress playing Mary rose from her place next to the manger and stood with one hand on her hip, her foot tapping in irritation. "It's not his turn yet." She crossed her arms and glared at the ill-timed trio. Then she swiveled and glowered unblinkingly at Todd as if to say, "You're the director—do something!"

Todd moaned softly and stepped up onto the platform. He stopped before the three boys and addressed their leader, a third-grader with bright red hair and a pugnacious jaw. "Come on," he entreated for what seemed like the thousandth time, "you have to remember to come in on cue."

The redhead stood his ground. "These guys," he said, jerking his head toward the shepherds, "always get to go first. It's not fair we always have to wait 'til last."

Todd scrubbed his face with his hands. He felt like he'd aged at least ten years since he agreed to direct the program, and that had been only two weeks ago. What condition would he be in by the time it was over?

"Look, Timmy—"

"Tommy," Meredith corrected gently, coming up behind Todd. "Boys, why don't we go sit in the back and go over the Bible story again? The wise men came from a faraway land, while the shepherds were close by. It makes more sense for the shepherds to get there first."

The three boys followed Meredith meekly. "Okay, Miss Blackwell," the leader said slowly. He threw a mutinous look over his shoulder at Todd and added, "As long as no one's just playing favorites."

"How do you do it?" Todd asked when they were seated in a nearby coffee shop for a post-rehearsal snack. "I try my hardest, and they barely listen to me. All you have to do is smile, and they're eating out of your hand. What's your secret?"

Meredith leaned back while the waitress placed two steaming mugs of hot chocolate on the table. "I don't know what the difference is," she said, choosing the mug without whipped cream on top. "I've always loved kids and they seem to love me back." She shrugged. "That's all there is to it."

Todd shook his head and gave her a crooked grin that made her heart skip a beat. *Thank You, Lord, for this friendship!* Only a few weeks ago she never would have believed she'd be having a conversation like this.

She was not used to opening up to others, saying what she thought without weighing every word. This, she thought, was relaxing. Comfortable. She breathed a sigh of contentment.

"I'm only sorry I won't be here for the performance itself," she said, her happy mood slipping a bit. Making reservations well in advance for her flight home to spend Christmas with her family had seemed like a wonderfully practical idea when she'd done it months ago. It would have been fine, she reflected, for the old Meredith, who had no commitments outside working hours. But the new Meredith was sorely disappointed not to see the end result of their labors.

Who would have thought things could change so drastically in such a short time? Those lonely days seemed far removed from her current busy existence. She was now busier and far happier. If she didn't have a nonrefundable ticket, she would never consider leaving the very day of the program.

"Would you like me to drive you to the airport?" Todd's voice brought her back to the present.

Meredith opened her mouth to say no, then reconsidered. Normally she would drive herself to the terminal and put her car in the long-term parking area. But Todd's offer prompted the memory of how vulnerable she always felt having to navigate the large parking lot by herself. Besides, it would be good to have a friendly welcome on her return, instead of having only an empty duplex to look forward to.

"I'd like that," she said. "If it's not too much trouble."

Todd dismissed the idea with a wave of his hand. "No trouble at all. That's what friends are for." A warm glow spread through Meredith.

"Do you really think it'll all come together in time?" Todd asked, his voice reflecting his concern.

"It will," she said with a reassuring smile. "The kids have their parts down pretty well now, and they're coming in on cue—"

"Now that you've persuaded the wise men not to trample the shepherds on their way to the stable."

Meredith chuckled and went on, "It was wonderful of Pastor Tompkins to move the evening service to the fellowship hall so we could use the auditorium for rehearsals. The kids will have a much better feel for the stage, and they won't be thrown by a change in location at the last minute."

Todd nodded in agreement. "My big concern right now is the donkey," he said, referring to the costume worn by two boys who were supposed to carry Mary to Bethlehem. "I keep trying to picture what will happen if Adam Wheeler hollers 'Oh, my achin' back!' during the performance."

Meredith sputtered with laughter. "That would be a problem," she conceded. "But I think we can convince him not to do it by then."

"We only have a couple more weeks," Todd reminded her.

"I know, but it's starting to gel. It'll be wonderful.

You'll see." Without thinking, she reached across the table and laid her hand on his, squeezing it lightly.

Todd's gaze locked on hers, and he turned his hand over and squeezed back. A long interval passed with the two of them staring into each other's eyes. The moment was broken by the waitress jostling the table when she left their bill.

Todd, looking as dazed as Meredith felt, swept the paper up in the palm of his hand and glanced at it. "I need to get some change for the tip," he muttered, pulling a bill from his wallet and leaving the wallet on the table. "I'll be right back."

Something fluttered to the floor and Meredith bent to retrieve it. A photo, obviously from Todd's wallet, lay in her hand.

Meredith stared at the woman pictured there, captivated by the luminous dark eyes above prominent cheekbones. Glossy brunette hair framed the delicate face. The picture was a full-length shot, and it only took a glance for Meredith to know this woman could trade places with any of the models in her magazines at home.

Meredith flipped the picture over, looking for a name, but the back of the photograph was blank. Feeling ashamed of her snooping, she tucked the picture back inside the folds of Todd's wallet.

Todd had never mentioned a girlfriend. Meredith had assumed he was unattached, since he seemed to have plenty of free time. Maybe this woman lived in another city, somewhere far enough away that they could see each other only occasionally.

Whoever she was, there was attachment enough for Todd to keep her picture with him at all times. And why wouldn't he be attracted to that beautiful face and model's figure? Meredith thought wistfully. Men were drawn to the ultra-slim; it was just that simple.

A pang of envy, as sharp as the twist of a knife, swept through Meredith, stunning her by its intensity. *What on earth is the matter?* she asked herself, blinking to keep back the sudden tears. She couldn't be jealous that Todd had a girlfriend! He was only her friend, her buddy. Her interest lay in Gordon.

She had absolutely no reason to feel so disappointed.

Chapter 6

Two tan suitcases lay open across the bed. Meredith folded a brightly colored holiday sweater and pressed it into the last available space. She took a deep breath, glad the job was completed.

Packing was one thing she did not do efficiently, and she would be the first to admit it. Her mind could catalog all too many possibilities, an overabundance of items she might need, and she had never been able to decide which things were necessary and which she could safely leave at home. The end result: she took them all.

Meredith picked up the list she had left on the dresser and began ticking off the items she had packed, wanting to make sure she had left nothing out.

Casual clothes to wear around the house with family. Check. A dressy outfit for the Christmas service at her parents' church. Check. Lingerie. Check. Cosmetics. Check. Shoes. Check. Meredith grinned, thinking of the pale blue walking shoes she had tucked into the bottom of one case. She could imagine her family's surprise when she declared her intention of walking the track at the nearby school every morning.

Family Christmas gifts. Check. She had shipped the

larger items the week before, but decided there was enough room to squeeze the smaller ones into her luggage.

She made a slow turn, mentally checking off the other things she had done, in order to leave the day after tomorrow. The post office had been notified of her plans and would hold her mail. Her paper boy knew not to leave a newspaper until New Year's Day. The timers she purchased for her lights were set to turn them on in the evenings and off at bedtime. Everything had been taken care of.

Meredith zipped her suitcases shut and set them near the front door. They would be ready to go when Todd came by to drive her to the airport. Turning, she noticed the slim notebook, neatly centered on the entry table, awaiting her return on New Year's Eve—waiting for her to begin work on her list of resolutions.

With a few minutes to spare before Todd was due to pick her up for the dress rehearsal, Meredith leafed through the pages of the notebook until she found the list. So much had been packed into the past few weeks that her memory of the items it contained were hazy. It would be a good idea to have them fixed firmly in her mind so she would be ready to start the program as soon as she returned. Meredith ran her finger down the numbered items with wide eyes, absorbing the fact that she had already made significant progress without even trying.

She had found a church she loved, one where she felt accepted and useful. Thanks to the Bible reading schedule Sheila had given her, daily Bible reading had once again become a habit. She had already read through most of the New Testament.

The symphony performance had been wonderful, she thought with a dreamy smile, remembering how Gordon spoke to her afterward, and she had thoroughly enjoyed the Impressionist exhibit at the museum. She and Todd had already made plans to visit the Museum of Natural History in early January.

The borrowed copy of C. S. Lewis's *Mere Christianity* had sparked a renewed interest in reading, and Meredith now made weekly forays to the public library.

What was left? Meredith scanned the list again. Surely her daily walks counted as regular exercise, and she could already see results. Four laps was her norm now, and she could step out at a brisk pace without puffing a bit. Only two items were left—losing thirty pounds and having a makeover.

Meredith mentally sorted through the different looks in her magazines, wondering which would be best for her. Instead of looming as a threatening experience, the makeover now filled her with anticipation. She could hardly wait until she could view her reflection in the mirror with pride.

As for losing those unwanted pounds. . . Meredith wrinkled her nose, thinking ruefully how dieting had always defeated her in the past. But not this time! Not with most of her other resolutions already producing results. This time she would succeed.

A giddy shiver ran through her. Was it possible she had done so much in only two months?

Meredith had to admit her life had changed drastically

since the motivational seminar. Her evenings and weekends were no longer spent in solitude. Other people's paths had crossed hers, and she knew her life was richer for it. Becoming involved in the children's program—seeing the joy on those young faces as they worked so hard to portray the Christmas story—had brought more satisfaction than any number of commendations on her job performance.

The clock on her mantel chimed, reminding her of the time. Meredith hurried to her dressing table and quickly applied blusher. She wanted to take special pains with her appearance for the dress rehearsal, since she would miss the actual performance. A lump formed in her throat at the thought that this would be as close as she'd come to seeing the finished product she had worked for so hard; she dashed away a tear.

"Don't be a baby," she said aloud. "There's always next year." But would she and Todd be involved with the program next year? Would she and Todd even be involved as friends? Meredith wondered gloomily if Todd planned to visit his slender girlfriend over the holidays. He hadn't mentioned any travel plans to Meredith, but then he hadn't made any mention of his sweetheart, either.

"And there's no reason why he should," she told herself sternly. "You may be his friend, but you have no claim on him. He's not required to tell you everything."

The buzz of the doorbell sounded through the duplex, and she still hadn't done a thing to her hair. Meredith hurried to the door and let Todd in. "Do you mind waiting for just a moment?" she asked. "I promise I won't take long."

Todd settled back against the wall next to the entry table and gave her his crooked smile, causing the usual turmoil in Meredith's emotions. She rushed back to her dressing table and began yanking the brush through her hair, trying not to rip it out by the roots.

"Did you say something?" she called, smoothing the hair back away from her face and fastening it in place with a new silver clip. Meredith hurried around the corner to the entry hall to find Todd thumbing through one of her fashion magazines.

"I said, can you believe how skinny these women are?" he answered, frowning.

The desire to share her goal stirred in Meredith. She had told no one of her plan to lose weight, of her dream of becoming as slender as one of the models Todd was scowling at. As slender as the woman whose picture he carried. Trusting anyone else with such precious knowledge was a risk Meredith wasn't sure she was ready to take.

But this was Todd, her trusted friend. Summoning up all her courage, Meredith reached for her purse, saying casually, "Actually, I plan to be that thin someday."

Todd's face was a study in disbelief. He thrust the magazine toward her, pointing to a model dressed in a peacock-blue jumpsuit. "You don't seriously mean you want to look like that, do you?" he asked harshly.

Meredith stood frozen in place, studying Todd. She thought she knew him so well, but his reaction couldn't have shocked her more if he had kicked a hole through her front door. How could he belittle something that meant so much to her? She had thought she could trust him, but look what happened the first time she shared one of her most cherished secrets.

Choking back the pain, Meredith swept past Todd and reached for the doorknob. "That's precisely what I have in mind," she managed to say through the sudden thickness in her throat. "Come on. We'll be late."

Todd planted an arm against the door, barring her way. "Rehearsal can wait. This is more important." He stared deep into Meredith's eyes, as if trying to read her thoughts. "Let me show you something," he said, pulling out his wallet and extracting a photo.

Great. Here comes the girlfriend. Meredith wanted to look anyplace but at the solemn, fine-boned face. That nasty twinge of jealousy flared up again, and she fought to contain it. *It is none of your business who Todd likes,* she told herself sternly. *None at all!*

"This is my cousin Sondra," Todd said, gazing at Meredith with sad eyes. "She's anorexic."

His cousin? Meredith took the photo and studied it. Maybe the cheekbones were a little too pronounced, the hollows under her eyes a little too deep. On closer inspection, Meredith could see the sharp outline of a hipbone under the fabric of Sondra's skirt. Granted she was thin, Meredith thought, but she still didn't think. . .

Todd's voice broke into her thoughts. "That was taken when Sondra weighed ninety-two pounds. She's now down to seventy-eight pounds, but she doesn't allow cameras near her anymore."

Seventy-eight pounds! Meredith felt her jaw go slack. She stared at Todd, compassion for both him and his cousin welling up inside her. "Will she be all right?" she asked softly.

Todd shrugged, his eyes filled with pain. "If she's left to herself, no. She won't admit refusing to eat is a problem, that it's life-threatening. She's an intelligent woman, but she can't—or won't—see that she looks like walking death. That's what makes it so frustrating.

"Right now," he added, his voice shaking, "she's in a treatment center, being monitored twenty-four hours a day. The family is hoping this will work, but. . ." His voice trailed off.

"I get so angry at all this," he said, waving his hand at Meredith's magazine. "Everywhere you look—magazines, TV, movies—women are being told they need to be thin to be acceptable. No, not just thin—emaciated!"

He ran his fingers through his hair and looked at Meredith with haunted eyes. "I've seen what that kind of thinking can lead to. Believe me, there is nothing attractive about looking half-starved!"

Meredith blinked her eyes against the sting of tears. The situation Todd's family was going through sounded like a nightmare. At the same time, all Meredith wanted to do was lose enough weight to be attractive. She didn't have an eating disorder like Sondra's.

"I'm so sorry," she whispered. "What she's going through must be awful, and I'd never want to put myself or the people I love through that. All I'm trying to do is slim down so I'm closer to my ideal weight, not starve myself."

Todd slapped his forehead with the palm of his hand.

"You're missing the point, Meredith." He gripped her shoulders, eyeing her intently, his face only inches from hers. "The question is, *why* do you think you're over-weight? Is it a question of health? Has your doctor told you to lose weight? Or is it because you think you have to look like that," he nodded toward the magazine, which had fallen to the floor, "to be okay?"

His question struck so close to home that all Meredith could do was stare back at him wide-eyed, her lower lip trembling. For all his legitimate concern about his cousin, Todd simply didn't understand. He didn't know what it was like to be invisible, to be overlooked because her fig-ure didn't conform to the accepted standard.

"Why try to be something you're not," Todd pleaded, "when you're perfectly fine the way you are?"

Meredith shook her head miserably, her eyes brim-ming with tears. "But I'm not. I'm. . ."

Todd turned her around so she stood face to face with her image in the large mirror. "Look," he said, his voice rough with emotion, "You're a lovely woman, Meredith. Can't you see it? Your beauty lies in the fact that you're a real person—a warm, caring woman with a wonderful sense of humor who anyone in his or her right mind would treasure as a friend." His hands tightened on her shoulders. "Who could possibly want something artificial when the genuine article is right in front of him?"

For a fleeting moment, Meredith stood in awe, star-ing through her tears at the person Todd described.

Chapter 7

Doors closed; the stage lights dimmed. Voices of excited children faded down the hallway.

"I wish you were going to be here for the real play, Miss Blackwell." Meredith looked down into a pair of solemn blue eyes. She knelt to put herself on the little girl's eye level.

"So do I, Kimmie. But I'll be thinking of you every minute." Meredith folded the little girl in a tight hug. "Do a good job and have a wonderful Christmas, okay?"

Kimmie nodded, flashed Meredith a gap-toothed grin, and scampered down the hall to her waiting mother. Meredith sat back on her heels and surveyed the empty auditorium.

The best thing that could be said about the dress rehearsal, she thought wearily, was that it was over. Nearly every member of the cast had bungled their lines at some point. Tommy Allen, jumping the gun on his cue even more than usual, led his band of wise men careening straight through the ranks of the heavenly host. Adam Wheeler, the rear half of the donkey, remained quiet about his aching back during the journey down the center aisle to Bethlehem. He had, however, added bucking to his repertoire and sent Mary sailing into a front-row seat.

Todd returned from storing the last of the props, dusting his hands on his jeans. He extended a hand to help Meredith to her feet. "What do you think?" Meredith thought he looked as dejected as she felt.

She tried to summon up an encouraging grin. "You know what they say—'Bad dress rehearsal, good show.' "

"Do they really say that?" Todd's tone was skeptical.

"My high school drama teacher did. Right after what was probably the world's worst dress rehearsal of *Our Town*." Meredith shuddered, remembering the mess they had made of Thornton Wilder's play. "He was trying to boost our morale for opening night."

"And how did the performance go?"

Meredith tried to stifle a giggle. "You don't want to know."

Todd groaned, switching out the lights and ushering Meredith outside.

They rode most of the way to Meredith's duplex in companionable silence.

"It's going to be lonely, doing the program without you." Todd spoke the words so softly, Meredith wasn't sure whether she had imagined them. She turned her head, studying Todd's profile. He looked away from the road for an instant and glanced at Meredith, one corner of his mouth curving up. "If you hadn't already told me you were leaving in the morning, I'd swear you were running out on me, after tonight."

"You'll be okay." Meredith's voice was equally soft, unwilling to break the gentle mood. "I'll be praying for you all day." Her voice dropped to an even fainter tone, and she added, "If I hadn't already made those reservations, I wouldn't have thought of leaving you to do the program alone."

Todd braked to a smooth stop in Meredith's driveway and turned toward her. He took one of Meredith's hands in his and squeezed it. Keeping her hand in a loose grasp, he held her gaze with his. "I know you wouldn't," he said, his voice husky. "I know."

Meredith gently extricated her hand and let herself out of the car, not wanting to prolong the discussion after the emotional roller coaster she'd been on today. Waving at Todd from her doorway to let him know she was inside and safe, she closed the door behind her and leaned against it, eyes closed. She needed time to think.

After Todd's outburst, they had hurried to the church, arriving just in time to greet their young performers. Making sure the right costume was on the right actor, doling out props, and keeping the rehearsal running in spite of the numerous goofs and glitches had left her without a moment to mull over the things Todd had said.

Meredith opened her eyes, her gaze dropping to the floor where the crumpled magazine lay near her feet. Reluctantly, Meredith picked it up.

The same finely-chiseled faces stared up at her, but Meredith studied them now from a different point of view. The delicate figures she had envied so long—did they look alluring or simply malnourished? Todd's outburst had shown her a whole new perspective.

Meredith had to admit even she had thought Sondra

looked remarkably like those models. But Sondra's figure wasn't just tiny; there was something terribly wrong that made her abuse her body that way.

Was it possible Todd was right? Had Meredith's view of herself been carefully molded by messages thrown her way at the rate of hundreds a day? Was using these women as her standard bound to force a comparison that would always put Meredith sadly short of the ideal?

Could she possibly be acceptable just the way she was?

Meredith hung her coat on the hall tree. Keeping her eyes focused on the entry table, she moved toward it, positioning herself in front of the offensive mirror. Her hands seized the edge of the table in a white-knuckled grip. Taking a long, shuddering breath, Meredith raised her eyes to face the mirror, afraid of what she might see.

For a long moment she stared in wonder at the reflection before her. Tears stung her eyes and a lump formed in her throat. The image Todd had shown her earlier was still there—a person of value, not because of how she looked, but because of who she was.

Because of *Whose* she was. A Bible verse she read earlier that week popped into her mind. Meredith's lips moved almost silently as she repeated the words: "I praise you because I am fearfully and wonderfully made."

Meredith pressed both hands to her mouth, trembling with the awareness that swept over her like a torrent. God had created her as a unique individual. In His infinite wisdom, He had chosen to make her the one and only Meredith Blackwell. She didn't have to pattern herself after someone else's ideal when God had already set the standard. All she was responsible for was being faithful to Him, being the Meredith He created her to be.

Warm tears spilled over to run down her cheeks, and Meredith's lips moved again, this time in a prayer of gratitude.

✿

Soft music and lively conversation greeted Meredith when the elevator door slid open on the top floor of the Lyman Building. The company Christmas party was in full swing, and the large meeting area had been transformed by glittering decorations and twinkling lights.

Meredith paused before a mirrored wall panel, discreetly checking her appearance. The deep green of her dress complimented her fair complexion and brought out hidden highlights in her dark brown eyes. The dress's flared skirt and popover top had a slenderizing effect on her waist, she observed, with an unfamiliar sense of approval.

Meredith glanced around the room, noting the appearance of the women in the various groups without her usual pang of envy. She still wasn't a size six. She would probably never be a size six, but that was no longer an issue. Like one from whose eyes the scales had fallen, Meredith now saw herself clearly as a child of God, a person of worth, and she had no intention of allowing her vision to become distorted again by the world's twisted thinking.

She moved past the tight knots of people, wishing Todd could be there with her instead of at the church men's fellowship that was meeting that night. But this was just an obligatory appearance, she reminded herself. She wasn't expected to be a social butterfly.

And it's a good thing, she thought, watching the groups grow more animated and hearing the chatter become louder, the laughter more raucous. Waiters passed through the crowd, exchanging the guests' empty glasses for full ones. From the looks and actions of most of the guests, Meredith felt sure those refills weren't their first. She threaded her way through to the refreshment table.

"What would you like to drink?" asked the young waiter who stood behind a pair of crystal punch bowls.

"Which is which?" Meredith surprised herself with the forthright question. Only a couple of months ago, she would have been too intimidated to ask, sure everyone within earshot would be laughing at her.

The young man's eyes gleamed with amusement, but not ridicule. "With. Without." He pointed to the punch bowls in turn. "Would you prefer leaded or unleaded?"

"Unleaded," Meredith replied, returning his smile. "Definitely unleaded."

She took the glass of frothy liquid and sipped it as she moved from group to group, nodding and exchanging greetings. More than once she encountered surprised glances at her uncharacteristic friendliness, and she smiled inwardly. What a difference it made just to be able to be herself!

Her circuit completed, Meredith was about to slip out and leave the others to their partying when she spotted Gordon Winslow on the other side of the large room talking to Martin Abrams, his buddy from accounting. Gordon threw back his head and laughed at something Martin had said. The light reflected off his wavy black hair.

Meredith worked her way through the crowd, taking up a position in an alcove behind the two men, but out of Gordon's line of sight. She would wait until he finished talking, then step around the corner and present him with the new, improved Meredith Blackwell.

Her stomach tingled with excitement at the thought of Gordon's reaction. The mirror told her she looked her best, and she knew her newfound confidence would give her a poise she'd never had before. There was no business to conduct this evening, no rush to leave. She and Gordon could have a leisurely conversation back here, out of the crush. What an opportunity!

Meredith leaned casually against the wall, as if taking a break from the social whirl, and waited.

". . .Strickland was not happy when he found out he was getting a new secretary." Meredith recognized Martin Abrams's voice. She rested her head against the dark-paneled partition, the better to keep track of the conversation. As soon as Martin went back to the party, she would make her move.

Gordon's rumbling chuckle sent shivers of delight up Meredith's spine. "But he changed his mind as soon as he took one look at the delectable Miss Emery, right?"

"Wrong!" Meredith heard Martin sputter with laughter. "The idiot keeps complaining she has no secretarial skills. He's worried about upholding his 'high departmental standards,' " Martin intoned with just enough slur in his voice to make Meredith wonder how many drinks he'd already consumed.

Martin snickered. "Can you imagine griping about

whether the woman types ninety words per minute when you can look at that incredible pair of legs all day? Departmental standards can take care of themselves."

Meredith glared at the wall, as if her gaze could burn a hole right through it and singe Martin Abrams. She knew he had a reputation for being a ladies' man, but hearing his viewpoint expressed so baldly made her furious. She pressed her head against the wall once more, eager to hear Gordon's response.

"If Strickland is so concerned about maintaining his standards," Gordon said, a trace of mockery in his voice, "I might be persuaded to take Miss Emery off his hands."

Meredith nodded her approval. It might be the best thing for this Miss Emery.

Martin gave a snort of laughter. "Yeah, off his hands and right into yours!"

Put him in his place, Gordon, Meredith pleaded silently. *Tell him he's a coarse, ill-mannered creep!*

Gordon chuckled again. "I'm sure that even if she's lacking in office skills, the woman has other. . .talents."

"And you're just the man to find them, aren't you?" Martin chortled.

"Let's just say I've had some modest success in bringing out the hidden qualities of some of our secretarial staff." Meredith blinked in disbelief at the self-satisfied note in Gordon's voice. Surely he didn't mean. . .

"Don't sell yourself short, buddy boy!" Martin's strident laughter turned the heads of several people who stared at him curiously, then resumed their own conversations. "Word has it you've branched out far beyond the secretarial pool. What about Lydia Myers and that luscious friend of hers?"

Gordon's laughter told Meredith more than she wanted to know. Thrusting her empty glass into the hand of a passing waiter, she elbowed her way through the crowd, not stopping until she reached the sanctuary of the elevator.

Meredith jabbed the button for the ground floor and rested her forehead against the paneled wall as the door hissed closed and the elevator began its descent. Pressing her hand over her lips, she was grateful she hadn't sampled any solid food. Keeping the foamy punch down would be challenge enough.

She rocked her head from side to side, wishing she could blot out the sordid conversation. If she hadn't heard the condemning words straight from Gordon's lips, she never would have believed him capable of them.

But she had, and the knowledge sickened her. The elevator door slid open and Meredith straightened, trying not to look as shaken as she felt. Stepping briskly through the lobby, she pushed through the heavy glass doors and escaped gratefully into the cold night, willing the crisp air to blow the clouds from her troubled mind.

This was the man whose admiration she had so desperately sought? The one she'd been willing to starve herself down to the size of a twig for?

Thoughts whirled through her mind on the drive home. *How could she have been so pitiful, so needy that she'd been willing to relinquish her own identity for a few scraps of his approval?*

Worse yet, what if she had actually gone through with her plan to look like those other women? She might have won Gordon's attention, but at what cost?

Meredith parked her car and hurried to her front door as if someone were chasing her. She trembled with relief when she closed the rest of the world out and stood just inside the door, relishing the security of her home.

"Thank You, Lord, for opening my eyes," Meredith whispered, grateful for His protection. All the time she was lamenting Gordon's lack of interest, God had been faithfully guarding His child. Instead of any lack within herself, it was Gordon's own twisted viewpoint that had been the problem all along.

The Gordon she thought she admired didn't exist. The women he laughed and joked with—women Meredith once envied and now pitied—didn't matter to him, beyond the way they looked on the surface. He wasn't concerned about the person underneath.

Not the way Todd is. The thought came unbidden and lingered in Meredith's mind while she got ready for bed. Comparing the characters and values of the two men, the difference between them was crystal clear. Climbing between her floral-printed sheets and switching off her bedside lamp, Meredith breathed a prayer of thanks for the wonderful friendship God had given her and for her new insight. *How could I ever have thought Gordon's opinion of me important?* she wondered, drifting off to sleep.

Chapter 8

Meredith stared out the plane window, watching the ever-changing patchwork of farms and fields below and wondering what was wrong with her. Normally, she would have been thrilled to spend a week with her family and pleased with her foresight in locking in her travel plans so far ahead. Today, all she felt was annoyance.

Booking her flight months in advance had been a great idea, back when each day followed the same dull pattern. But life had taken on a rich new texture, and Meredith chafed at her inability to rearrange her plans.

If she had known she would be involved with the children's program, she never would have scheduled her departure for the day of the performance. She hadn't known, though, and she would have to live with things as they were. Meredith sighed, wishing with all her heart she could be there to share the excitement with Todd.

Todd, who loved God wholeheartedly. Todd, who enjoyed life to the fullest. Todd, who was her friend.

And who, only an hour earlier, had shocked her right down to her depths.

He had arrived at her duplex as planned, effortlessly

stowing the heavy suitcases in the trunk of his car. On the drive to the airport, they talked about the program, Todd speculating on everything that could possibly go wrong and Meredith reassuring him it would all be fine.

Todd had ignored her insistence that he drop her and her luggage off outside the terminal; instead, he had parked the car and accompanied her all the way to the gate, despite her protests.

"It doesn't seem right, not having someone here to see you off," he told her after they checked her bags. "You need a proper sendoff, and I'm here to see you get it." Meredith had recognized the stubborn gleam in his eyes and decided it was no use arguing.

Hearing her flight called, Meredith had turned to Todd. "You're right," she admitted. "It does help to have someone to say good-bye to. Thanks for being here." She smiled and impulsively held out her right hand. Instead of the simple handshake she'd expected, Todd grasped her right hand in his left, then slid his right hand around her left shoulder.

He studied her face intently, as if memorizing every feature. "I'll miss you," he had said solemnly, then he tilted his head toward Meredith's.

Startled by the realization Todd was about to kiss her, Meredith had prepared herself for a friendly peck on the cheek. She was totally unprepared for her reaction when Todd's lips touched hers and clung, and his arms tightened around her, pulling her close to him.

Time stopped, and the two of them existed in a world apart—floating, spinning, whirling through space.

Meredith's heartbeat thundered in her ears as she returned Todd's kiss, leaning into his embrace.

An authoritative tap on her shoulder had brought her back to earth with a jolt. "Ma'am, are you on this flight?" The attendant smiled sympathetically, gesturing toward the passenger tunnel with a handful of boarding passes. "I'm sorry, but you'll have to board now."

Meredith blinked slowly, taking in Todd's proximity, her arms wound securely around his neck, and the grinning onlookers. Her mouth went slack and she stared at Todd, mortified by her behavior.

Todd had stared back, expressionless. "I'll meet you here on New Year's Eve," he said.

Meredith nodded, shoved her boarding pass into the attendant's hand, and fled down the tunnel.

Even now, an hour later, she could still feel the warmth of Todd's kiss. Her face flamed as she remembered her unrestrained response. How could she have acted like that? Todd had meant the kiss as a friendly gesture, nothing more, and she had overreacted beyond belief. In front of a crowd of people, no less.

Meredith closed her eyes and shook her head slowly. She would have to apologize as soon as she got home. Or would it be better if she didn't mention it again? That was probably the best choice. She had already embarrassed her dearest friend in public; there was no need to rub salt in the wound by rehashing the incident. The last thing she wanted was to drive him away.

*

"Aunt Meredith!" Three small bodies hurtled down the

driveway as soon as Meredith stepped from the taxi. She opened her arms in a hug big enough to include them all and held them tight.

"Hey, Sis, good to see you!" Pete and Janice, her brother and sister-in-law, followed their young brood. They distributed Meredith's bags among themselves and carried them inside in one load, with Pete and the children all talking nonstop.

"Mom's in the kitchen with Gram. They decided we didn't have enough pies, so they're whipping out another batch."

"If I get a bike under the tree tomorrow, will you teach me to ride it, Aunt Meredith?"

"A bike won't fit under the tree, silly. Besides, Aunt Meredith is going to spend time with me."

"Come on, kids," Pete said. "Give your aunt a chance to catch her breath before you run her ragged." He shooed them into the backyard and ushered his sister into the kitchen, where she was met with more hugs from her parents and grandmother.

Meredith basked in the warmth and love of her family throughout the afternoon, reliving the holiday activities of her childhood by eating her dad's fabulous popcorn, drinking cinnamon-spiced apple cider, and looking through family albums. This was what she'd come home for.

As evening approached, she found herself checking her watch frequently, realizing the time for the Christmas program—*her* program—was rapidly approaching. She opted out of the traditional Scrabble game at the kitchen table, choosing instead to curl up in her father's recliner, where she could join Todd and the children in her imagination.

Meredith knew the exact moment the program should start. She pictured the first scene, where Gabriel appeared to Mary, hoping Gabriel would remember to face the audience instead of speaking to the wall behind him.

She could recite the script word for word from memory and followed along in her mind. How she wished she were there beside Todd, to encourage and prompt and worry right along with him!

Would the sheep remember to enter on cue? Would the wise men wait for theirs? Would Adam Wheeler buck Mary off on their way to Bethlehem?

"Where are you, honey?" Gram's voice broke into her thoughts. "You look like you're a million miles away."

Meredith started and grinned at her grandmother. "Why aren't you in the kitchen, clobbering everybody at Scrabble?"

"They thought I was too good for them. And they're right." The older woman settled into a nearby rocking chair. "But let's talk about you. We hardly get to visit anymore, since you moved away. Is anything bothering you?"

"No, no one. . .nothing," Meredith corrected. "Everything's fine. I was thinking about the children's program at my church. It's going on right now. I helped direct it," she added shyly.

Gram beamed. "I am thrilled to hear that. Your getting back into church is an answer to prayer. Is anything else going on?" she asked, giving Meredith a shrewd look.

"Not really," Meredith replied. *Except for having made an utter fool of myself today,* she added silently, remembering her behavior in the airport. Should she call Todd later to ask how the program went? Her pulse beat faster at the thought of hearing his voice. No, better wait until she got home. It would give him a chance to forget what she'd done. Meredith hoped Todd would be able to forget. She knew she wouldn't.

Lost in the memory of the kiss they'd shared, Meredith didn't notice when her grandmother slipped off to bed.

❧

Christmas Day came and went, and for the first time in her life, Meredith didn't feel her usual joy in the holiday. Thoroughly disgruntled, she laced up her walking shoes, donned a heavy jacket, then headed for the school track, hoping a good dose of exercise would help clear her mind and banish her blues.

Meredith strode along briskly, trying to sort out her feelings. This was the town where she grew up, where the rest of her family still lived. Coming back always meant coming home. . .until this trip. Now she felt an aching homesickness for her new life. She missed her church. She missed working with the kids.

She missed Todd.

Without him, life seemed flat and empty, and that scared her. Thoughts of their last moments together at the airport did nothing to ease her mind. Being held in Todd's arms had made her feel like she had finally come home after traveling a long, weary road.

That was a feeling she couldn't afford to dwell on, Meredith scolded herself severely, walking even faster. No matter how she felt about Todd, she knew he considered them friends, nothing more. If she wanted to keep that friendship intact, she'd better get a grip on her emotions before her return on New Year's Eve.

❧

Todd picked up the phone and punched in the number he'd gotten from Information. Before it could ring, he set the phone back in its cradle. "This is ridiculous," he muttered, running his fingers through his sandy hair. All he wanted was to hear Meredith's voice and assure himself she was doing well. She was, after all, his ministry project.

Yeah, right. His actions when Meredith was preparing to board her flight went way beyond a friendly interest.

Todd thumped the heel of his hand against his forehead. What had possessed him to do that? All he'd intended to do was shake the hand Meredith offered. Then he'd looked into those soft brown eyes and found himself pulling her into his arms, kissing her with increasing fervor.

He could have sworn she'd returned the kiss with equal gusto, but when the attendant's summons interrupted them, one look at Meredith's stricken face showed him he was wrong. She'd hurried off like a frightened deer, and he wasn't sure how to repair the damage he had done.

No more kisses, that's for sure. The last thing he wanted was to scare her off. But the truth was, he had enjoyed that kiss—enjoyed it a lot. It was going to be an uphill battle not to repeat it.

Todd picked up the phone and weighed it in his hand. One call couldn't hurt. Just one simple call to tell her how smoothly the children's program had gone. The kids had sailed through without a hitch. Todd fielded congratulations from the congregation, but the praise seemed empty without Meredith there to share it. One little call, just to let her know how pleased he was.

And how much he missed her.

Todd set the phone back down with a thud. If he took that course, he'd frighten her away for sure. He buried his face in his hands. How had a simple ministry action turned into a relationship he couldn't bear to lose? More important, what was he going to do about it?

Pushing his chair away from the table, Todd walked to his living room and knelt by the couch, determined to storm the gates of heaven until he had the answers he needed.

When he finally rose to his feet, he knew there was only one solution.

Chapter 9

Glistening like jewels against the night sky, soft flakes of snow were falling when Meredith's plane taxied up to the terminal.

Meredith squared her shoulders on her walk through the passenger tunnel. She would not—repeat, would not —make an idiot of herself again. Lifting her chin, she entered the waiting area, determined to maintain a pleasant air of friendliness.

Her step faltered when she spotted Todd waiting with a welcoming smile, and her resolve to play it cool almost went out the window. He didn't offer a hug, merely took her carry-on and headed to the baggage carousel. Meredith breathed a sigh of relief, knowing if he had taken her in his arms at that moment, her self-control would have been undermined completely.

Take it one step at a time. She walked beside Todd, trying not to stare at the handsome profile she had missed so much. *You'll be home before you know it.*

After Todd put the luggage in his trunk and opened the car door for Meredith, he slid behind the wheel and turned to look at her. "Is there any reason you need to go home right away?"

Meredith gaped at him. *Only to get away from you, so I don't have to fight for control.* "Why?" she asked cautiously.

"I thought we might see in the new year together." Todd put the car in gear and pulled out of the parking space. "If you don't have other plans, that is."

"I'm not dressed for—"

"You're fine," Todd said, nodding in approval at her heavy sweater, slacks, and boots. "You don't need to change."

Warning signals went off in Meredith's brain. Spending more time than necessary with Todd was a bad idea in her vulnerable state.

She knotted her fists in her lap. The more she was around him, the more she wanted to repeat their kiss and tell him how much she cared. She stole a sidelong glance at Todd, and he chose that moment to look her way, giving her a smile that melted her heart.

Was she crazy to turn down the chance to spend a few extra hours with him? *No, you're crazy if you put yourself through this. Don't risk your heart!*

"I'd like that," she said, telling her heart she'd start behaving tomorrow. It would be a new year, after all.

Todd pulled up next to the curb at the edge of a residential district. "I thought we'd walk," he said.

The snow had stopped falling, and a full moon emerged from behind the clouds, lighting their way. Todd led Meredith across the street to a large park, deserted at this time of night. "It opens up even more beyond the playground area," he explained. "Just like a walk in the country, but we'll be near enough to hear the church bells ring in the new year." He reached for Meredith's mittened hand, holding it firmly in his own.

Meredith's breath caught in her throat. Their tracks were the only ones in the newly fallen snow. They were alone, she and Todd, walking hand in hand through a snowy, moonlit wonderland.

It would have been the most romantic moment in Meredith's life, if only Todd shared her feelings. *You are here with your friend,* she reminded herself. *He's your buddy, your pal. Keep that in mind.*

As Todd promised, the back portion of the park opened up into a large, meadowlike area. They left the shelter of the trees and wandered across the broad expanse, their footsteps crunching in the snow. When they had nearly reached the other side, Todd stopped.

"I have something for you." He reached into his coat pocket with his free hand and produced a small, gift-wrapped package. "Call it a belated Christmas gift."

Meredith's momentary embarrassment at not having something to give him in return disappeared in the thrill of knowing Todd had bought her a gift. *He must have forgiven me for that kiss.* Eagerly she tugged at the shiny ribbon.

Inside the paper lay a small notebook. Meredith looked at Todd quizzically. *It's the thought that counts. After all, a gift is a gift.* But it was awfully. . .practical. The kind of impersonal gift you'd give an acquaintance from work. If she'd needed confirmation she and Todd were only friends, this was it.

Todd smiled, oblivious to her disappointment. "It's a replacement," he told her. "You need a new one for your list of things to do."

Meredith's eyes widened. "And how do you know about my list?" she demanded. She was gratified to see Todd squirm slightly.

"I found your notebook the day you dropped it a couple of months ago," he admitted. "I saw your name inside, so I put it on your desk."

"You saw more than just my name, didn't you? You saw my list of resolutions."

"Is that what they were? Resolutions? But why?"

It was Meredith's turn to squirm. "I wanted to make myself a better person," she mumbled. A new thought struck her. "But the other notebook is practically brand-new. Why would you think I need a replacement?"

Todd stepped closer, brushing her cheek with the backs of his fingers. "How many things do you still need to do to make yourself better?" he asked with a tender smile.

Meredith tried to remember what was left on the list. "Only a couple."

"Wrong," Todd corrected gently. "You don't need to do any of those things. You're wonderful just the way you are. You don't need the old list any longer, but I didn't want you to start the new year without a goal."

Meredith stared at him, confused. Hadn't he just said she didn't need to do any more of the things on the list?

"You're a wonderful person," Todd repeated. "There's only one more thing you need to do to be just about perfect. I've taken the liberty of writing it down for you." He tapped the notebook with his finger. "In there."

Meredith looked down at the notebook to hide her disappointment. Just when she thought Todd liked the real Meredith, he wanted to remake her, too. Some present!

Slowly opening the cover, Meredith turned the pages one at a time until she found one that contained a line of writing in a bold, masculine hand. In the moonlight, the carefully printed letters were plainly visible: *Marry Todd*.

A surge of joy rushed through her and tears filled her eyes. Looking up, she had to blink them away to see Todd's face clearly, sending them streaming down her cheeks. Her own sense of wonder was reflected in Todd's eyes.

"Will you marry me?" he asked in a husky whisper.

Unable to speak, Meredith nodded; she felt Todd's arms encircling her, drawing her into a tight embrace. When he lowered his head to hers, she gave herself up to his kiss, a kiss that assured her she was everything he wanted, just the way she was.

This was one New Year's resolution that would be easy to keep. . .and keep. . .and keep.

CAROL COX

Carol makes her home in rural northern Arizona. She and her pastor husband minister in two churches, so boredom is never a problem. Family activities with her husband, college-age son, and young daughter also keep her busy, but she still manages to find time to write. Since her first book was published in 1998, she has eight full-length titles and eleven novellas to her credit, with more currently in progress. To learn more about Carol and her books, visit her Web site at www.carolcoxbooks.com. She'd love to have you stop by!

Beginnings

by Peggy Darty

For Darla

Chapter 1

Erin McKinley lay in a hospital bed, staring solemnly at the snow drifting past her window. Tears filled her eyes as she fought back a wave of self-pity. It was two days before New Year's Eve, and unlike most New Yorkers out enjoying the holidays, she was nursing two fractured ribs and a bruise that resembled a plum on her left cheek. And. . .her "friend," the IV and its stand, went everywhere she went, which wasn't her idea of a great date for New Year's Eve.

She closed her eyes, and again the nightmare of the accident rushed through her mind. She had hesitated at the green light, waiting to make a right turn. Impatient over the ceaseless flow of traffic, Erin had misjudged her timing, and the white truck had slammed into the left side of her little black Honda. The airbag had popped out and the seat belt held her tight, as her little car spun in a full circle, landing in the parking lot of a video store.

Clinging to the steering wheel, she had stared into space, dazed for several minutes, aware only of the sharp pain in her left side and the crowd gathering around her car, staring curiously through the windshield.

For the next horrible hour she had been unable to think. Who should she call? The ambulance attendant wanted to know. Her parents in New Mexico? No, not yet. Her landlady in the apartment house? She didn't know how to reach her without her address book, which she had foolishly left on the desk.

She recalled Eleanor Sullivan's invitation for Erin to call if she needed anything; but she had already called once. She couldn't intrude again during the holidays.

No, she would endure this ordeal alone.

The tears she had been fighting now rolled freely down her cheeks as she turned to face the window. The move from New Mexico to New York had depleted her funds; she couldn't afford to go home for Christmas. So she had spent Christmas Day with the family of her law school counselor. Watching Eleanor's little daughters squeal with delight over their doll houses brought back memories of her own childhood. Erin had been one of seven children raised in a Christian home by wonderful parents.

She swallowed hard and lifted a corner of the crisp sheet to wipe her cheeks. She mustn't think about home now. She would start squalling so loud that a nurse might note on her chart: *patient extremely depressed.* Then—horror of horrors—she might be forced to stay another day for observation.

"Hey, man, you gotta get outa here!" a male voice shouted from the hall. Her head rolled on the pillow and she stared out at a thirty-something guy with long brown hair, scruffy beard, and weird-looking earring. Erin's eyes widened.

Another male voice from within the room made some reply, and soon rousing male laughter overflowed into the hospital corridor. Erin watched an older, stern-looking nurse rush into the room and close the door. The laughter died away.

What luck, Erin thought with a sigh. It was bad enough that she was stuck here; now she also was to be tortured by noisy, questionable neighbors—the kind who laughed a lot. The last thing she wanted to hear was the sound of happy voices.

The gray-haired nurse stepped into her room and shook her head disapprovingly. "Sorry about the guy across the hall. He has lots of visitors, but I've asked them to keep it down."

"Thank you." Erin forced a grateful smile and turned back to the window.

New York City was still half asleep at 8:30 in the morning, with many people taking the week off from their jobs in the tall skyscrapers that seemed to reach to the heavens.

She felt the blues creeping back. Here, at long last, she was in New York, fulfilling her big dream of attending law school at New York University. But where would she be spending the much-anticipated New Year's Eve? Not in Times Square watching the silver ball drop. No, she would see the festive crowd on television once again, from within the confines of her cramped apartment; but at least that would be better than this hospital room.

She willed herself to forget her problems and go back to sleep, but suddenly her senses were sharpened by the floating aroma of a wonderful perfume. She looked again toward the hallway and saw a tall, beautiful woman, dressed in a red silk pantsuit, carrying an armload of roses and colorful balloons.

Erin watched in fascination as the woman tossed back her long black hair and knocked gently on the rowdy neighbor's door.

A loud appeal for her to enter filled the air, followed by a clear baritone voice singing: "I'm looking for someone in red. . . ."

There was another roar of laughter and the door closed.

Who in the world is in that room? Erin wondered. The woman didn't fit with the mental image she had of the patient, whose guests so far had looked as though they had wandered in from the nearest bar or one of those body-piercing shops around Washington Square.

Now even the woman was laughing. Erin could distinctly hear her soft peal of laughter through the closed door.

She stared at the blank screen of her television. At least she had something to occupy her active mind now. She could try to figure out what sort of person her neighbor was, and she could gawk at the variety of guests. With that in mind, she slipped carefully out of bed, hugged the IV stand, and slowly rolled the stand with her toward her bathroom.

She was standing directly in front of her door when the door opposite her's opened and the pretty woman in red emerged, smiling back at the males in the room. Her dark eyes swung to Erin and widened.

Erin turned suddenly, trying to escape into the bathroom. Her bare foot caught on something, and she toppled, bringing the IV pole down with her. The crash was horrible, but at least she had fallen on her right side, not the left, where her ribs still ached.

"Are you all right?" The young woman had rushed in, and Erin was instantly enveloped in a cloud of perfume. "Don't move. I'll get the nurse," she said, looking younger than Erin had guessed from a brief glance.

"Wait. . . ," Erin began helplessly, before realizing she should not, in fact, try to get up on her own.

In the fall she had managed to loosen the needle in her arm, and now her plain white hospital gown was about to be trimmed in bright red. At about the time this catastrophe registered on her confused brain, two nurses were upon her, asking all sorts of questions.

"I'm fine," Erin managed to respond with as much dignity as she could muster.

With a nurse clutching each arm, she was ushered back to bed, the needle properly reinserted and her gown changed.

"Please don't try to get up without help if you feel lightheaded," she was cautioned by one of the nurses.

She bit her lip, nodded, and watched them leave. Her gaze stopped on the face of what she would have guessed was yet another homeless person, who gaped at her before hurrying into the room across the hall.

"Who's the dish next door?" she heard him ask loudly. "She's really zoned out."

The blood shot to her face and her temper boiled

over, confirming her father's philosophy about the red-hair-temper thing.

"At least I'm not rude," she yelled back.

Silence answered her before a door closed softly.

She whirled over to face the window. Why had she taken the bait? Now she had a fuss going with her neighbor, when what she needed was to ignore the characters in that room.

Another nurse entered her room and reached over her bed for the blood-pressure cuff. Erin offered her arm and forced a limp grin as the nurse slipped the cuff around her arm and began to pump. The white-haired little woman could have been her grandmother, and Erin wished, in fact, that she were.

"Your blood pressure is up a bit," she said, removing the cuff from her arm. "Try to relax. You may get to go home tomorrow."

Erin's eyes widened. "Do you think so?"

The nurse smiled patiently, her brown eyes warm and caring. "You seem to be doing okay."

"Yes, I'm doing fine," Erin agreed with a nod. "I just sort of tripped over my own clumsy feet," she said, trying to make light of her embarrassing sprawl.

The grandmotherly nurse made a note on Erin's chart, then smiled pleasantly. "Have you made your New Year's resolution?" she asked.

"To be less clumsy," she answered with a mirthful grin, then she added more seriously, "I should try to have more patience. That's my biggest problem."

The nurse laughed. "I think that's everyone's problem.

See you later," she said, hurrying off to spread more cheer.

The room was silent again; even the hall was silent. She slumped into her pillow, trying to nurse her wounded pride. Suddenly, the pleasant silence was interrupted by a slight creaking sound. *Something needs oiling*, she thought wearily, trying to relax. The creaking grew nearer, and she identified it as a rhythm, the rhythm of wheels turning. Her eyes flew to her open door, and she saw a white cast extended on a footrest. Her eyes moved up the wheelchair to a very handsome guy, looking silly in his pale green hospital gown.

"Hi, I'm Luke Mitchell, your neighbor," he said in the same deep baritone that had serenaded the beautiful woman.

She took a deep breath and tried not to stare at the face—she saw chocolate brown eyes, exactly the color of his hair, and a beguiling smile, all set in fair skin. He needed a shave, and the back of his hair popped up in a cute little wave, as though he had just risen off a pillow.

"I came to apologize for my rude friends," he continued pleasantly. "They obviously forgot their manners."

"It's okay," she said, rather stiffly. Then she noticed there was no wedding band on his left hand, and she perked up. "What happened to you?" she asked, studying the thick ankle cast, covered with signatures and humorous art, that stretched from his foot midway up his calf.

He followed her gaze to the cast. "A skiing accident in Vermont. It was my first day off in weeks. I broke my ankle and had to have some minor surgery, so I came back to NYU hospital. It's close to my apartment."

"Mine too," she said, tilting her head to look at him in a different way. He seemed like a nice guy, and it was too bad that he, too, had ended up here during the holidays. "I'm sorry about your ankle," she said, finding it easier to smile now.

"What about you? Aside from a nasty bruise on your cheek, I don't see any casts or bandages. What happened?" he asked, then frowned slightly, as though worried he was being too personal.

"A car accident."

His dark brows peaked curiously. "Really? I'm sorry. Anyone else hurt?"

She shook her head. "No, just me. I have a couple of broken ribs here on the left side, but I'm doing okay." Her hand crept up to smooth down her rumpled red hair. "I was impatient to get home and made a right turn when I should have waited. I'm not hurt, not like you," she said, pointing toward his ankle.

"Well, I was impatient too. Hadn't been on the ski slopes in awhile and just couldn't wait to go zigzagging down that trail. I should have made a few trial runs first."

They were both smiling at one another, saying nothing. He blinked, glanced down at the wheels of his chair, and began to roll backward. "Well, I hope you get outa here soon."

"Thanks. I'm sorry I yelled back earlier," she said, hoping to continue the conversation.

"Oh, you had every right." He grinned. "From now on, I'll try to keep the noise level to a minimum."

"It's proven to be pretty entertaining," she said, smiling into his eyes. "I've been bored to death here."

He paused, looked around the room, then back at her. "No company?"

She shook her head. "No flowers or balloons," she teased. "I just moved to New York and haven't made many friends yet. And I didn't want to alarm my folks in New Mexico. I'm okay, really. There's no point in upsetting anyone else's plans."

He paused and stared at her for a moment. "That's very thoughtful of you. You can tell me it's none of my business if you'd like, but may I ask what you're doing in the city all alone?"

"Going to law school at NYU," she replied. "I'm starting winter semester, but I came in December to get settled in an apartment and try to learn my way around. This city is a culture shock after living in a town of twenty-two thousand, pets included."

He chuckled. *A pleasant sound,* she thought, *complete with nice white teeth.* Her breath caught as she realized how much she enjoyed his laughter and the conversation they were having.

"I got my degree in criminal justice after I went through the police academy," he said, inching forward again.

"Really?" Her eyes widened, and her heart beat faster. At last she could have a conversation with someone who shared her interests. "So are you a policeman here in New York?" she asked, not wanting him to leave.

"Actually, I'm an investigator."

"Oh." The memory of his guests rose in her mind.

Were they ex-cons or people he had helped? What was the story?

"Hey, do you get up and around?" he asked suddenly. "I guess you have to drag the IV stand with you."

"Yeah, but it's getting to be my closest friend."

He laughed again. "Well, if you get lonesome, come on over to my room. I have more boxes of chocolate candy than I can possibly eat. And a game that requires two people." He hesitated. "Or I could roll back over here, and we could play Chinese checkers here." He grinned. "Something I learned as a kid to please my grandmother. It's her favorite game. She's in a nursing home in New Jersey now, but when she heard I was in the hospital, she had a Chinese checkers set delivered here. She thinks I still get a kick out of checkers at twenty-eight; can you believe that?"

"I certainly can."

"Why is that?" he asked, his brown eyes dancing.

"Regular checkers and Chinese checkers are a big pastime at the police station in Rock Cliff. That's my hometown," she added. "My father's the chief of police."

"Really?"

"Yes, but the point I was making is that my grandfather is the champion checkers player there. Nobody can beat him. He always used me as a guinea pig for a new strategy."

He grinned at her. "Then we definitely must have a game. Maybe you could teach me some of your grandfather's strategies."

"Okay," she said, looking into his dreamy brown eyes.

She smiled and sighed, unable to help herself.

"Well, bye for now," he said, glancing back at the hall. "I hear the heavy tread of Nurse Rutherford. She plays warden for my cell."

He turned and the creaking began in earnest, as though he were making a quick dash back to his room.

"Now Luke. . . ," a stern voice sounded down the hall.

Erin chuckled, amused by his little-boy antics. And yet . . .what a fun guy he seemed to be. And nice. And then she remembered the beautiful brunette with the balloons and roses, and reality crashed in. *The dream could turn into a nightmare,* she thought, sinking deeper into the mattress. But for now, it might be fun to play checkers and talk with him about his work. She was passionately interested in criminal law and all phases of police work.

She heard footsteps in the hallway, and this time she noticed a dignified, middle-aged man. He was carrying a Bible. When he spotted the number on the room across the hall, he entered.

Erin stared after him. Luke's parade of visitors never ceased to amaze her. At least he had a minister, or maybe this was some minister who had decided this was the perfect time to convert Luke. Either way, her interest was piqued again. Everything about Luke Mitchell fascinated her.

She was replaying in her memory all she had witnessed in the hallway since coming to her senses in the hospital room. She was actually grateful he was over there, if for no other reason than because the activity had kept her from being bored to death. She didn't want to watch all the holiday festivities on TV—she found that too depressing, given her present situation.

As she was gazing into the empty space of the corridor, the man with the Bible stepped out of the room on the other side of the hall and walked over to knock on her open door.

She tried to sit up straighter in her bed. "Hi," she said, smiling.

"May I come in for a minute?" he asked pleasantly. He was of medium height, was rather thin, and had graying brown hair and kind blue eyes.

"Of course," she said, glancing at the Bible he carried.

"I'm Luke's minister, Jim Wallace," he said, extending his hand.

"It's nice to meet you," she replied, shaking his hand and smiling. "I'm Erin McKinley. Would you like to sit down?" She indicated the armchair nearby.

"Thank you. Luke suggested you might appreciate a quick visit."

"Yes, I would. And I wouldn't mind a verse or two of Scripture and a prayer," she said, suddenly homesick again. "I'm from New Mexico, and I couldn't go home for Christmas." She bit her lip, unable to say more.

He nodded, seeming to understand all she wasn't saying. He told her about the church where he ministered and invited her to join them, and she was pleased.

"I would love to come visit sometime," she said, careful not to obligate herself. "I don't have a church home yet."

He nodded. "Then let us be your home until you find one that suits you. If we aren't quite what you're looking for, that's perfectly all right."

She smiled at him, pleased by his kindness, as he lowered his head and turned the pages of his Bible. "Why don't I read the same passage to you that I just read to Luke?"

"Fine," she said.

"I'm reading the NIV version of Isaiah 40, verses 28 through 31. I think the passage is appropriate for anyone going through a difficult time," he said, and began to read:

> *The Lord is the everlasting God, the Creator of the ends of the earth. He will not grow tired or weary, and his understanding no one can fathom.*
>
> *He gives strength to the weary and increases the power of the weak.*
>
> *Even youths grow tired and weary, and young men stumble and fall; but those who hope in the Lord will renew their strength. They will soar on wings like eagles; they will run and not grow weary, they will walk and not be faint.*

She listened intently as he read the words that were so familiar to her. It was a passage her father had read often during their family devotions.

When Pastor Wallace finished and looked up at her, she smiled warmly. "Thank you. May I see your Bible for a moment?"

"Of course." He handed the Bible to her.

She scanned down to Isaiah 41:13. "This is my favorite verse: 'For I am the Lord, your God, who takes hold of your right hand and says to you, Do not fear; I will help you.' "

She took a deep breath, closed the Bible, and handed it back to him.

"Well," he said, smiling at her. "You obviously know your Bible."

"Yes, I do."

He did not ask her what had happened or why she had landed in the hospital. She appreciated his gentle tact as he stood up, tucking the Bible under his arm.

"Now would you like to pray?" he asked.

She nodded, closing her eyes; she felt the warmth of his hand as it closed gently over hers. His prayer was short—a simple word of praise that she was healing and a request that she be restored to good health soon.

When he finished the prayer and she opened her eyes, she was touched nearly to the point of tears. "Your visit has brightened my day," she said. "I can't thank you enough."

"I'm glad to be of service. And you can thank Luke for sending me over. I'm afraid I don't go from room to room as some ministers do; I go only where I know the patient."

She nodded. "I'll be sure to thank him. Happy New Year," she said on impulse, recalling that was what everyone was wishing one another these days.

"Thank you, and the same to you."

After a few more words of encouragement, he left. Erin stared after him, feeling warm and loved. Amazing what a fellow Christian could do, and having the Bible read to her soothed her frazzled nerves.

He's right, she thought. *I should be praising God that I wasn't seriously injured. A broken ankle right now would have been a real nuisance.* That thought led her back to Luke Mitchell.

She decided it didn't matter about the brunette today. He was just a friend who had been very nice, and she didn't feel so alone anymore.

A nurse came in to check on her, and Erin asked for her makeup kit in the dresser drawer. "I think there's a hairbrush somewhere, too."

The nurse opened the drawer. "Your purse is in the safe, but someone has thoughtfully removed the things a woman needs," she said with a wink as she pulled the lap tray around and placed the makeup kit, hairbrush, and a hand mirror on it. "Anything else?"

Erin took a deep breath and decided to plunge in. "After I freshen up, I'd like to get out of bed and try walking around. I know that the sooner I prove I'm strong, the sooner I'll get to go home. And of course you'll note that on your chart, won't you?" She grinned at the nurse.

"Of course. We encourage patients who are willing to get up and move around to do so. You're right. When we're sure you're strong enough, I think you'll be dismissed. But be careful," she added. "In fact, I'll help you out of bed when you're ready. Just ring the bell."

"Thank you," Erin replied, diving into her thick kit.

She was well organized when it came to having what she needed wherever she went. Soon, she had foundation, blush, mascara, and lip gloss in place, and then she tackled her thick hair. Wincing, she dragged the brush through the tangles and tried to coax the wild red curls into submission. At last, when she felt she was presentable, she rang for the nurse.

"I brought a robe," the nurse said thoughtfully.

"Oh." Erin looked down at the thin hospital gown. "Good idea. I wasn't exactly planning a trip to the hospital when I left home."

The nurse seemed to understand. "We try to keep a few of these around for emergencies," she said as she helped Erin get out of bed and pulled the plain white robe over her gown. Then she slipped Erin's feet into the soft scuffs the hospital provided.

"Thanks for everything." She smiled at the nurse, who steadied the IV pole while Erin stood up and gained her balance.

The nurse returned her smile. "You're welcome. You look very nice. Where are we going?"

Erin was embarrassed to say her eventual destination was the room across the hall, so she merely smiled at the nurse. "After you're sure I'm steady on my feet—and I do feel steady—I'll just wander around."

The nurse seemed to understand. "Fine."

They slowly entered the hall, walked halfway up toward the nurses' station, and then she turned to the nurse. "I can make it on my own. I'm not lightheaded or unsteady," she said confidently.

"Okay. You seem to be the determined type," the nurse added with a grin. "Just call if you need anything." She patted her arm, then hurried into another room.

Erin moved cautiously down the corridor toward her

room. Once she reached Luke's door, closed for a change, she tapped softly, hoping he didn't have a visitor.

"Come in," the deep voice rang out.

She pushed open the door, careful to hang onto her IV stand to prevent another disaster. Slowly the room came into view, and she had a fleeting impression of a cozy gift shop. Red, purple, and green balloons floated in the air. Green plants filled the window sill, and one hanging basket of lush ferns dangled from a corner. A sweet fragrance filled the air, and she spotted the bouquet of huge red roses prominently displayed on the wall dresser.

She looked back at the hospital bed where Luke reclined lazily, his arms propped over his head on the pillow.

"Hey there," he called, looking pleasantly surprised as he absently brushed through his thick dark hair. "I just had the door closed to keep the warden from breathing down my neck. And I've been on the phone," he added.

She glanced at his bedside table, where the yellow page of a legal pad was ink-scribbled with numbers, then she looked back at him.

"I came to thank you for sending your pastor over. It was nice to have someone read the Bible and say a prayer for me."

"Pastor Wallace is a great guy," he said.

"He seems to be."

"Still want to play a game of checkers?" he asked, his dark eyes challenging her.

"Sure," she said, moving slowly toward the bed.

"Here, have a seat," he said, indicating an armchair beside his bed. Then he began to wrestle with the metal rail on the side of the bed facing her. He stopped suddenly and sent an aggravated glance toward the cast on his ankle, propped on a pillow. "This cast is coming off later in the afternoon, thank God. And it's possible, by begging and pleading, they'll give me a pair of crutches and let me out on probation."

"Then who'll be your warden?" she teased, gripping the back of the mauve leather chair and inching around to take a seat.

He chuckled. "Nobody. And I'll be perfectly happy to be alone."

Alone. Her smile deepened. That meant the brunette wouldn't be around. "So where's the board and marbles?" she asked, trying to lower herself gracefully into the chair while keeping a sturdy grip on the IV stand. The last thing they needed was the warden rushing in to scold her, too.

"Right here." He turned to a side table, drawn up close to his bed, and began to lift the board and the zip-top plastic bag that held the marbles.

She reached over and pushed the button on the side of the rail, then put the palm of her hand on the railing and pushed. It finally moved, but her injured ribs responded with a sharp pain, and she grit her teeth and turned loose. Then her IV cord began to dangle precariously.

"Got it," he said as his arm shot out to steady the stand. His face was dangerously close to hers for a moment, and she inhaled the tantalizing scent of aftershave. She could see he had shaved since his visit to her room earlier.

His gaze locked on hers for a moment, then he reached back for the extra pillow under his head. "If you put this in your lap, it will steady the board. There's nothing wrong with my ribs, so I can do the maneuvering here."

"Okay." She situated the pillow on her lap, and he placed the colorful game board on the pillow. Then he opened the bag of marbles.

"What's your favorite color?" he asked, looking up from the assortment of colored marbles.

"Green," she replied.

He grinned. "Mine too. But I'll take the blue as a personal sacrifice for your visit."

She laughed softly as they began to put their marbles in the little holes on the board. She could hear the low melody of Christmas carols from his radio, but she no longer felt sad. In fact, she was feeling pretty good.

"Well, at least I don't have to tell you how to play," he said, a twinkle in his dark eyes.

"Nope. Just be careful. I'm warning you in advance: I'm good," she said, challenging him with a mischievous grin.

"I have no doubt of that," he said, looking equally mischievous.

She turned her attention to the checker board, and they began their game in earnest. The quiet sound of music and the tap-tap of marbles being moved around the board filled the room. Their concentration was fully centered on the game. After a couple of moves, which he immediately checked, she could see that he was a tough opponent. She stared at the board, contemplating the best moves; but for every jump she took, he had a strong defense. The game slowed down as each fought to win.

By the time they were down to six marbles each, he

heaved a sigh and leaned back to look at her. "Man, I didn't know how tough this was going to be. I'll need a sedative after this."

She half grinned, her eyes never leaving the board. She racked her brain to think of one of her grandfather's tricks and saw a solution. She kept her eyes and hand centered on the right side of the board, and she could see that he was relaxing, thinking he had her. When he moved a marble to block her, she quickly jumped the lonely little marble in the left corner over two of his.

"Hey," he yelled, "you tricked me."

"Sure; that's part of the game," she shot back. "You're the one who's heading in the wrong direction."

He stared at the marbles in amazement, then looked at her with a begrudging respect. "You really are good. If it won't sound too egotistical, may I say you're the first to beat me since Granny?"

They both were laughing when the "warden" came marching in, halting abruptly beside Erin's chair, her square, no-nonsense face looking over the situation. "I was just about to leave," Erin said meekly as Luke quickly scooped up the remaining marbles. She suspected it was to conceal the fact that she had defeated him, rather than to appease the stately RN he referred to as his warden.

The woman cracked a smile at Erin. "I hope you beat him." Then she looked wickedly at Luke, who made a face at her as he deposited the bag of marbles back on the table, then reached for the board.

"I did," Erin said, grinning and gloating over her hard-earned victory.

"She cheated," he objected loudly, suddenly looking as spoiled as her brothers when she had beaten them at shooting hoops.

"I did not cheat," she said, tossing the pillow at him.

"Okay, you two. Let's not get our blood pressures up." The nurse reached down to help Erin from her chair. "Congratulations. Not everyone is sharp enough to show this young man he's not as smooth as he thinks he is."

"I don't think. . . ," Luke began; he finished with a sigh. He was obviously outnumbered and overpowered.

"Yes, you do," the nurse called over her shoulder as she put her hand under Erin's elbow, steering her and the IV stand from the room.

When they reached the door of Luke's room, Erin looked at the nurse. "Just a second, please," she said, turning slowly to face Luke. "Thanks for letting me beat you. I'll be happy to play again. Maybe it won't be so difficult for you next time."

The tall, heavy-set nurse threw back her head and laughed so hard that Luke's muffled words were drowned out as they crossed the corridor to Erin's room.

"He really is a nice guy," the nurse whispered, as she helped Erin back into bed and smoothed the covers.

"I know," Erin whispered back, "but I beat him fair and square."

The nurse was still laughing when she left the room.

Chapter 2

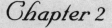

Erin was propped up in bed, waiting for the doctor; today she would prove she was healthy enough to be dismissed. After all, this was New Year's Eve; surely the man had a heart.

A *thump-thump* preceded Luke as he entered her room, dressed in navy sweats and white sweatshirt. He looked extremely proud of himself, with new crutches tucked firmly under his arms and his left foot hoisted slightly as he swung himself over toward her bed.

"I'm leaving in a few minutes," he gloated, his dark eyes twinkling mischievously.

"Oh, you are?" She grinned at him. "Well, I'll be going home later in the day, unless the doctor decides to be unreasonable."

His eyes swept over her freshly brushed hair and clean, smiling face. "I don't think he'd have the heart. I assume you live in the vicinity, since you're going to NYU and you're in this hospital."

"I live off Washington Square in one of those old townhouses that has been chopped up into a dozen apartments." When she mentioned the street, his grin widened.

"You only live a few blocks from my place. Washington Square is my beat."

"Oh, really? Are the students that notorious?" She enjoyed teasing him.

He gave a wry grin. "Have you spent much time around the square at night?"

She thought about it. "Not much. What have I missed?"

"Drug dealers and prostitutes," he whispered. "But I don't think you'd fit either category."

She lifted an eyebrow. "I should hope not."

"Don't worry. My work covers the broader Washington Square area, which includes some of the other streets. You're in a good location."

"But I planned to walk to school. . . ."

"That's okay. I'll tell you the areas to avoid when I check on you."

"You're going to check on me?"

"I feel it's my duty."

"Your duty?"

"Well. . .maybe I just want to. Could I have your phone number?"

She hesitated.

"Don't tell me you're one of those people who won't give out a phone number?"

"It's a new phone. I have to stop and think."

At that exact moment a female voice called out, "Luke?"

"In here." He turned and glanced toward the hall. "I'm across the hall," he announced to the world.

The pretty dark-haired woman, the woman of the

roses, popped her head in the door, wearing a black, belted trench coat with a hood. Erin had stared longingly at one just like it in the window of Macy's.

"Hey, good looking," Luke grinned. "Come on in."

Erin caught her breath, glancing from one to the another.

"Would you mind introducing yourself to Erin McKinley?" he asked, looking from the pretty brunette back to Erin.

The girl entered the room, smiling. "Hi. I'm Lane Mitchell." She looked from Erin to Luke, then back to Erin. "I happen to be this character's twin sister." The girl smiled adoringly at Luke.

Erin sighed. "Tell me something. Do I look gullible? My left ribs are broken, not my brain."

The girl stared at her in a way that made Erin feel she was the only one in on the joke.

"She's starting law school at NYU," Luke explained patiently.

"Then I know you are not gullible. In fact, you must be very intelligent. I probably couldn't score high enough to get into undergrad over there."

Erin could feel the blush creeping up her cheeks. "I. . . I didn't mean to be impolite. I thought. . ." She faltered, still not sure if this was a joke.

"She thinks we're kidding her about being twins," Luke whispered loudly, grinning at the confused young woman.

Lane's dark eyes flicked back to Erin, and suddenly Erin was struck dumb by the resemblance shared by the two.

"I am Lane Mitchell," she said, opening her shoulder bag and pulling out her wallet. "See?" She flipped open her billfold and thrust her driver's license in Erin's face.

Erin looked sheepishly at the identification that proved who she was. "It doesn't do you justice," Erin replied meekly.

"Thanks. Now shall I go get Luke's billfold or should we just call Mom? And by the way, we have an older brother, Bryan."

"Maybe you should call Bryan. He's the most practical member of our family," Luke offered helpfully, as though they were dealing with a very serious matter.

"I'll call Mom," Lane decided, turning for Erin's phone.

"That isn't necessary," Erin said, touching Lane's hand. "I'm sorry."

The girl grinned, looking exactly like her mischievous brother. "It's okay. I realize this guy is a prankster. You probably don't know when to believe him. But I assure you, we're twins." She swatted at him playfully. "Besides, he isn't my type. I prefer the Nordic look."

"Blond hair, blue eyes. Sounds like Scott," Luke sighed.

"Lane, how do you put up with him?" Erin asked, trying to laugh away her embarrassment.

"I don't," she answered honestly. "Until he goes off hot-dogging on a ski trail and ends up being dependent —like this." She waved at his crutches.

"They make me less dependent now," he said, patting one crutch.

Lane was not smiling. "Are you ready to go? That's why I'm here, you know." She looked back at Erin. "Sorry if he's been giving you a hard time."

Erin shook her head. "He hasn't." She cupped her palm to the side of her mouth and loudly announced, "I've already beaten him at his favorite game." Luke ignored the comment as he hobbled toward the door.

Lane was laughing, looking from Luke back to Erin. "He may have met his match in you," she said, her dark eyes flashing approval.

"I think we've both just been fighting boredom." She watched Luke turn back at the doorway and glance in her direction. "He's a nice guy. And I'm pleased to meet you, Lane. I must have seemed pretty rude."

Lane shook her head, and the dark hair swirled. For the hundredth time, Erin wished she were a brunette instead of a redhead.

"What happened to you? Or do you not want to talk about it?" Lane added quickly.

Erin had to laugh. "I don't know why I ever doubted you two were twins. Not only do you look alike, you even seem to think alike. He asked the same question in almost the exact same way."

"Oh," Lane replied; yet there was still a look of confusion in her eyes.

Erin explained about the accident and ended by apologizing again to Lane.

"Do you have someone to take you home from the hospital?" Lane asked with concern.

"Yes, I do. Thanks." It would be a taxi driver, but no way would she admit that to these two who were probably nice enough to insist on coming back for her.

"Well, good luck," Lane called, following her brother out the door.

Luke's head popped back around the door a few minutes later. "You didn't give me your phone number, but I can always call information."

Before she could answer, the *thud-step-thud* continued on down the hall. She wanted to shout the number out to him, but he was already gone. And she had already made a fool of herself.

Impulsively, she pressed the call button for a nurse. She was going to demand her doctor stop by as soon as possible.

Chapter 3

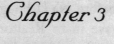

Erin stood in her studio apartment, suddenly feeling confused, disoriented, and alone. Her eyes rushed to the small Christmas tree at the window—a tiny thing, sparsely decorated. Underneath the tree, the presents from home were unwrapped but remained in their boxes. It was a pleasant reminder of her loved ones in New Mexico.

She blinked and tried to pull herself back to the present. She had done the paperwork in her hospital room, propped up in a chair. Then a nurse had wheeled her down to the hospital entrance and helped her into a waiting taxi, which drove her home. Since she had taken little with her, there was little to bring back, so that wasn't the hard part. Being here was.

Her eyes roamed over the cramped apartment which did not yet feel like home. She had rented it furnished. When Mrs. Brantley, her landlord, told her this apartment was compact, she had used the right word, for sure. The rent had been the one thing she liked, and the fact that it was in a respectable neighborhood. Mrs. Brantley had bragged that the home had been built in the 1830's, when the area was quite exclusive.

"But that was before NYU bought up the property and homeowners gave in to Realtors' offers; now look what we have," Mrs. Brantley had said as she flung an arm toward the window.

Erin knew the sixty-something landlady was referring to the boxlike structures so numerous around campus. She was glad she had followed the advice of a college friend and had gone through a broker to get this place.

"My grandfather never gave in, and we've kept the house in the family," she said proudly, straightening her tiny frame to its maximum extent.

Mrs. Brantley had omitted the fact that the heating system was antiquated, along with the plumbing. And there were stained spots on the ceiling that had been ignored. Still, Erin had a fondness for old brownstones and this type of architecture, which was rare in New Mexico.

She took a deep breath and tried to see the possibilities of what could be done here.

The living area was near the door, with a tiny burgundy velvet love seat that had seen better years. A slightly scarred end table and lamp huddled beside it, with the one redeeming feature being a small, sturdy desk with a good reading lamp for studying. She sauntered toward the end of the living area to the kitchen. The dining area was a small counter with bar stool. Next to it was an apartment-size refrigerator and a small microwave on a tiny cabinet. If she dropped a knife between the refrigerator and counter, there would be no hope of getting it out of the crack between them. She tilted her head to the side, wondering how Mrs. Brantley had managed to squeeze so much into one corner.

She turned toward her "bedroom" on the opposite wall. A dresser/bureau were combined, and a twin bed adjoined an ample closet.

She walked over and carefully stretched out on the bed, still very protective of her sore ribs. She closed her eyes and felt a rush of silence closing in over her. Well, at least the mattress was comfortable. When she regained a bit of strength, she would simply have to occupy herself with making the place feel like home. Her mom was the one with the knack for doing that. She smiled at the memory of the little tricks Mom had used to convert a simple stucco house into a pretty home.

Erin opened her eyes and stared at her little tree. Despite the shiny little balls and the personal ornaments she had brought from home, without the lights turned on, the tree looked pathetic. Time to take it down. Then she would get some plants—lots of plants.

"Plants are the best way to spruce up a room," her mother's words echoed in her mind.

She tried to force herself to think positively. She had prayed over her decision to go to law school. Particularly at NYU. When she got a stipend, that sealed her decision. Yes, she felt she had made the right choice. The rent suited her budget, and she could walk the eight blocks to school until her car was repaired.

The car! She turned her head on the pillow and stared at the beige phone on the dresser beside her. What had she done with the business card the tow truck driver had given her? She had called from the hospital and learned the name of the garage where the car was towed, but she hadn't the courage to go further.

Just thinking made her feel more weary than ever. Everything was suddenly requiring a huge effort. As she stared at the phone, trying to summon the energy to do something constructive, a shrill ring broke the silence. She jumped, flinching when her ribs reacted as the phone rang again. By the third ring, she had stretched across the pillow and managed a weak hello. Surely someone had the wrong number.

The deep baritone voice she had first heard across the hall in the hospital vibrated over the wire to her.

"Erin?" he asked doubtfully.

"Hi. Yes, it's me."

"You made it home okay?"

"Yes. And you?"

"Oh sure. I felt guilty for not waiting around to see that you got home, but to be honest, I'd had enough of those four walls, not to mention my well-intentioned nurse who will give me nightmares for weeks."

Erin laughed. "You mean the 'warden'?" she asked, remembering the way he had described his nurse when Erin first met him.

"None other. But to quickly change the subject, I wanted to let you know I've checked on your car for you."

"You have?"

"I spoke with the service manager, and he promised to have it ready for you as soon as possible."

"He did?" she gasped. "How bad is it? Or maybe I don't want to know," she said, her spirits dropping again.

"Yes, you do want to know, because the car was not that badly damaged. You'll come out fine. After your deductible, your insurance will take care of everything."

He spoke with such confidence that Erin smiled. Thank God she'd had the presence of mind to contact her insurance company. Then she remembered the older couple in the big truck, and her heart raced in panic.

"Those people. . .the truck? I couldn't find out anything. I mean, they weren't admitted to my hospital. I checked that."

"They're okay. They were only shaken up with some bruises from the air bags. He wasn't going fast, and since the front of his truck hit you on the driver's side, you were the one who was hurt. Those big all-service vehicles are built sturdy and high. There was some damage to the front bumper, but nothing that can't be easily repaired. I'll call them if you want."

She sighed. "I would appreciate it. And then I'll phone them and apologize."

"You already did," he answered gently. "The tow truck guy told me you kept saying over and over how sorry you were. The couple was more concerned about you. They didn't even have to go to a hospital; they just went to a small clinic near their home to be checked out. So don't worry; God was with all of you."

"Boy, don't I know that!" She remembered little about the accident after the truck struck her. She only remembered telling the ambulance attendant that she didn't need to get in, that she was okay. Then she must have passed out.

"You're suddenly quiet. Are you okay?"

She sighed. "I'm getting there. Thanks for all you've done. I had been trying to think where I should call about the car. By the way, how did you get these details so quickly?"

"I'm an investigator, remember? It wasn't complicated to get a copy of the accident report faxed to my apartment. From the report, it was easy to track everyone down."

Easy for you, she thought, still amazed by what he had accomplished.

"As for your car," he continued smoothly, "The front and back door on the driver's side will have to be replaced, but otherwise it's fine."

She swallowed down the egg-sized lump in her throat. "I'm so relieved to hear that. I was afraid it was totally wrecked."

"Nope. But you are going to need transportation until your car is repaired. Your insurance covers a rental car, you know."

She blinked, unsure of what her insurance covered and feeling stupid. From now on she'd read every word in those thick policies.

"What kind of car do you want?"

She shook her head. "It doesn't matter. Just something economical—whatever my policy allows," she answered and frowned. Where had she put the policy?

"There'll be some paperwork, but I can arrange to have a car delivered to you."

"Well," she said with a smile, "you are a top-notch investigator. Since you're so good at handling this type of situation, I'll just ask you to choose the car, if you don't mind."

She felt as though the heavy blanket of gloom had magically disappeared, and now she was almost overwhelmed with relief and happiness.

"Luke, I don't know how to thank you. I mean. . ." She remembered his ankle. "Could I run an errand for you? I'll be happy to pick up anything you need, once I get the car."

"Actually, I do have a craving for some fresh boiled shrimp."

Fresh boiled shrimp! Her mind raced to the location of the nearest seafood market. "You mean now?"

He chuckled. "Mom's already been here with her special double fudge brownies, my favorite, and roast beef and vegetables."

"Oh," she said limply. Then why did he need shrimp? Or why didn't he ask his mother to get it? Maybe his mother lived over in New Jersey. If he was asking her a favor, the least she could do was comply. If he craved fresh boiled shrimp, well, she'd find some!

"Okay, assuming you're all set for meals today, will tomorrow be soon enough for the shrimp? And is there anything else, sir?" she added impishly. "Imported caviar, perhaps?"

He chuckled. "As a matter of fact, there is. I don't like taking pain pills."

"Neither do I," she admitted. "I am now to the aspirin stage. Have you tried—"

"Aspirin won't make me forget the pain. But. . .you know what would?" he asked.

"Uh. . .no."

"Seeing a certain redhead with big hazel eyes and a beautiful smile would make me forget about my ankle."

She laughed again, appreciating his sense of humor and trying not to allow the compliment to go to her head. "Okay, give me your address. And what time do you want the shrimp?"

"Hey, not so fast," he chuckled. "To be perfectly honest, I already have the shrimp."

"That was sneaky of you," she said, trying to pout but failing miserably. He really just wanted to see her?

"I know. Sorry. And please don't think I'm asking you to hail a taxi and come find me. JJ—that's the rude character from the hospital—can actually be very polite. He's promised to be a perfect gentlemen when he comes to pick you up. And he'll take you back home whenever you want to go," he added, as though she needed to know he was making no demands on her.

She took a deep breath, recalling JJ, with the long brown hair and scruffy beard. She tapped her fingernail against the phone as her mind replayed the conversation.

"Something tells me I should be wary of you," she said, trying to act suspicious, although she felt she could trust him.

"Why?"

"You're pretty smooth. And by the way, I don't like to feel that I've been manipulated. Not that I don't appreciate what you've done about the car and all. . . ."

"Smooth? No. Manipulative? Absolutely not. Stubborn, yes. I'll honestly admit to that. Remember when I said I would see you again? Well, I meant it. But if you feel you're being manipulated, I'll package everything up, come to your place, and prepare dinner for you. Is that being manipulative?"

She had to laugh. "No, it's called being nice. We could wait a couple of days on dinner, don't you think?"

"In a couple of days I may be stuck on a case that's a twenty-four-hour job. Unfortunately, in my line of work, time off is a luxury usually afforded only to those who have been with the department long enough to have seniority. And have you forgotten this is New Year's Eve?"

She blinked. Actually, she had. She ran her hand through her hair, grateful she had shampooed it in the shower before she left the hospital. "Then I guess I can't say no."

"You could," he assured her. "It's strictly up to you. You really don't owe me any favors," he added in a gentle voice.

The voice reached through the phone to her, making her feel warm and special all the way down to her toes.

"I'd love to have shrimp with you. And I'll be ready around six, if that's when JJ can pick me up."

"Great!" He sounded genuinely pleased. "Wear your most comfortable outfit."

Her most comfortable outfit. That would be her red flannel pajamas. She smiled to herself. Maybe her other jeans were clean. "Is there anything I can bring?"

"Just your sense of humor. I'll need a laugh or two after I tackle the paperwork on this desk."

"I keep it with me at all times," she quipped, and they both laughed before he hung up.

Chapter 4

A s Erin rode the dozen or so blocks to Luke's place, she had a totally different impression of JJ than she'd had earlier. Meticulously polite and conservatively dressed, his hair and his beard were neatly groomed. And the huge gold hoop earring in his ear was gone.

"Amazing how close you two live," JJ commented as they drove past the purple flags symbolizing NYU.

Erin looked at the streets, alive with street vendors, as JJ's sleek black sports car zipped along beside the grassy park in Washington Square. The carolers were gone now, along with the Santas and the bell ringers at the Salvation Army booth.

"Seen any of our famous sites since you've been here?" he asked, attempting another conversation.

"Well. . ." She leaned back against the smooth leather seat. "I've only been here a couple of weeks. After getting moved in, the most memorable thing I've done is walk over and take a picture of the house where Mark Twain once lived."

"I forgot about that. He lived on 10th, right?"

Erin nodded. "Mark Twain is my father's hero. Aside

from that, I've just been hanging out at the Strand, wandering around staring at all the books there. Did you know they have more than two million books in that place?"

"No, but I don't read much. Luke says you're going to law school at NYU?"

"Yes, I am." She glanced through the window as he turned down a cobblestone alleyway and slowed before one of the boxy little brick buildings.

"These were once the stables for the fashionable homes of the 1830s," he said. "Of course, everything has changed now."

"Even the stables," Erin said with a smile as he cut the engine and came around to open the door. As soon as they reached the wooden doorstep, the door swung open and Luke was staring down at her.

"Hi," she said.

"Hi. Told you I'd be casual." He indicated his deep-green sweatshirt, the expensive kind, and navy sweat pants.

"How's the ankle?" She looked down at his bare feet. The left one was wrapped in an elastic bandage.

"Just as I had expected. When you arrived, the pain disappeared."

Erin laughed while JJ cleared his throat from behind them. "I'll come back for Erin when you page me," he said, backing down the steps.

"Thanks," she called over her shoulder as Luke took her hand and led her inside. "I'm afraid it looks as though Scrooge lives here. No Christmas decorations," he explained, grinning down at Erin. "I spent Christmas with the folks in New Jersey, then took off for the ski slopes of

Vermont. Didn't see any point in putting up a tree before I left, only to be taken down when I returned."

"Wish I had followed your plan, only there isn't much to take down at my place," she said as her eyes ran over the living area. It was small, with a brown suede sofa and a few green-striped pillows. Her eyes moved from the pillows to the same pattern in the flanking club chairs. Then her attention was captured by the sound of gurgling water, and she turned to see a copper fountain on the coffee table. Water played over three leaf-shaped tiers and dribbled down to tiny pebbles.

"Like it?" he asked.

"I adore it." She knelt on the dark wooden floor to study the little fountain. "I know this is a silly question, but how does it work?"

"A pump recirculates the water," Luke explained. "I enjoy the sound."

"Mmm." Erin nodded dreamily. "Sounds like a mountain stream trickling over smooth rocks."

"Mountain streams in New Mexico?"

"We vacationed in Colorado every summer when I was growing up."

"I've never been to New Mexico," he said, helping her to her feet. "What's it like?"

Erin hesitated, thinking about her home state. "It certainly doesn't have the drama of New York or the spectacular mountains of Colorado, but it does have a rugged kind of beauty, with huge mounds of red rock, wide open spaces that stretch for miles between the towns, and most of the towns are small. The sunsets are beautiful, and sometimes the clouds are so close, it seems you could reach up and touch them."

"Sounds nice. Would you like to come into the kitchen? I'm just putting the finishing touches on dinner."

"That has a nice ring to it," she said, following him into a U-shaped cubicle of black and white. "I'm not accustomed to a man in the kitchen. Cooking, I mean. My three brothers are disasters when it comes to cooking, and Dad isn't much better, with the exception of his Sunday morning omelet."

"Oh, he does that?"

"With pride. I think the challenge for him is holding out the skillet to flip the omelet over like a real chef. Naturally, he requires an audience for this performance, and we were all hauled out of bed to watch." She laughed. "I think it was a sneaky device on the part of our parents to get us out of bed so we could start getting ready for Sunday school."

She glanced from the black and white interior across to the eating bar, open to the living room.

"I like the color on those walls," she said, pointing. "Do you know what shade of paint that is?"

He was tying the long strings of an apron that featured a large cartoon of a chef in white apron and cap, gaping in frustration at the flames coming from his oven.

"The paint? Actually, I'm not sure, even though I was the master of the mix. I painted the place when I first moved in. The walls were a dull beige, just like the carpet. I discovered hardwood floor under the carpets, ripped up the carpeting, sanded and varnished the floors, and—but you asked about the paint."

"But I love hearing what you've done," she encouraged.

"Okay. Well, since there weren't many windows here and the mood was sort of depressing, I found myself longing for sunlight. I accomplished the look I finally arrived at by mixing a soft gold paint with a cream-colored one, experimenting with a patch on the wall until the patch looked like pale sunlight when it dried."

"Great idea! Are all the walls like that? Except for the kitchen?"

"Yep." He was opening the door to the refrigerator. "When I find something I like, I usually stay with it." He was watching her as he spoke. "Want to set the table?" He opened a cabinet where dishes were kept.

"Gladly." She reached for two sturdy white plates rimmed with a thin stripe of green and gold. She turned to the eating bar, which obviously was their dining area, for two mossy-green place mats sat on the white vinyl surface, and a fat green candle gave the pleasant aroma of fresh pine.

"The silverware is in the drawer to your right." He had removed a huge crystal serving bowl lined with lettuce leaves and topped with mounds of huge pink shrimp from the refrigerator and placed it on the eating bar. Tucked down in the center of the shrimp was a tiny dish of cocktail sauce.

"Looks great," she said, placing the silver flatware beside the plates as he returned from the refrigerator with another crystal bowl, this one full of fruit salad.

"Compliments of Mom," he commented, with a glance at Erin.

"All of this?"

"Just the fruit salad. I peeled the shrimp and opened the jar of sauce. Oh, and I opened the box of crackers and put ice in the water goblets." He hesitated. "Or would you rather have juice or milk?"

"Water is fine. And I appreciate your efforts," she added as he hopped around the kitchen attending to every detail.

"Then have a seat on the bar stool and I'll join you."

She went around the partition into the living room, where four bar stools lined the eating bar. As he took his seat, there was a momentary pause.

"May I say grace?" she asked politely.

"Please do."

She offered a brief prayer of thanksgiving, to which he added an amen.

"I'm glad you're a Christian," she said, wondering if she was assuming too much; yet it seemed obvious.

"And I'm glad that you, unlike many women, do not feel that living in a liberal society requires you to hide your faith. Some have no faith at all, of course."

"I know. But that's true in New Mexico or anywhere, I guess. That's why I was so pleased when you sent your minister over to my hospital room."

"I'm glad you appreciated his visit." He held the bowl of shrimp up for her while she used the silver tongs to remove two servings of shrimp, then she picked up the relish spoon and dipped out the sauce.

"Tell me about yourself," he suggested as she finished spooning out the fruit salad. "Why did you decide to go to law school? And why did you choose NYU?"

"Those two questions require very long answers," she replied, enjoying the sweet, delicate flavor of the shrimp. "By the way, dinner is fantastic."

"Thanks. New Year's Eve seems like a good time to ask and answer questions. I mean, well. . .you know, getting the new year off to a good beginning."

Erin nodded in agreement. "Okay, I'll have a go at it." She took a deep breath, still chewing her fruit salad, then reached for her water goblet.

"I've already told you Dad is chief of police in Rock Cliff, New Mexico. Well, I grew up with his frustrations being aired over the dinner table. He complained about how hard he and his officers worked night and day to keep our area safe. New Mexico is at the top of the list, nationally, for alcohol and drug abuse. Our area is second worst within the state.

"I got my undergraduate degree in secondary education from the University of New Mexico in Albuquerque. I wanted to help young people, and I thought that by becoming a teacher, I could emphasize to kids the importance of staying in school, keeping their grades up for college, and filling their weekends with wholesome activities, like church functions. But gangs continued to pop up, driven by the lure of drugs, and I saw so many good kids get caught up in that. I learned about peer pressure," she sighed, taking another sip of water. "It was hard enough when I was growing up, even though I was the daughter of the police chief. But now it appears to be even worse for kids."

He nodded. "I know about that. The initiation rites for becoming a gang member are unbelievable. My life here is a continual process of trying to stop drug dealers."

"Are you succeeding?"

"The statistics for my area this year are better than last year. Part of the credit goes to the drug testing we now have in place in schools and workplaces, and part to the endless efforts of my undercover guys. People like JJ."

As she listened, she felt ashamed for judging JJ without knowing him, and she made a mental note to be extra nice.

"So go back to your story," he said, popping a shrimp into his mouth. "What made you decide to quit teaching to attend law school? And why did you choose NYU to study law? Why not someplace closer to home?"

She gave him a wry grin. "I'll answer those questions in reverse order. Dad's last case, and the most important one of his career, was one that we had worked on together, finally nailing the kingpin of drug deals in our area. Through my kids at school, we followed the trail from a small supplier to a bigger one, and finally we backtracked to the really big guy. It took months to accomplish this. When he was arrested in Albuquerque and brought to trial, a slick defense attorney shot holes in Dad's case. The guy got off, and it almost killed Dad, since one of his most dedicated policemen was killed during the arrest."

She turned to Luke. "And guess where that hotshot defense lawyer was educated?"

"I'd venture to guess NYU."

"Right. I'd had three frustrating years of teaching, so in anger, and almost as a lark, I applied to law school here. Nobody was more surprised than I when I received a scholarship."

"That's very impressive. NYU is one of the top law schools."

She had to laugh. "I realize that now, but I didn't in the beginning. I hadn't even researched the schools. But to my surprise and pleasure, at the time I applied here, NYU was ranked number three in the nation. The scholarship and that knowledge sealed my decision to become the best prosecution lawyer I can be. So here I am." She lifted her palms up in a humorous gesture.

"I think you're doing a very noble thing. And you're planning to go back to that area when you graduate?"

"Absolutely. I want to help prosecute the criminals who are going free because some attorney didn't do his homework or didn't have enough education." She sighed and looked down at her plate. "I know I'm only one small player in this great big game, but I can do something to make a difference."

"Of course you can. That's why I work so hard."

She nodded and stared at him. It occurred to her that this was the first date she had truly respected and appreciated. The fact that he was handsome mattered little now; she had learned, the hard way, that behind the good looks often was a dark soul, or at least a person who was not right for her to love.

Love? She dropped her eyes. Why had that word popped into her mind?

"At least what you're doing is making your own start in the war against drugs," Luke said. "That reminds me

of something. Let me show you what my nephew made
for me."

They got up from the bar stools, and he limped over
to the coffee table and opened a drawer.

He removed a sheet of red construction paper marked
JANUARY, with a cutout of a calendar and numbers for
each day of the week. At the bottom of the page, in the
same bold silver print, were the words "Happy New Year.
David."

"He sent this in with Mom when she came from New
Jersey to visit me at the hospital. David said to tell me
that a new year is a new beginning. Apparently the
teacher has been stressing this to his kindergarten class,"
he said in a tender voice as Erin gently touched the silver
lettering on the little calendar.

"How sweet," she said.

He placed the calendar back in the drawer and
turned to face her. "So. . .let's make the new year a new
beginning."

She smiled warmly. "Sounds fine to me. Happy New
Year, Luke."

"And to you, Erin McKinley." He leaned forward,
kissing her lightly on the forehead.

She smiled up at him. His eyes moved over her face
slowly, and he smiled back. Then he glanced at the video
clock mounted on the computer. "They'll soon be dropping the ball in Times Square."

"Already?" she gasped, looking amazed. Where had
the time gone?

"Actually, it's still an hour away. We're at countdown."

He lifted the remote control from the coffee table, and instantly the crowd and confetti of Times Square came to life on the screen. "I wish I had been able to take you to a nice restaurant for dinner or—"

Erin put up her hand to silence him. "Believe me, I've enjoyed this more. Let's do the dishes before we watch TV."

"No, I insist that we sit down and talk." He hobbled around to the sofa, and she followed.

Sinking into the plush sofa, she sighed. "I'm glad we're not out in all of the traffic of New Year's Eve."

She looked at him, more interested than ever, as he grinned back and sat down beside her on the sofa. He started to prop up his feet, then hesitated. "Do you mind?"

"Of course not, silly," she laughed as he carefully lifted his bandaged foot, then hoisted the other one. "Now it's your turn to talk about you. You asked two questions, and I practically gave you my life history."

"Okay, one more question for you, then you can grill me," he said, his dark eyes twinkling in that way she had come to adore.

One more question. She couldn't imagine what she had left out during her extended babble. "What's the question?" she asked, tilting her head sideways to survey him curiously.

"You didn't mention a guy. There has to be a guy back home waiting for a girl who is as smart and witty as you are."

She noticed he omitted "beautiful," which she thought made him seem more sincere. She was not beautiful, although she knew she was striking. As her mother often said, she had just missed beautiful and hit striking and cute. "The Reba McIntire of New Mexico," her dad often teased.

"There's no guy waiting back home or anywhere else," she informed him proudly. "I was interested in someone in Albuquerque when I was attending UNM, but we were going in different directions spiritually."

Doug, with his exuberant personality, would not attend church with her, and he had been less than trustworthy, even though he had tried to be faithful. He simply was plagued with a wandering eye when it came to women.

"Care to elaborate?" Luke pressed.

"Well. . .let's just say he would never have sent his pastor over to visit me in the hospital," she replied, looking into Luke's deep brown eyes and somehow forgetting everything.

"Since he didn't send flowers when you were in the hospital, I take it this guy is history."

"He's been history every since I graduated from college. When I went back to teach junior high, the pickings were slim, to quote an often-used Rock Cliff expression. There was a nice guy in my singles' class at church, but I just couldn't bring myself to feel anything more than friendship for him, even though I really tried."

He took her hand. "I think that when the right person comes along, you don't have to try. It just happens." He hesitated for only a moment, allowing her to ponder that philosophy, then he pressed his head back against the sofa and stared at the ceiling.

"You asked about me," Luke said, taking a deep breath. "I'm one of three children—you already know that. Born and raised in Hackensack, New Jersey. My older brother, Bryan, married a sweet girl, Patricia, and he's an insurance broker. Pat's a stay-at-home mom and loves it. Lane, my twin, is. . .between jobs. Hasn't found the right career since graduating from college. I think she's waiting on Scott to propose, and he probably will soon. He's a great guy and crazy about her.

"As for me, after college I tried to get into insurance, like Dad and Bryan. Hated it. Then I got a public relations job in an investment firm. Hated that, too. Other than softball and spy novels, I couldn't get excited about anything.

"Then my cousin in Newark invited me to visit him while he was attending a law enforcement academy. After following him around for a couple of days, I felt an intense excitement that had eluded me before. So I went through the academy, started out as a patrolman, then got a day job here in the city. I worked my way up to investigator after going to night school, changing my major to criminal justice. Since I've been in investigations, I haven't even thought about slowing down for the last two years. Which reminds me—" He glanced toward the telephone on an end table. "I guess I should check my messages and turn on the phone and beeper."

His eyes flicked back to her and he smiled. "I didn't want us to be disturbed."

"Oh, then by all means, check your messages," she insisted.

"Excuse me."

Her eyes followed him as he moved away, and soon he was on the phone. She tried to concentrate on the crowd in Times Square, so it would at least appear that she wasn't listening.

"No, I'm off. Remember?" His tone had taken on a defensive note.

Erin glanced at him. He was standing with his back to her, his crutches propped against a chair, and his left hand firmly gripping the back of the chair.

"No way. But I'm willing to listen to your ideas and try to help come up with a solution."

Obviously he was needed at work. How unfair that he couldn't even recuperate in a relaxed atmosphere.

The soothing gurgle of the little fountain on the coffee table calmed her nerves, and she sank deeper into the sofa, while Luke grew more anxious in his conversation. After a heated debate with the person on the other end, his tone of voice sharpened even more.

"You can't handle him that way!" he snapped. "Look, I'm going to page JJ and get him in on this." He hung up the phone, then began to redial.

Was he calling JJ? And if JJ was about to take on a job, how would she get home? Oh, of course—by taxi.

"We're about to lose our star witness." He cupped the mouthpiece and looked across at her.

Quickly she got up and walked to his side. "Do what you need to do. I can go home now."

"Wait a minute," he said, pressing the phone against his shoulder as he put the person on hold. "I hate for our evening to end this way, but I need to go on this ride with JJ. It's very important."

She nodded. "I understand, believe me. Just get me home."

He lifted the receiver and spoke briefly. "Hey, JJ, come pick up Erin and take her home while I change clothes. Then you can come back for me and we'll get right on it."

He hung up and raked a hand through his dark hair, the look on his face was one of total frustration.

"Do you have plans for tomorrow?" he asked. "We could do something."

"And miss all the ballgames on television?"

He frowned. "Yeah, but—"

"I happen to be a football fan as well. And remember, I grew up with three brothers and a father who were all avid sports fans. My sisters were sissies," she added, wrinkling her nose. "If you want, I can come over and we'll pop popcorn and drink sodas. Maybe I'll even whip up a batch of my classic fudge, which is about the best treat I can prepare."

"A great plan." His eyes lit up, sending a glow to the depth of her soul.

In the background, she could hear the shouts from the crowd in Times Square via the television screen: ten. . . nine. . .eight. . ."

He glanced at the TV. "I was in that crowd last year. They're much too rowdy for me."

"And I thought I was really missing something!" Erin said with a sigh.

"Maybe you were." He reached out to smooth back the lock of red hair that dipped onto her forehead. "Maybe you were missing me and just didn't know it."

She laughed as her gaze roamed from his even white teeth up the smooth nose to his soft brown eyes. Maybe she was missing him, but it was too soon to know if Luke was Mr. Right, although she had a feeling. . .

And then he lowered his lips to give her a gentle kiss, and the joy of his smile was nothing compared to the thrill of his kiss.

The doorbell rang, interrupting the sweet moment, and with a sigh, Luke left her to open the door.

JJ wandered in, his hands shoved deep in his pockets. A question mark could have been written on his forehead as he looked from Luke to Erin, then back to Luke.

"We're going to continue this celebration tomorrow," Erin explained good-naturedly.

Both men heaved a sigh of relief.

"You be careful taking her home," Luke warned, helping her into her coat. "What time can you come over tomorrow?"

"Just give me a call," she said as he kissed the top of her head.

JJ stared in bewilderment, then snapped to attention. "You are one lucky guy," he muttered to Luke as Erin walked out the door ahead of him. She merely laughed. She understood this time, or at least she thought she did.

Chapter 5

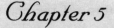

The phone rang the next morning at 9:15, and Erin rolled over in her bed and glared angrily at the clock. She was not a morning person. The caller was persistent, however, and she was forced to pad across the cold floor to silence the offending instrument.

"Good morning. I hope I'm not calling too early," Luke's voice rang out cheerfully.

"As a matter of fact, you are," she said, although her anger was already fading.

"Oh. Then when should I call back?" he asked meekly.

She sank down on the floor, drawing her knees up to her chin. Even in her thick pajamas, her apartment was cold. She sighed. "It's okay. I'm awake now. Or rather, my eyes are open. My brain doesn't function until I get a jump start from caffeine."

"Well, I have plenty of that. And cinnamon rolls. For the ballgames, there's popcorn and soda, and we still have roast beef and vegetables for a solid meal."

She laughed in spite of herself. "Got it all figured out, huh? Have you dispatched JJ yet?"

"He's sitting on go."

She rolled her eyes and shivered against her knees.

"Well, tell him to turn off the engine and give me an hour. There are a few minor details to take care of before I leave."

"Such as?"

"A shower and. . . Aren't you being a bit personal?"

His rich chuckle vibrated over the wire, and she had to smile.

"Yes, I am. I just mean you do not have to bring anything."

"Okay," she replied, her eyes flitting to the refrigerator.

"An hour from now would be around ten. Want to make it ten-thirty, just to be sure you have enough time?" he asked politely.

"That would be better," she said, slowly pulling herself up from the floor. "Casual again, as in a sweat suit? It's really cold out, isn't it?"

"In the twenties, I think, so dress for warmth. Wear a ski mask if you like. Ooops, let's not mention the word ski. It shouldn't be in my vocabulary for a very long time."

"Well, at least not in your plans," she said, staring across at the coffee maker.

"Right. See you later, Erin."

Promptly at ten-thirty, she was picked up and delivered by a polite JJ to Luke's doorstep, where the football games of the day had already begun.

"Hi," she said, smiling at Luke, who was wearing a different sweat suit, a white one this time. Despite his casual attire, he still managed to look better to her than any guy she had ever met.

He smiled back. "Hi." He looked a bit tired as his

eyes swept her pale blue turtle neck, jeans, and hiking boots. "I'm glad you could come."

"How did last night go?" she asked as she pulled off her coat and scarf and draped them on the coat tree. "Or should I ask?"

"I'd rather forget it," he said, his dark eyes filled with misery for just a moment. She couldn't bear that, so she lifted the container in her hand.

"Then we'll forget it. Here is my prize-winning fudge."

She knew her fudge would be good for a laugh. Unfortunately, it had been a total flop, just when she needed it to turn out right.

"What is it?" he asked curiously, eyeing the square plastic container.

"It's supposed to be fudge, but it decided to be taffy instead. I thought we could eat it with a spoon. Correction, make that chew it on a spoon."

He threw his head back and laughed, a laugh so deep that his eyes crinkled, and even Erin had to smile at her joke. He needed her sense of humor, that was easy to see. Or at least he needed something humorous, and the fudge would certainly accomplish that.

They settled down on the sofa to get involved in a bowl game. Luke was rooting for one team, so Erin decided to make things interesting by pulling for the opposing team.

They had a lunch of cold roast beef with vegetables; later in the afternoon, they snacked on popcorn. Finally, when she had no choice, she pulled her container of fudge from the refrigerator.

"I thought you should sample my culinary talents," she said, proudly opening the container.

"Taffy! Just what I wanted on New Year's Day."

"I knew that! Taffy is kind of like, well, it's like a challenge. It's a challenge to the teeth. And we need to have a challenge to start us off on the right foot for the new year, right?"

"Right. Just the right beginning," Luke agreed.

They were both laughing as they spooned into the stubborn fudge, laughing even harder when, as Erin predicted, they practically had to chew it off the spoon.

The only problem was a constant barrage of phone calls and beeps from Luke's pager.

"Can't you just turn everything off?" she asked, trying to hide her irritation.

Luke sighed. "I'm afraid not. Look, if we can catch this guy, your neighborhood will be a lot safer."

"At the moment, I'm not interested in my neighborhood," she shot back tartly. "I thought this was supposed to be a date, not a screening process by phone while you pretend to entertain me."

"Who's pretending?" he asked, frowning at her.

And then the phone rang again, and Erin decided she had had enough.

When he finally hung up, she reached for her coat. "While you're doing your phone work, please page JJ to take me home," she snapped.

She knew she was acting like a spoiled child, but she couldn't seem to help herself. She liked Luke, really liked him, and that bothered her more than the interruptions by his work. This was bad timing for her; she couldn't afford to get distracted by a guy at a time when her mind needed to be sharp. In fact, she had to be sharper than ever to do well in law school at NYU.

The dark eyes turned cold, as he looked at her for a long moment, then turned and punched a number into the phone. After he barked instructions to JJ and hung up, he hobbled toward the kitchen.

"Sorry. The last girl couldn't take it either," he said over his shoulder as he opened the refrigerator and reached for a soda.

"Well, I'm not the last girl!" Erin stormed. "In fact, I'm not like any other girl."

"I'll agree to that." He turned and looked her over.

"The fact is, when I have a date, I assume that I will have the other person's attention, at least part of the time. You've taken thirteen phone calls—I counted—and five beeps, and the light on your answering machine was already flashing when I got here." She pointed an accusing finger at the machine.

"Frankly, Luke, I don't think you have time for a social life; you seem only to have time for your job, which is obviously the most important thing in your life."

His lips were pressed in a thin hard line as he placed his soda firmly on the cabinet and helped her on with her coat; someone knocked on the door.

"Maybe you're right," he said, his voice low and hard. "My job has been the most important thing in my life. But somehow I hoped that you would understand since you—"

"Since I'm starting law school. Well, you're right,

school is the most important thing in my life, so I do understand. That's why we don't need to see each other any more," she said as she dramatically flung her scarf around her neck. The startled JJ stood in the doorway, watching the argument in silence.

"Maybe someday," she said, buttoning her coat decisively, "when I'm a lawyer and you're a top-notch investigator who has caught all the bad guys, we'll bump into each other again. Hopefully in court. Until then, good luck. And you can keep the fudge," she added as she turned on her heel and hurried out the door, JJ meekly trailing along behind.

Chapter 6

When Erin's temper finally had cooled, she sat and stared out her window. The streets were grimy with slush and trash after the celebration of New Year's Eve and New Year's Day. The rental car had been delivered this morning so she now had transportation, but there was nowhere she wanted to go, nothing she wanted to do.

Her gaze inched toward the telephone. She felt miserable for the things she had said to Luke. But it was true; two dates in two days, and each time he had deserted her to take care of work. And he was supposed to be off duty!

"The last girl couldn't take it either," he had said.

Well, she could understand why. To divert her thoughts, she picked up the phone and dialed her parents' home.

"Happy New Year," she said as her dad answered.

"Erin! We tried to call yesterday but you were out."

She took a breath, trying to keep her tone light. "Yes, I was invited to a friend's place to watch the ballgames."

"Good. Glad to hear it. Your mother worries about you being alone, and so far away. But I keep telling her you're a survivor!"

She nodded. "I try to be," she said, hoping she sounded

more convincing than she felt.

"I gotta tell you something," her dad rushed on. "Remember our famous Mr. X?"

"The kingpin we nailed who got off? How could I forget?" she asked bleakly.

"Well, guess what?"

"What?"

"He made the mistake of bragging to the wrong person after he'd had too much to drink at a bar one night. We've set him up again. This time, he won't get off!"

"How do you know, Dad?" She clutched the receiver tight, her senses sharpened by his words. Her adrenaline was racing now. "Oh, Dad, I wish I could be there!"

He chuckled. "No, you don't. We've worked around the clock tailing him, setting up situations, placing the right men at the right place. I've had three hours sleep in two days, but it will be worth it. And God bless your mother; she didn't complain about having to cancel plans for New Year's Eve, and I even missed the football bowl games yesterday. I just wish you were here to share in the celebration with us."

Tears stung her eyes. "So do I," she said quietly. "I've met someone here," she said, surprising herself with her admission. "A police investigator who is just like you, Dad. Totally devoted to his job." She smiled sadly. "Maybe that's why I like him."

What was she saying? It was the exact opposite of what she had told Luke.

"Really?" His tone of voice changed. "He'd better not neglect you."

"But you neglect Mom."

He cleared his throat. "Well, er, it takes a special woman to live with people like us. But then, you're about to jump into the same boat by educating yourself to prosecute these criminals. Honey, I can't wait to see you in the courtroom!" His voice boomed with pride, and the tears Erin had tried to choke back flowed down her cheeks. "Dad, something's boiling over," she said in a rush.

"We'll call you back," he said eagerly, before she hung up.

Something was boiling over all right: her emotions. She dropped her face into her hands and began to sob. It was true. She was as dedicated as her dad and Luke. Once she started law school, nothing else would matter. She would not let herself get diverted by romance. Never again.

She got up and went to the kitchen and dried her face with a paper towel. Work. She needed to get busy on this stupid-looking place. Reaching into the cabinet, she hauled out her small box of cleaning supplies. Mrs. Brantley, the landlady, told her the apartment had already been cleaned, but to satisfy herself, Erin got busy. By the end of the afternoon, there was not a speck of dust in sight. Every piece of wood had been polished, and the bathroom and tiny kitchen gleamed.

She had taken down her tree, hauled it out for the garbage collectors, and boxed up her meager supply of Christmas decorations. She had hung the new sweater and slacks sent from home in the closet, and the various items given by brothers, sisters, nieces, and nephews were tucked away in the dresser drawer. Wisely, many had sent gift certificates or cash, which she preferred. Two of her little nieces had made a beaded necklace and bracelet for her.

"Now what?" she asked herself, hands on hips, as she appraised her new living area with satisfaction. She decided on a long, hot soak in the tiny tub, followed by a late afternoon nap. With that in mind, she headed for the pint-sized bathroom. The ringing of the telephone caught her halfway there.

That would be Dad calling back. She hurried over and grabbed the phone, trying to sound more cheerful than she felt. To her surprise, the deep voice on the other end was not that of her father, but of Luke Mitchell. Luke, the investigator.

"Hi." He sounded sheepish.

"Hi," she replied, trying to switch her tone from cheerful to indifferent.

"I am so very sorry," he said. "I've treated you terribly, and I was hoping you would give me the chance to make amends this evening."

This evening? Her gaze flew to her soiled jeans, and automatically her hand shot to her tumbled hair. Before she could form a response, he continued on, as though fearful she would hang up on him.

"It's going to be a beautiful night—a crystal clear, starry sky with a big full moon. I thought it would be fun to take a buggy ride around Central Park, maybe go to the Rockefeller Center and watch the skaters, or have a meal, or. . . If you don't want to see me, I understand," he finished quickly.

She sighed and sank down on the bed, gripping the

receiver. "I haven't even been to Central Park," she said limply.

"Then you have to go. You can't possibly start law school and admit to your peers that you haven't seen Central Park!"

"I suppose that would be embarrassing to admit," she conceded. "We're playing a very childish game, you know." She could no longer keep the humor out of her voice. After talking with her dad, she was ready to forgive Luke. And she was dying to see him again.

"And Erin, I promise. No phone calls, no interruptions."

"Did you catch the guy?" she asked, unable to suppress her curiosity

"I'm surprised you even asked. But yes, we did. You can read all about it in today's paper. But I don't want to talk about that, I want to talk about tonight. I've threatened to quit my job if anyone, I mean the police chief, the mayor, or even the president, calls. I am not to be interrupted." His tone had sharpened with that declaration, but the next words he spoke were as beautiful as a New Mexico sunset.

"Please give me another chance."

She couldn't control the smile that spread across her face until her cheeks ached. "I'm sorry I lost my temper," she said, feeling all warm inside.

"You had every right," he said, sounding more relaxed. "Hey, it's a new year; let's make a new beginning. Again."

She laughed. "Okay. What time?"

"When can you be ready?"

She calculated the preparations necessary. "Two hours."

"Great. I'll be at your door at—"

"Look, there's no elevator in this house, and I don't expect you to climb two flights of stairs with your ankle."

"Well, no more sending JJ. I'm calling for you myself. I'll hail a cab and be there in two hours."

"In that case, I'll meet you down at the front door. My landlady appears to thrive on the actions of her tenants. I've noticed her posted at her window as I come and go. In fact, her expression was priceless when JJ and I left together." She laughed, remembering the parted lace curtain, and Mrs. Brantley's face at the window. The woman's mouth had opened and formed a perfect *O*. "Since I am presently her source of entertainment, why don't you have the driver sit on the horn while you wave out the window? I'll rush out the front door and skip down the steps like an eager sixteen-year-old on her first date."

He laughed, a full, deep laugh. The kind of laugh her dad would make after she beat one of his opponents at Chinese checkers.

Chapter 7

Erin buttoned up her green woolen coat and wrapped her new plaid scarf—a Christmas present from her sister—around her neck. Pulling on the matching gloves, she could not resist the excitement that soared through her as the taxi pulled up to the curb before her building. As planned, the driver laid on the horn, and she saw the window come down as Luke's grinning face peered out at her.

"Hurry up, honey!" he shouted.

Giggling, she ran down the steps, but to her disappointment, Mrs. Brantley was not at the window. He was laughing as she jumped into the backseat and glanced toward the downstairs bay window. The room was dark.

"All our efforts were in vain. Mrs. Brantley apparently has gone out. I can't believe it."

She turned to Luke, and her heart beat faster as her eyes met his. He was wearing a navy pea jacket, and the look on his face was one of pure delight.

"Doesn't matter. Our little act was kind of fun. Like the Chinese checkers." He glanced toward the driver. "Rockefeller Plaza at Fifth." He turned back to her. "By the way, when do I get another chance to beat you?"

"Whenever you feel you're up to the challenge." She couldn't deny the happiness she felt at being with him again. "You know, I'm actually putting into practice one of my New Year's resolutions."

"Giving a guy a second chance?" he said, putting his arm around her shoulder and pulling her closer.

"On the same level, I suppose. Patience." She snuggled into the warmth of his arms and sighed. "Actually, I'm glad you called. You see, this has put my resolution to the test."

He chuckled. "I'll test mine later."

"What is it? You have to play fair since I've told you mine."

"I promise to tell you later. By the way, I thought we'd go to the Rockefeller Center first, if you have no objections. They'll soon be taking down the Christmas decorations, and I'd like to see them one more time."

"I'd like to see them for the first time," she admitted.

He was obviously surprised. "You mean you haven't seen *the* tree?"

"I haven't seen anything beyond Washington Square and NYU hospital. I haven't had the chance. By the way, the economy car was delivered today."

"Has anyone told you it might be smarter to take a taxi around town?"

"I was only going a few blocks to investigate another parking garage when I had the accident. The prices are ridiculous. The monthly fee for parking my car is going to blow my budget. In fact," she chewed her lip, "maybe I should sell my car."

"Or maybe you should keep it at my garage. Or better yet, in my brother's driveway in Jersey City. They have a big house in the suburbs with lots of parking space. It's just a suggestion. Until you learn the city, I think it would be wise to travel by taxi—or even the subway, which is relatively safe."

"It's nice of you to make that offer," she said, turning to look up at him. "About leaving a car at your brother's house, I mean."

As she looked at Luke, the lights of the city played over his face in the shadows of the cab's interior, and again she was struck by what a handsome guy he was. She often forgot that, because she had forced herself to concentrate on the other person's inner being. More than once, looks had proven deceiving, but she had a feeling Luke Mitchell was the exception.

"Well, the offer stands," he said. "In fact, I think it would be a very good idea, once your car is repaired, for us to take it over to my brother's home. It'll be safe there, and you need to learn the city first." He frowned suddenly. "Where are you keeping the rental car?"

"In the same expensive garage I was keeping my now wrecked car—which, by the way, I should have left there. The parking fee would have been far less expensive than my little fender bender."

He reached over and gently pushed a wave of red hair back in place. "You know what? If you hadn't had that little fender bender, I wouldn't have met you."

"And if you hadn't taken off to the ski slopes hot-dogging, as Lane put it, I might not have met you."

They stared at one another in thoughtful silence as the cab jerked to a halt, both of them pondering the what-ifs. "I might never have met you," he said, looking amazed.

"I doubt that I would have been picked up as an offender."

"Life is strange, isn't it?" Luke said, scarcely aware the driver was waiting impatiently for his fare until the man awkwardly cleared his throat. "Oh." Luke glanced around them. "Here we are."

He paid the fare and helped her out of the taxi, while Erin gawked at the enormous Christmas tree before them. "There must be thousands of lights on that tree," she said, scarcely able to drink in the vast beauty of the magnificent tree.

"I happened to be here for the ceremonial lighting," Luke said casually, as he slipped his hand under her elbow and they began to walk.

"What fun." She turned back to him, shoving her hands into her pockets as they moved into the crowd on the sidewalk.

"It would have been a lot more fun if you had been with me," he said, glancing down at her.

"Thanks," she grinned. "I'm sure I would have enjoyed watching the tree being lit far more than I enjoyed cleaning out closets and loading up my boxes. Not that I brought that much stuff. I go by the three-box organization method."

"The three-box organization method? How does it work?" He looked questioningly at her as he pushed open the door and they began to walk through the city within a city that was the Rockefeller Center.

"Here's the three-box method. You organize your belongings in three boxes: one to keep, one to give away, and one to throw away. My problem is, I'm a pack rat."

He laughed. "And I'm just the opposite."

She stopped herself just before saying, "Then we'd make a good team." The thought, however, lingered in her mind. She had always looked for a relationship in which one's strength was balanced by another's weakness, and vice versa. Her parents had that, and at times they seemed to be worlds apart in the little things, but in the important matters, they were always in agreement.

"Being a little bit opposite in some respects is what keeps our marriage interesting," her mom had joked. Erin understood what she meant now, as she dragged her gaze from Luke and forced herself to concentrate on all the shops along the promenade.

"I have a very favorite hot chocolate I get here." He indicated a café overlooking the skating rink.

"Terrific. I adore hot chocolate."

With huge mugs of hot chocolate topped with a mound of whipped cream, they took a seat to watch the skaters. Erin was absolutely fascinated with the sites and sounds and wonders that the city offered. Without thinking, she took a sip of the hot chocolate and burned her mouth.

"I should have warned you." Luke frowned over the rim of his cup.

"I should have known, but I do it every time, no matter where I am."

They laughed at that, and he began to recount a story of his dad bringing the family here during Christmas holidays one year, and what a blast everyone had.

"Until I overdid it on my new skates and fell and busted my you-know-what."

"Not your ankle," she teased, as he reached over to wipe a tiny wisp of whipped cream from her lip.

"No, not that."

"In New Mexico we went up to Colorado every winter to ski; rather, my church group went. It was always fun. I must have taken a dozen sprawls before I learned to ski."

He grinned at her. "But you conquered it?"

"Sure," she answered, as confident as ever.

"Why did I ever doubt that? You're quite a lady," he said, leaning back in his chair. "And the fact that you stand up for yourself makes me admire you even more."

"I take it you're referring to my display of temper yesterday?"

"I'm not trying to start—"

"I know. And I refuse to take offense. I pride myself on being independent. It was a trait I learned early, or maybe it was a matter of survival in a house with six siblings."

"I wish Lane were more independent," he said, toying with the handle of his mug and staring at the hot chocolate. "She's pretty dependent. In fact, the last guy she dated was an athlete on steroids. He almost got violent with her, but she had enough sense to get out of the restaurant before he hit her. He completely lost it, though. If he would do that in public, I hate to think what would have happened if they had been in her apartment."

For a moment a look of sadness crossed his face as he continued to stare at his mug. "In my line of work, I come across all types. Domestic violence is something that's been hard for me to understand. My dad always taught us to respect a woman."

"And it shows," Erin replied softly, silently thanking God for that quality in him.

"I hope so. I'm amazed at how much domestic abuse takes place. And it's not always the guys. Even women claw and scratch and slam guys over the head with skillets." He shook his head, looking back at her in bewilderment. "I'll admit, when I hear their stories, I can see how it would be tempting to do something back, but they go way too far with their retaliation."

She nodded. "There's a lot of domestic abuse in New Mexico, too, but when Dad attended a national conference of police chiefs, he discovered that's a crime that is common in every state. At least now more legislation is being passed to stop abuse."

"And you are educating yourself to be one of those people who help to put a stop to it."

She nodded, warming to her favorite subject. "I really do want to be a good attorney. I guess I always have wanted to be an attorney, but it just seemed like such a long and difficult road. Not to mention the expense. I went through UNM on a scholarship, but I still had to take out a school loan before I graduated. Once I got out of school, I thought that was the end of it. I convinced myself that being a teacher was the right thing to do."

She paused, looked out at the merry skaters, then back at Luke. "I now realize I needed a few years on the job to get my life into perspective, to see what I really want to be when I grow up," she said, grinning at him. "I prayed about it a lot," she added softly, growing serious again.

"You'll make an excellent attorney," he said with conviction. "And when God leads in a choice, the choice is always right." He hesitated for a moment, then reached across to squeeze her hand. "Erin, I'm really glad that you and I met."

The merriment enveloping them seemed to fade into the background, along with the music and the shrieks from the skating rink. For a moment, she was lost in his gaze, and suddenly she couldn't believe she was in New York, about to embark on a new life with a new and wonderful man.

"I'm glad we met too," she said, dropping her eyes to her mug. It was empty. Where had the time gone? Had she talked that much?

"If you're ready, we'd better go out and grab a buggy," he said. "The longer we wait, the harder it will be, since it's the holidays."

"Sure."

They walked hand in hand back down the promenade as she gazed again in wonder at all the various displays. Once they were outside, Luke managed to get a driver just before another couple caught up.

"Sorry," Luke said, glancing over his shoulder at the disappointed couple.

"It's okay," the guy answered, a smile on his face. "You were first."

Erin looked at the girl with him and saw the glow in her eyes. They were obviously in love and enjoying a beautiful evening in the city, with all its glittering entertainment.

Luke tucked a blanket around the two of them, and the driver tapped the reins of the horses. They were off at a smooth trot, and Luke hugged her tighter against him.

"Are you cold?" he asked, a note of concern in his voice.

She gazed up at the sky, looking for the Milky Way, as her father had always taught her to. "No, I'm fine. There are so many skyscrapers here," she said, thinking of the huge open sky in New Mexico. "But you were right," she said, spotting the full moon. "It's a perfect night. . ."

"Watch it!" The driver shouted at a pedestrian who had stepped out in front of them.

The buggy lurched and Erin was thrown against the front seat. Her left ribcage sent a surge of pain through her body, and for a moment she was tempted to join the driver in yelling at the careless pedestrian. What if she had reinjured her rib? Then she remembered Luke and his ankle, and she reached out to him.

"Are you okay?" She was the first to ask.

"Yeah, I think so. And you?"

She took a deep breath and settled back into the warmth of his arms. "I'm just fine. I think my resolution is working, for now."

"Then I'd better start working on mine," he said, looking down into her eyes.

"Which is?"

"To make a change in my life. Or rather, my work habits. My goal is to steal the heart of a certain special redhead who has completely stolen mine," he said, his face closer to hers, his eyes watching her face carefully as he spoke.

Erin's breath caught in her throat. Was she really hearing what she hoped to hear? What she wanted with all of her heart to hear? She didn't know what to say, and as usual, Luke interpreted her silence as a challenge.

"I think I better get started," he said, lowering his lips to hers and warming her mouth with a kiss that thrilled her. *It is going to be the best year ever,* she thought, as her arms slipped up his shoulders and she clasped her hands at his collar.

She pulled back from him for a moment and smiled up into his eyes. "I would say you were off to a great beginning. . . ."

As a soft night wind drifted over them, and the street sounds of New York City swirled about them, the driver glanced back over his shoulder and shook his head. Then he smiled. It was as if he was thinking, *Another couple in love; well, that's what makes my job worthwhile.*

PEGGY DARTY

Peggy has been spinning wonderful tales of romance for several years-and winning awards along the way. She had her first inspirational romance published by Zondervan in 1985. She started writing articles of inspiration about family life, but fiction was her real joy. After an editor suggested she try inspirational fiction, she found it to be a way to share messages of hope and encouragement that she feels are desperately needed in these difficult times. She loves to hear from her readers and says, "When I get a letter from a reader who tells me one of my books touched her heart, lightened her load, or helped in some way, I feel my goal had been accomplished." At home in Alabama, Peggy has been married to her college sweetheart for more than thirty years, and she is the mother of three and grandmother of two little boys.

Never
Say Never

by Yvonne Lehman

Dedicated to Lori

Chapter 1

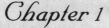

Amy Treadwell's excitement turned to trepidation as she entered the creative writing class at Greenland Junior College and saw the other students' expectant faces and heard their animated conversations. She took the nearest available seat, in the first row, at the front. *What have I gotten myself into?* she wondered, as she turned sideways so she could view the other students.

At least she looked like most of the students, dressed in jeans, shirt, pullover sweater, and tennis shoes; she had even pulled her long blond hair back into a ponytail. Her appearance was a far cry from how she had looked earlier in the day when she left the office where she worked as secretary to the dean of the college. She'd been glad to get out of her heels and dress casually.

As she waited for the class to begin, she thought back over her reasons for being here in this writing class. At the beginning of the year she'd made a resolution to write a synopsis and three chapters of a book to send to a publisher. By mid-August she had realized that her chances were getting slimmer and slimmer of being able to keep that resolution. She didn't like the idea of failure. That's why she had jumped at the chance to take this course offered in Continuing Education.

"Hi," said a pregnant woman behind her, interrupting Amy's thoughts. "I'm DeeDee Jones."

Amy barely had time to introduce herself before a tall, thin man in a suit rushed in, eager to relieve his arms of a cardboard box that he set on the desk. "Good evening," he said. "I'm Dr. Prince and I suppose you're all aspiring writers."

Perspiring writers might be more like it, Amy thought, glancing sideways at the rest of the class. None of them looked too confident about being writers.

Dr. Prince smiled, peering over his half-glasses at the students, then looked down while he took papers from the box. "I'll check roll as you introduce yourself to the class, tell something about yourself, what you've written if anything, and why you're taking this class."

Amy's heart thudded; she had sat in the wrong place. She could have said his next sentence for him. He looked straight at her and said, "We'll start with this young lady in the front row."

Amy cleared her throat and swallowed hard. "I'm Amy Treadwell. I'm secretary to the dean of the college, and I live in Pine Valley. I've written a few articles for the school paper." Self-conscious about sharing her dream, reluctance crept into her voice. "I'd like to write a romance novel."

Dr. Prince smiled and nodded. "Next," he said.

"I'm a stay-at-home mom," DeeDee Jones said. "I had a story published in *Little Baby Magazine*. It was about my two-year-old painting my one-year-old with chocolate pudding."

Everybody laughed, and Dr. Prince said, "That's good. Many publishers are looking for humor."

"It wasn't humorous when it happened," DeeDee said. "I only got fifteen dollars for it, but when you have two in diapers and another on the way, every little bit counts. If I can write about life with babies and laugh instead of crying, I figure I can maybe survive these hectic years."

Amy watched the students as they spoke, realizing they were all beginners who were afraid they couldn't write. Dr. Prince's expression never changed. Wearing his glasses on his nose, he just peered at each one with friendly eyes, smiled or laughed when appropriate, and nodded, gestured, or said, "Next," when someone was reluctant to speak up.

"You all seem to be at about the same place," he said when the introductions were finished. "By the end of the course, I want each of you to write a short story, a poem, or an article and send it away for publication. Now notice I didn't say, 'get it published.' That's out of your hands once you send it out. Those of you writing a novel need to complete a synopsis."

"Sir?" asked a young man a few rows over. "Can you explain exactly what a synopsis is?"

"Briefly," Dr. Prince said, "it's an overview of what your book is about. It's not a '1-2-3, A-B-C' kind of outline, but it lets the editor know what your story elements are, like time, setting, characters, conflict, plot line, and ending."

"If you tell everything," the young man asked, "don't you have to worry that they might steal your idea?"

"Son," Dr. Prince said pointedly, "a writer's problem is

getting an editor to like your idea, not steal it. For instance, um. . ." He looked down at his roll and the notes he'd made while the students introduced themselves. "Amy. I suspect you gave your articles to the college paper. Is that right?"

She nodded. "I didn't get paid."

"That's a good start, though," he said. "The titles can go on your résumé. You're published. If you get paid even a dollar, you're considered a professional writer. Ask the school to give you at least a dollar for each article."

Wow! Before the class even got started she'd become a professional! It didn't matter that she would get only four dollars. She felt encouraged already.

Dr. Prince was still talking. "An interviewer once asked Ernest Hemmingway what was the hardest part of writing. Do you know what he answered?"

Nobody did.

"Hemmingway replied, 'The hardest part of writing is getting the words right.' "

They all laughed, but Amy had already realized that. Even writing those articles for the school paper caused her to sometimes stare at her computer screen so long without typing anything that she felt sure it would develop eyeball imprints.

An older woman near the back raised her hand. "I heard *The Wizard of Oz* was rejected over and over."

"That's right," Dr. Prince confirmed. "*A Tree Grows in Brooklyn* was rejected twenty-nine times. Finally, it was accepted, became a best-seller, and a movie was made of it."

After the first hour of learning that it was all right to

be rejected, Amy felt less apprehensive. The second hour was a delight. Dr. Prince had them do exercises in getting ideas on paper. They tried pre-writing, clustering, brainstorming, and listing. What she liked best was clustering. Out of a list of words Dr. Prince gave them, she chose the word "night" to put in the middle of the blank sheet of paper, then clustered any thought that came to mind. Hers turned out to be "knight, shining armor, romance, damsel in distress, and castle." Then she wrote a paragraph, using those words.

She felt the creativity flowing, until to her horror, Dr. Prince collected the paragraphs and said he'd bring them back next week.

On the thirty-minute drive home to Pine Valley, Amy again felt that mingling of excitement and trepidation. But Dr. Prince had said emotions like that were common to writers. They wanted to succeed, but sometimes fear of failure prevented their even trying. He also said that having a desire to write was a good indication that they should.

Her desire to write had been born after she'd received many compliments from teachers and students about her articles in the school paper. Was that just her ego—wanting more compliments?

Or was God nudging her to break out of her comfortable, well-organized lifestyle to pursue something more challenging? She thought of the parable in the Bible about the servant who hid his talent in the ground. Yes, it was time to shake the dirt off the ideas that had been buried in her brain for so long.

God, she prayed as she drove, *if You have given me any writing talent, then help me to develop it and use that gift for Your glory.*

※

During the first week in October, Amy thought her prayer was answered when Jason Barlow joined her singles' Sunday school class. He was a dream to look at. Not only was he wearing a designer suit over his tall, lean frame, but he had dark, wavy hair, a handsome face, vivid blue eyes, a confident air, and a slightly crooked smile that gave his otherwise polished exterior a roguish appeal. He'd make a perfect hero for a romance novel.

But the crowning point was when he revealed he was an editor with a major publishing firm in New York, then said, "I'll be working out of my home for a while."

Amy's heart thudded. A real live editor. Up there in the Barlow mansion on Little Piney Mountain! Right above their little town of Pine Valley, South Carolina! Pure joy washed over her. Dr. Prince was a wonderful teacher with two novels and a hundred articles published, but even he said you had to please an editor if you ever hoped to be published.

After Sunday school Amy said to her best friend as they made their way to the sanctuary for the worship hour, "Jason Barlow is the ideal person to help me with a synopsis and three chapters. Maybe on Resolutions Day, I'll be able to say I kept mine after all. Can you imagine anything more perfect?"

"Yeah," Janice said, putting her hand to her heart in an exaggerated gesture. "One of his crooked little smiles just for me."

Amy laughed. His smile was captivating, she had to admit. But her thoughts were on a more serious level at the moment. Jason Barlow just might be her own personal miracle.

Amy's euphoria lasted one week.

She came to the Sunday school class early the following Sunday morning, hoping to have a few words with Jason Barlow. With a real editor's input, there was nowhere to go but up, up, up, she told herself.

After she descended the steps leading to the singles' class, she stopped suddenly in the hallway outside the door. She heard Buddy, a freshman college student, talking about writing. "I'm not even good at writing essays," he said. "I wouldn't want to tackle a whole book. Sometimes I have trouble just reading one."

A light laugh followed. "That's refreshing," said Jason Barlow's voice. "I'm accustomed to everybody and his brother wanting to write a book. Most of them seem to think they can retire from their jobs, sit down, and the words will flow magically. And many seem to think that I'm their ticket to publication."

The voice of Jason Barlow that had just last week made her feel so hopeful and encouraged, now sounded to Amy like the voice of doom. Her hope dropped to her toes, and her feet felt like lead as she made her way back up the stairs. She wouldn't dare go into that room just yet.

From that moment on, every time she saw him or thought of him, she thought of the phrase, *You can't judge a book by its cover.* Her mind always added, "And you can't judge an editor by his appearance."

She couldn't help but think of him fairly often, since he came to the singles' class every Sunday morning. And his appearance was unquestionably appealing.

But he wasn't what he seemed. He apparently didn't have any desire to help a struggling writer. She might be able to complete the class assignment of writing a synopsis, but there was no way, considering her work schedule, she could keep her resolution of writing an additional three chapters.

I will never make another resolution as long as I live, Amy vowed to herself. *And I will never mention a word to Jason Barlow about my trying to write a book.*

A couple of weeks later, Jason made a point of stopping her after class, in the hallway. "Amy," he called. "I hear you're interested in writing."

"You hear?" She stared with her mouth open. *Who told him that?*

Trying to regain a level of dignity, she closed her mouth and stepped back so others could ascend the stairs. "Oh, I'm taking a creative writing course and dabbling a little with articles," she said with a slight shrug as if it weren't important. She couldn't resist adding, "Maybe someday when I'm retired and can't do anything else, I'll just plop down at my computer and crank out a book in a week or two."

His smile spread over those straight white teeth. "Maybe I could help you and speed up the process." He laughed.

Amy didn't laugh. Her ambition was no laughing matter. "I'll keep that in mind for when I retire," she quipped. Instantly, his smile vanished. Amy walked away, ashamed of herself. Silently, she asked the Lord to help her control her bad attitude.

She didn't need to resent Jason Barlow. She was doing fine in her writing class. After filling two pages with possible titles, she had hit upon the perfect one: *Knight of Dreams*. The class loved it and so did Dr. Prince. Now, all she had to do was write a synopsis and then work on "grabbing" the reader with a great first line. After that, she could get on to writing a scene, then another, and another, and that would be a chapter.

It might take years, but she could do it! She had lived happily for twenty-five years without a published book or the likes of Jason Barlow.

Chapter 2

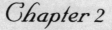

After church, driving his granddad's Bentley through Pine Valley, Jason thought of the many times he'd scribbled a note for his secretary to return a book manuscript that his company couldn't accept for publication. He had an inkling now how that must feel to a prospective writer. Maybe the way he felt when Amy Treadwell's eyes had flashed in neon letters, "Rejected—Jason Barlow doesn't meet my format!"

For the life of him, he couldn't figure out what he'd said to offend her. He mulled it over in his mind. She was taking a course in writing—yet she wasn't serious about writing. That sounded contradictory to him.

Then when she'd made the "write when I retire" remark, he'd thought she had a sense of humor. He had tried a little of that himself, but she hadn't found his remark amusing.

Did she think his comment was a ploy just to talk to her? Suppose it had been? Wouldn't that be all right? After all, Buddy had said she was single and had no special boyfriend.

He'd noticed her the first time he'd walked into the

singles' class. She'd reminded him of approaching autumn in a silky suit of yellow, green, and brown threads running through a cream-colored background. Her dark brown eyes and olive skin were a striking contrast to her straight honey-colored blonde hair that hung below her shoulders.

He'd felt her eyes had a special glow when she'd looked at him, and he'd thought, *There's a woman I'd like to know better.* But after that first Sunday, she'd become distant. Was she one of those "dyed in the wool" Southerners who wouldn't be caught dead talking to a Yankee?

If she gave him the chance, he could tell her that he had been born and raised in Pine Valley. His granddad had started *The Pine Valley News*, and after his three sons grew up, they worked with him. Ultimately, they owned a chain of newspapers across the southeast, extending into New York.

Jason himself had ridden his bicycle and delivered newspapers up and down the streets of Pine Valley. He'd known just about everybody in town back then. But after his dad moved the family to New York, he felt like he'd gone to a new world.

His dad trained him in just about every department of newspaper work, but after his college courses in communications, literature, and creative writing, he learned his expertise lay not in writing of materials as much as in critiquing and editing. He'd landed a job with a major publishing company, started as a first reader, and worked his way up to the position he'd wanted from the beginning: senior editor of the religious department.

He'd discovered, during the past month, that his

return to the area hadn't been as inconvenient as he'd imagined. In fact, his work went even more quickly. He kept in touch with the company through conference calls and he could fly up to New York whenever necessary.

That thought was both comforting and disturbing. The disturbing part was his uncertainty about what the future held. After being diagnosed with Alzheimer's, his granddad had given Jason the house and local newspaper. Granddad had wanted to settle his affairs while he was still able to function mentally. The dementia had progressed, however, to the point that his granddad had to be placed in a health care center.

Jason wouldn't even consider selling the house yet. After all, on good days his granddad wanted to come back here. This was home to him, although his affairs had all now been turned over to Jason.

Pulling in at the back of the house, Jason glanced at the dead leaves on the tarp covering the swimming pool. He couldn't escape the memory of a few days ago, when his granddad had stood at the sliding doors, looking out at the swimming pool, with tears streaming down his face.

"Nobody's fault," Granddad wailed. "Nobody's fault." He held out his arms to Jason as if he were still a child. Against Jason's shoulder the old man shook with heartbroken sobs. Jason felt his own warm tears wash his face and a terrible ache in his chest. He knew what his grandfather was thinking of; the same memory haunted his own life, casting its shadow on all he did.

Finally, his granddad pulled away and looked at Jason as if to say, "What's going on here?" That just added to

Jason's feeling that his own cracked heart might just break.

Trying to escape the unpleasant memory, Jason quickly exited the car and entered the silent house through the back door. He focused on pleasant memories of the past and thought of the panoramic views from all the windows of the mansion. How refreshingly different it was from the concrete and steel structures he viewed from his apartment window in New York, where pleasant evening scenes of lights being turned on in tall buildings and a small glimpse of the East River had to suffice.

He'd always held a fondness for Little Piney; he was already regretting that he'd have to leave.

※

He was not on a sabbatical from God, so he had decided to participate in the church's activities as much as possible. This would be the first time he'd ever gone to a singles' meeting, and he didn't know what to expect. He looked forward to it, however, already realizing that the diverse group of ages and backgrounds were as interesting, if not more, than seeing a play on Broadway.

That thought intensified when he pulled into the church parking lot and recognized Amy, Janice, and Buddy getting out of a small blue economy car. Amy said "Hi," to his "Good evening," and kept walking.

Janice, a girl shorter and slightly heavier than Amy, greeted him enthusiastically. She had a pretty face, surrounded by closely cropped short hair. Jason smiled, seeing the vivacious girl spread her arms and lift her head toward the darkening sky, as if embracing the world. "Isn't this such a beautiful evening?" Without waiting for a response, she ran to catch up with Amy.

Buddy waited and walked with Jason. Jason tried to concentrate on the young man's words and push aside his strong feeling that Amy Treadwell was giving him the cold shoulder.

Jason sat at one of the long tables with Buddy, several college students, and a middle-aged widower named Bob, who had joined the class a week ago. He estimated about thirty-five singles were in the room, the majority of them female.

After a devotional period, the teacher, Lydia Fortner, said there were two main items of business. One was "Resolutions" and the other was "Christmas Colors." She took a stack of bright pink envelopes from her purse, big enough to serve as an overnight bag, and laid them on the table.

"I've brought back last year's resolutions," Lydia said. "You have about two months to continue working on them. Forgive yourself if you failed to keep them. At our New Year's party we will talk about this and concentrate on beginning again."

Jason had come to admire Lydia, a middle-aged widowed woman with a profound knowledge of Scripture and a gifted teacher and leader. He listened as she explained the resolutions project for the benefit of new members. Each New Year's Eve the singles met and made resolutions for the coming year. Lydia would then pair them up according to their goals.

"The most popular resolution," she said, "including my own, has been to lose a few pounds."

After the understanding mutters of agreement, she continued. "All those making that resolution will be placed together and will work on the resolution and encourage each other during the year."

Jason liked the idea of making a resolution, although the last one he made was when he fell in love with Janie Carter in the first grade. He had resolved to be her boyfriend. Unfortunately, Janie Carter hadn't cared for the idea. Now, he did pretty much what he wanted, and he saw no reason to make a resolution.

He was more interested when Lydia called on Amy for the explanation of "Christmas Colors."

"She's the one who developed this project," Lydia said.

Jason thought Amy looked especially beautiful tonight in a slack suit of light blue, his favorite color. She stood in front of the group with a warm and friendly smile.

"At Christmastime, instead of planning a big party, we like to sponsor the 'Christmas Colors' project for the church. This is the third year, and it's been a great success." She explained that the singles would choose the project that interested them, then seek volunteers from other classes, organize the groups, and complete the projects.

Jason liked being able to look at her without seeming to stare. Her dark, intelligent eyes moved from one person to another, and she spoke with ease about projects obviously close to her heart.

"You may volunteer for the project in which you would like to participate." Her long blond hair fell softly around her animated face as she leaned forward to take several squares of colored papers from a box on the table.

She straightened. "This green stack is for needy families, the blue stack for the Christmas cantata, the yellow stack for children's needs, the white stack for the interstate project. Any questions?"

Jason halfway listened to the questions and answers. He had his favorite charities and always did something special for needy children at Christmastime. He'd already talked to the administrator about doing something for the residents at the health center.

Amy returned to her seat and Lydia got up. "So pick your cards, and while you're having refreshments you can gather around, choose a leader for your group, and decide how you're going to proceed." Lydia and a couple of the older women went into the kitchen. Jason kept his seat, and Buddy leaned his chair back precariously on the two back legs.

"I've already kept my resolution," he said. "I made a C in Sociology last December, so I resolved to bring that up to a B. I did that in the spring semester." He grinned proudly. "Guess I should have made two resolutions." He allowed the chair to return to its four legs. "I deserve a cookie for that," he said. "Oh, I need to choose my card too."

"Amy, are you doing the Interstate again?" Jason heard Janice ask as he neared the table.

"Yes, that's my favorite," Amy said, taking a white card from the stack, then Janice did the same, and the two of them moved toward the cookies.

That little stack of white papers drew Jason's hand like a magnet.

❧

While getting refreshments, Jason talked with several members. When Bob said he lived twenty-five minutes away in Greenland and had to leave early, Jason considered doing the same.

However, Buddy called to him. "Hey, Jason. You took a white card, didn't you?"

"Oh, yes, I believe I did," he said, as if he'd forgotten. He took a seat where Janice patted, beside her.

Amy stared at her bright pink resolution envelope, making Jason wonder if she'd forgotten what resolution she'd made at the beginning of the year. Then she sighed and stuffed it into her purse.

Janice spoke up. "I don't think there's any question about who our leader should be. Amy's done the interstate for three years.

"Hear, hear," Buddy said and applauded. "I've never done it and I don't guess you have, Jason."

"Never." He had no idea what was involved. "It sounds unanimous to me. Amy's our leader."

"Well, how can I refuse, now that you've all volunteered me?" Then she launched right in, confirming they'd been right to choose her as leader.

"Since we're all busy, the best time to meet might be thirty minutes before Sunday school, for as many Sundays as we need." She looked around and each of them agreed.

"Fine," she said. "Now, since you two haven't done

this before," she began, "I'll explain what the Interstate Project is about."

Jason sat back, enjoying the sound of her voice. "What we do is go out on the Interstate the first week in December," she said. "At that time everybody is thinking about Christmas and we want to remind them that the holiday is a celebration of Jesus' birth. We give the travelers coffee, orange juice, roadmaps, and Christian tracts."

She tapped lightly on her white card with a pen, accentuating her words. "The main point is to witness to them. Let them know the reason we're out there is because we're concerned for their souls."

Buddy spoke up. "Are they going to stick around long enough for all that? I mean, most people on the Interstate speed, instead of slow down."

Jason noticed, over the rim of his coffee cup as he lifted it to his lips, the warmth that glinted golden in Amy's dark eyes. "You're right and that's our whole purpose—to get them to slow down," she said softly. "We need to think about this, so we can impress upon them that life is a journey and the Bible is a roadmap that guides us on our way and leads us to our final destination."

Amy spoke with such feeling about the project that Jason began to realize this was not just a Sunday school activity. She had a sense of mission and cared deeply about lost souls. He witnessed a beauty about Amy Treadwell that reached far beyond skin-deep.

Her passion about this project could work well in a book. Thousands of Christians all over the nation could sit in their own homes and read such a book, becoming more conscious of their journey of life, and many might be inspired to go out on the road and talk to travelers about their souls.

Too bad Amy wasn't serious about writing.

After 10:00 P.M., Amy parked in Janice's driveway and switched off the motor. Janice had just said, "Don't you feel better about Jason now?"

Amy faced her friend. "I'm confused," she admitted. "He gives the impression of being a wonderful, dedicated Christian man."

"Wonder why he chose the Interstate project?" Janice asked innocently.

Before Janice could imply anything more, Amy quickly said, "Maybe because you did, Janice."

"No," Janice said wistfully. "I've looked deep into his pools of blue and felt myself about to drown. But it's like watching Brad Pitt on the big screen. I like to just stare and eat my popcorn. I'm not up to the challenge of taking it any further." She grinned. "Give me a down-home guy any day when it comes to getting serious." Her grin turned to a grimace. "Looks like I might have to move to another town."

Amy laughed. "Your Mr. Right will come along one of these days."

"Yeah," Janice said offhandedly. "I'm okay."

Amy knew she was. They'd been friends all through school, and the two of them were alike in many ways. Neither was in a hurry to get serious, and both still enjoyed living with their parents.

"Anyway," Janice said, "don't you think you could forgive Jason for making that one remark you overheard?" She snorted. "Goodness knows, I've heard worse."

"Oh, I know it's nothing earth-shattering. Except. . . it sort of was for me. And I'm not holding it against him. I'm just always aware of it. I wish I'd never heard that remark."

Janice reached over and patted Amy's hand. "He likes you, Amy."

Amy was shaking her head before Janice could even finish the sentence. "No. If anything, he probably wants to know why I'm not making eyes at him like the rest of you single gals."

Janice giggled and Amy joined in. Each of them always kept the other from staying too serious about anything for too long.

"Just think," Janice said, "you can use this in your book."

Amy saw her point. "You're right," she exclaimed, then went into a dramatic oration:

"Lady Heather simply couldn't decide who was the right man for her, handsome Knight Xavier or Royal Prince Rupert. Both had asked for her hand in marriage. Unable to sleep with such a troubled mind, she stole down the stone steps and went out into the courtyard. Perhaps a turn in the garden would help. Just as she stepped onto a darkened path, she overheard voices and saw two figures walking into the courtyard, lighted by torches."

"The figures or the courtyard were lighted by torches?" Janice interrupted.

"Janice! I'll revise and do grammar later. Now do you want to hear this or not?"

"By all means," Janice said, folding her hands and trying to look demure.

"Lady Heather hid behind a tree, afraid to make her presence known. Then, as she heard them talking, she realized the men were Xavier and Rupert. Her hand covered her mouth as she stifled a gasp. The secret she overheard changed everything. She would rather spend her days locked in a castle tower, existing on bread and water, than spend a moment with a man who had such a dreadful secret in his life."

Janice leaned close. "What does she hear?"

Amy shrugged. "I don't know yet."

Janice's voice became shrill. "Well, who had the secret? Xavier or Rupert?"

"I don't know that either. I'm just now getting the idea. It has to germinate."

"Germ. . ." Janice shook her head. She reached for the door handle. "I'm going to bed. You go write your book."

That's exactly what Amy intended to do. Dr. Prince had said, "Incorporate daily living into your characters. You have a problem, work through it with your characters."

She didn't think there was a way to approach Jason Barlow and say she really did want to write a book. What good would that do, since he wasn't interested in helping "everybody and his brother" write a book?

Her resolve to work on her book lasted one night.

Early the next morning the teacher-editor of the school paper was waiting in her office. "I have a young woman you might like to interview, Amy," he said. "She's a remarkable student. Besides working to pay her way through college, she's made the dean's list her first semester and has started a deaf-awareness class at her church. I can have her come down here and talk to you, if that's all right."

"Sure," Amy said. "Send her down here."

The editor extended his hand and Amy shook it, which meant *Knight of Dreams* would fade into the background. . .again.

The editor started to walk out of the office. Amy stopped him, then hesitated. She couldn't bring herself to ask for four dollars. "Could you pay me a dollar for the article?"

His immediate response came without her having to explain the reason. "No problem." He grinned. "Looks like you're learning how the writing business works."

Chapter 3

At the meeting before Sunday school the following week, Amy handed Jason and Buddy a list of what needed to be done for the Interstate project. Quickly, each one agreed to accept certain responsibilities. Jason and Buddy would contact the department of transportation for permission to set up a tent at two Interstate rest stops, obtain road maps, and take responsibility for seeing that needed supplies were taken to the rest stops. Amy and Janice would make up posters, contact all the Sunday school classes for volunteers, obtain Christian tracts, see that supplies were available, organize schedules for helpers, post them on the bulletin board, and include an announcement in the church bulletin.

Jason was amazed at how much the four of them accomplished in that brief meeting. He looked forward to others, wanting to learn if he were mistaken about Amy's coolness toward him or if that was just a part of her personality. Perhaps she was just more cautious than Janice and Buddy were about accepting new friends.

Although Buddy was much younger than Jason, during what little spare time Jason had, the two of them related well as they carried out their assigned chores for the project.

After volunteers were lined up, Amy made up the schedule. They would all need to be at the church by 5:00 A.M. Those assigned to the rest stop beside the westbound lanes, from 6:00 to 10:00 A.M., were Jason Barlow, Buddy Fields, Nelson Howard, Ann Hill, Darrell Hill, and Martha Grayson. At the same time, beside the eastbound lanes were Amy Treadwell, Janice Taylor, and two married couples.

Pretending to read other names assigned to other times, Jason kept his eyes on the schedule for a moment. Had she deliberately put the two of them on opposite sides of the Interstate? He forced the thought away. Amy probably never thought of him at all. And she'd never said or done anything against him. She was just. . .distant.

He looked up and his eyes met hers. "Any questions?" she asked.

Jason stared for a moment and she quickly looked away. Why had she been looking at him? Was it to see his reaction? "I have a question," he said.

He thought she stiffened as a guarded look came into her eyes. No, he would not let her know that he cared if they were on opposite sides of the Interstate. . .or the world, for that matter.

"Could I give anyone a ride on the morning of the project?" he asked.

Her glance fell to the schedule. "You could pick up Nelson Howard," she said. "He lives the closest to Little Piney."

Jason agreed, and at 4:45 A.M. on the first Saturday morning in December, Jason drove along the quiet street in the dark and fog, looking for the address of Nelson Howard. He saw a porch light, and a tall, lean man who looked to be in his seventies stood in the driveway, waving and gesturing for Jason to pull in.

"Looks like we got up before breakfast." The man chuckled as he got in the car.

"Before daylight too." Jason extended his hand. He'd talked with Nelson Howard on the phone but hadn't met him until now.

"Just call me Nelson." The man shook Jason's hand with a strong grip. "It's mighty sportin' of you to pick me up."

"No trouble," Jason said, backing out his car.

"I had a stroke after my last heart attack and lost part of my vision," Nelson said. "So I don't drive anymore. My wife takes me everywhere I need to go. But she doesn't mind. She's a young woman. Only in her sixties."

Jason smiled. While Jason concentrated on easing through a foggy intersection, Nelson launched into stories about his "young" wife. "I always said I married a woman young enough to take care of me in my old age."

Jason figured if she had any more vitality than Nelson, she could run a marathon.

"But I warned her when she turned forty and got kinda sassy, if she didn't straighten up I was going to trade her in for a couple of twenties."

Nelson laughed at his own jokes and just as Jason wondered if he was going to be entertained for the next four hours, Nelson grew serious. "I knew you when you were just a little tyke. Your grandfather used to bring you to the same church we're going to now. I often wondered whatever happened to ol' Seth Barlow."

Jason told him about his granddad being diagnosed with Alzheimer's. "The rest of the family have their own homes and didn't want the big house up on the mountain," Jason said. "So it's mine now."

"You plan to stay or sell it?" Nelson asked.

"The future's uncertain," Jason said. "But for now, I want to be near Granddad as much as possible and bring him home on his good days. Those are becoming fewer. He's at the health care center."

"Maybe I'll get my wife to drive me out there to see him," Nelson said.

"He'd like that." Jason was glad he had been asked to pick up Nelson. "I believe he knows more than his unresponsiveness indicates."

"That's what happens when you start getting old." Nelson sighed, then said what Jason didn't want to hear. "I remember that awful time. That was hard on ol' Seth. On all of you, I reckon."

"Yes," was all Jason said. Then quickly he asked, "Let's see. I turn up here, I believe."

Nelson began to give him directions, although Jason didn't need them. What he needed was to keep his mind off that childhood experience to which Nelson had alluded. Jason did not want to think about "that awful time."

❧

Once the youth director stopped the bus on the westbound side, there wasn't time for Jason to think about anything but the mission at hand. After unloading the equipment, they were all busy setting up a tent and tables, unloading coffee urns, running long extension cords from the waiting room between the rest rooms, and setting out signs that read WELCOME! REFRESHMENTS! at the entry and GOD BLESS YOU! at the exit.

"Who all can make coffee?" asked Mrs. Hill.

"I can drink it," Nelson laughed. "Have to fill myself up on caffeine and crank myself up before I can get started."

"I guess Jane and I are elected," said the woman.

Jason surmised Nelson must have drunk a lot of coffee that morning. The man never slowed down. He was the first to grab a handful of tracts and head for the vehicles pulling in.

Jason never dreamed he'd be shivering in the fog at a rest stop on the Interstate. He knew that New York would be covered with snow and be much colder than here. However, in New York all he had to do was step out of his apartment into a cab and be driven to work, the theater, or anyplace of his choice. He never stood out in the weather and certainly not before daybreak.

He thought of how he might be sitting in his office, with the odor of freshly brewed coffee wafting his way. His secretary would appear at his doorway, smile, and ask, "Would you like a cup of coffee, Mr. Barlow?" If anyone had told him he'd be involved in a project like this, he'd have said they were out of their minds.

But he wasn't doing it out of fondness for cold, dank, early-morning fog. He wanted to also be actively involved in some physical capacity.

Once he got the hang of things, following Nelson's

lead of saying, "God bless you," and "Drive carefully," he began to mean it. He realized he'd never done anything like this before. People who knew he was a religion editor seemed to take for granted that he was a deep Christian. Jason supposed he did too. But now he realized the joy of reaching out, doing something physical for the Lord, bringing a smile to the faces of weary travelers, and reminding them of the "reason for the season" coming up.

During a lull in the traffic, Jason poured himself a cup of coffee. He walked over near the edge of the rest stop, looking out across the Interstate in the approaching dawn. This was the first opportunity he'd had to even wonder how things were going over at the eastbound rest stop.

Amy stood near the GOD BLESS YOU exit, sipping orange juice and staring across the Interstate. All morning, distance and thick fog had prevented her from seeing anything beyond her own frosty breath and the headlights of cars making holes in the haze.

Now she took a moment to revel in the scene before her. The world became a canvas on which an impressionistic picture began to emerge. A pastel orange sunburst made an opening in the lightening sky, turning the distant treetops to yellow and the morning mist to shimmering gold dust.

How could she describe it? *It was like. . .like. . .looking at a beautiful setting while looking through tinted glass. Yes, like looking through a glass. . .darkly. That's what the apostle Paul wrote in the Scripture: "Now, we see through a glass darkly. Then we shall see face-to-face." He was talking about our life on earth, compared with when we see Jesus in heaven.*

Oh, that would be a perfect quote on the teaser page before the first chapter of her book. It fit with a plot she had in mind.

"Hey, no sleeping on the job," Janice called as a couple of vehicles pulled in.

"I've got to do this, Janice."

Janice moaned. "Not your creative juices again."

"This is priceless, Janice. Really. Take over for a minute." Without waiting for a reply, Amy went to the table where a record was being kept of how many travelers stopped. She took one of the pencils and grabbed a tract. There wasn't much blank space, but she began to write the verse of scripture and a couple of words to remind her of the plot ideas floating around in her head.

After a few notes, she folded the tract and put it in her jeans pocket for safekeeping. "I couldn't help it, Janice," she said between travelers, "doing things, like coming out here, gets my adrenaline flowing and I want to write. I'm getting some really good ideas."

"Your mom said washing dishes always brings on your writing urge."

"That's the truth, Janice. I sit in front of the computer with my mind blank. I get up to do something and all sorts of ideas jump into my mind."

"Well, hold onto those thoughts. You can tell me about it on the bus. Here come a row of cars."

Amy quickly finished jotting down her ideas. She had finished the sign-language article, and Dr. Prince said that could be her final project since she wouldn't have time to finish her book synopsis. He encouraged her to keep writing down any ideas about it, however. He'd be teaching a novel-writing class next semester if there was enough interest.

⁂

After ten o'clock, when a new crew of scheduled volunteers relieved the early morning workers, Amy and Janice slid into the bus seat behind the driver. The early morning group from the other side of the Interstate had already been picked up and had taken seats further back. Amy took out her notes and Janice listened wide-eyed as Amy related her ideas.

"How's this for a first sentence?" she asked. "Lady Heather dreamed of Xavier again last night."

"Perfect," Janice said. "It fits with the title and makes me want to know what happens next."

"Great! Then I'll tell you," Amy said. "It was a lovely dream of his kneeling before her, holding her small pale hand in his strong bronzed one, vowing his eternal love. Upon awakening, she threw open the shutters, hoping to see him riding up on his steed. But she could not see beyond the dense fog that lay on her skin like a wet cloth."

"Oh, that's good," Janice said. "Fog on her skin like a wet cloth. I like that."

Amy nodded. "That's kind of how it felt, wasn't it? Do you like that better than having her go outside and stand in the morning mist as thick as gravy?"

"I like the wet cloth better," Janice said. "Where is this? London? Scotland on the moors?"

Amy shrugged. "I don't know yet. Could be either. I'm trying to get my characterization down right now."

"Okay," Janice said. "Tell me more. What does Xavier look like?"

Amy described him. "He's handsome, strong, brave, good, kind, and even calls on the Lord for strength."

"Oh, to have a man like that." Janice sighed. "He sounds perfect."

"Right. But Dr. Prince says the hero and heroine should have some kind of flaw. It doesn't have to be big, but something so he isn't perfect. He's got to seem real."

"What's his flaw?" Janice asked.

"Well, I don't know if it's what Lady Heather overheard, or something else. That's still buried deep in my subconscious."

"Well," Janice said. "Maybe another trip to the Interstate—or washing dishes—will bring it out."

❧

Jason parked at the back of his house next to Selma and Slim Martin's car. He still employed the older couple who had seen to the care of the house and grounds for his granddad.

"You must be starving," Selma said when he went into the kitchen. "I'll whip you up some breakfast."

"Great. I'll wash up."

When Jason returned to the kitchen, bacon was sizzling in the pan. A cup of hot coffee was already waiting for him at the table. So was Slim, who set his own cup down, motioned for Jason to take a seat, and said, "Well, tell us all about it."

It was good talking to this couple like they were his grandparents. It took a little of the sting out of not having his own granddad around. "Over three hundred cars stopped." Jason pulled out a chair and sat. "We served at least five hundred cups of coffee and juice and gave out five hundred Christian tracts." Satisfaction tinged his voice. "Not one person refused the tracts."

Selma brought over his plate filled with bacon, hash browns, and two sunny-side-up eggs. "You'll probably want to nap after this," she said.

"I feel more exhilarated than exhausted," Jason replied, much to his own surprise. "But I don't think I could sit down and edit effectively. Since it's a clear day, I thought we might go out and find a couple of Christmas trees."

"I'll get the chain saw," Slim said.

Jason had other ideas. "I'd like to try and do it the old-fashioned way. Bring the axe."

Slim glanced at Selma, as if to say Jason had lost his mind. "I'll get the truck," he said, "and the chain saw, just in case."

After Jason finished his breakfast, he walked out back, waiting for the truck. Breathing in the cold air, he thought about how productive the morning had been for him. He felt more alive than he had in a long time. He'd even been reluctant to leave. He'd felt good talking to strangers, giving them coffee or juice, giving them tracts about salvation. It was good spending four hours thinking about other people.

He had always considered his job his mission: making Christian books the best he could so that the gospel message went out to strengthen believers and plant seeds in unbelievers. But there was something different about the personal contact, shaking someone's hand, sharing a smile, a kind word, and wishing someone God's blessings and a safe trip.

He'd watched Amy and Janice take a front row seat on the bus, and he had seen how animated they were as they laughed and talked. Maybe someday he'd get the chance to tell Amy how impressed he was that she had come up with such an effective way of witnessing.

As he walked on out to the truck, he realized that in New York, everything had been rush, rush, rush. Here, he had time to go out in the woods of his own property and cut trees like his granddad used to do.

With Slim beside him, Jason drove along the narrow rutted dirt road into the woods. When he was a teenager, his granddad had taught him how to notch one side of a tree with an axe, then whack away at the other side. Jason wanted to remove that skepticism from Slim's eyes.

With a sense of accomplishment, he downed the biggest cedar he could find to go in front of the living room window. "Selma always wants fresh pine and holly boughs," Slim said. "And mistletoe." He went off to find them while Jason cut a smaller tree for the great room.

When they arrived home, Selma already had the colored lights and family heirloom decorations out for the big tree. "Decorate any way you want to in the living room," Jason said. "But I want this one to have small colored lights and lambs on it."

"Lambs?" both Selma and Slim said in unison. While

Selma stood speechless, Slim cleared his throat and asked in a dubious tone, "You mean lambs like in *maa-maa?*"

"Slim, I think you have goats on your mind. Let's try the *baa-baa* kind, as in 'Black Sheep.' But let's make these white."

"Could I ask why you want lambs on the tree?" Slim asked.

"Christmas! Jesus!" Jason replied, beginning to feel embarrassed. "Okay, so maybe it's not a creative idea, but it's symbolic. You know, the Lamb of God. And 'feed My lambs.' It's all scriptural."

"Hmmmh," Slim grunted and looked at the tree.

Selma came back to life. "You might have trouble making them stay on."

"I'm not talking about real ones." Jason laughed.

Selma snickered behind her hand. "I know, but I was thinking plastic. But. . ." She stared at the tree. "Maybe Beanie Baby lambs."

"There!" Jason said, as if the matter were solved. But he went away wondering, *Beanie Baby lambs?*

It only took Selma three days to gather all the available Beanie Baby lambs in Pine Valley, which came to the sum total of four. "But, I thought the little lambs could use some guardian angels," she explained to Jason, "so I found some nice ones."

"That's fine," he said after seeing the size of them. If she'd found many more, he could just dispense with the tree." But once she decorated it, he was quite pleased. She set the cream-colored lambs and the larger white angels back into the tree limbs, and at the forefront she hung small crystal stars that reflected the colored lights.

"Perfect," Jason exclaimed triumphantly. "And you two thought I didn't know what I was doing."

Chapter 4

At the last writing class, which ended in mid-December, Dr. Prince returned student papers with suggestions for revisions. Although Amy's article had already been printed in the school paper, that didn't mean it would meet the standards of a writing teacher. She saw a lot of red marks.

"Good," he'd written beside her title, "Nancy Supports a Silent World." He'd also written, "Your beginning catches the reader's interest."

She'd begun with:

> *The little boy didn't heed the woman's shout for him to stop before he darted out in front of the approaching car. . . .*
>
> *The speaker turned his head and the woman in front of him never heard the end of the story. . . .*
>
> *These are but a few instances of those who live in a world of silence, the world of the deaf, isolated from hearing people who do not understand and cannot communicate with them.*

In the body of the story, he'd marked a couple of

grammatical errors, a typo neither she nor the computer had caught, and a few places where she could delete or tighten. "Excellent ending," he'd scribbled next to where she'd written:

> *With her little finger, index finger, and thumb held up, Nancy made the symbol of the universal language that all understand. "This," she said smiling, "means 'I LOVE YOU.'"*

She received an A–. Maybe it would get accepted when she sent it away to a magazine. She recalled a quote she'd heard somewhere. "Reach for the sky, and be happy if you land in the treetops."

She'd just begun to reach. Maybe writing magazine articles was the treetops for her. Maybe she wasn't a novelist. But she was not a quitter, and she'd take that novel writing class next summer.

But for now, she would concentrate on spending Christmas with her family. She could return to her *Knight of Dreams* after the first of the year.

But, she wouldn't make any resolutions about it.

❧

"A fire started in the kitchen and burned out part of a wall. They won't be able to get the soot cleaned up in time for our New Year's party," Lydia informed the class on Sunday morning. "All the other restaurants are completely booked up. I have company," she said, "but—"

When she spread her hands in a helpless gesture, Jason interrupted and volunteered, "We can meet at my house if you'd like. I have plenty of room."

He didn't know why he said it, but the moment the words came out of his mouth, the class members all seemed in favor, making comments like, "Oh, neat! Thanks, Jason. Great!"

Lydia accepted immediately. "That is so generous of you, Jason. We can bring covered dishes."

"No, just bring yourselves," he said. "I'll handle the rest."

Janice smiled broadly and nudged Amy, looking delighted. Amy smiled at her friend, giving Jason the impression that even she liked the idea. He'd noticed a particular exuberance about her lately and wondered if someone special had come into her life to bring that excited glow to her eyes. How fortunate a fellow would be to have won her affection.

Although he'd just received acceptance from the entire group, he felt a stab of aloneness and stared down at the floor. What brought that on? Maybe it was the fact that he'd spent most of the Christmas holiday alone in the big house. For several years, he and his associate editor, Martha, had gone to parties and special events together. He'd visited with her family and she with his. This year had been different.

Realizing he was staring at the floor, he raised his eyes and looked straight into Amy's. She lowered hers to her Sunday school quarterly. Jason turned his attention to the teacher.

"Now don't forget," Lydia was saying, "bring your resolutions already written out. Now we'd better get to the lesson."

Jason tried to concentrate on the lesson and on the worship service afterward, but his mind kept wandering to the party coming up in just a few days. Would he be able to get a caterer at this late date?

He needn't have worried. By Monday afternoon Selma and Slim had secured the caterers, the servers, and all the help he'd need.

❧

A light snow was falling on New Year's Eve, turning the landscape into a holiday greeting card. But as Amy drove up Little Piney Mountain, she couldn't enjoy watching the barren forest sprinkled with white soft snow. She felt apprehensive.

She felt guilty accepting Jason's hospitality when she hadn't been very free with her own. She hadn't readily accepted him like the others had. Buddy obviously hadn't minded Jason's remark about writers. Maybe she was just being too self-conscious about him and her writing. He'd certainly proved to be a giving person by going out on the Interstate, then inviting everyone to his home.

"Look at that," Janice said. "I've seen the mansion from a distance but never up close. I wonder if he lives up here all alone."

Amy had assumed he did. But if so, who was helping him with the party?

As soon as Amy stepped inside the great room, she saw an elderly man in black trousers and white shirt taking coats. An elderly woman was passing around hors d'oeuvres, and she realized this was the "proper" way to greet guests—that is, if you had a mansion.

Jason walked up and greeted them, then said to Amy, "You look like a snow bunny—all dressed in white."

Amy flushed. Janice eased the awkward moment by saying, "You have a lovely room here, Jason."

"Thank you," he said. "Make yourselves at home. Look around if you'd like. Excuse me." He left to greet other arrivals.

Janice poked Amy with her elbow. "Why didn't you say thank you?"

Rather than admit Jason Barlow had a way of making her tense, Amy feigned innocence. "Thank him for what?"

"For saying you look like a snow bunny."

Amy shrugged one shoulder. "Was that a compliment?" At Janice's stare, Amy asked, "What part of me resembles a bunny? Was he saying I have big ears? Or that I look like an animal that ought to hop around on four legs? Do I have a rabbit face? Or facial hair that looks like whiskers?"

By that time Janice was cracking up and Amy couldn't hold back the giggles. When she and Janice were together they often acted like little kids with big secrets and giggled like schoolgirls.

Actually, she hadn't known what to say. Should she say he looked like a blue bird because he was wearing a blue sweater that made his eyes look like a Carolina sky in summer? How fond was he of snow bunnies anyway? Even if he liked them, was that a way to compliment a woman? Why, oh why, did she have to question everything?

"Oh, look at that," Janice said, and the two walked over

to where Lydia was standing in front of a beautifully carved crèche.

"Hi, girls," Lydia said.

"Isn't that beautiful?" Janice looked at the lifelike nativity scene figures. She picked up a wise man.

Lydia nodded. "Jason was telling me he got that in Bavaria where he spent the Christmas holidays one year. I asked how much it cost, and he said just one of those hand-carved lambs cost over three-hundred dollars."

Janice carefully replaced the wise man, then glanced at Amy, who immediately felt the giggles again. Janice turned to the tree. "Now this is unique, Jason," she called when he came near. "I like your tree. It's different."

"Thank you," he said. "I have to admit Selma is responsible for most of it."

"Now, don't you go blaming me for that," said the woman with a tray of hors d'oeuvres.

When Jason responded, "I thought I was giving you credit," the woman grinned and moved on.

Soon, Selma rang a little bell. "Dinner is ready," she said.

The dining room doors opened and the most fabulous aroma of meat, cake, and spices floated down the hallway and into the room, beckoning the guests to come and partake. Beneath a magnificent crystal chandelier, the long table looked fabulous. It seated eighteen, and three round tables handled the overflow. Two low centerpieces of fresh white carnations against dark green leaves graced the big table and smaller ones were on the smaller tables. White china plates with a gold edge sat on larger green plates, flanked by gold knives, forks, and spoons that gleamed in the light of the chandelier. Long-stemmed goblets, one filled with water and another one filled with a green napkin, sat above each plate.

"If you gather around and stand behind your chairs," Jason said, as the guests filed into the dining room, "we can ask God's blessing on the food."

How it happened, Amy wasn't sure. What she thought was the foot of the table turned out to be the head of the table where Jason eventually stood. Lydia was on his right, Janice on his left, and Amy beside her.

Amy felt the silence. Everyone was in awe as much as she. They'd been to nice restaurants before, but this was a home. Jason had really done it up big. But she supposed it wouldn't do to live in a mansion, invite people in, then have them sit on the couch, at card tables, or the floor as they'd done at her house. She couldn't imagine what the food might be.

"Our Father God," he began, "at this season when our hearts turn to You and the greatest blessing that could be given to mankind, we thank You for Your love, Your mercy, and most of all Your Son who saves us from our sins. We ask Your blessing upon the food of which we are about to partake, and may our lives be an example of Your Spirit living within us. Guide us through the evening, and we give You the praise. Amen."

After the "Amen" they all sat. A man, wearing black pants, white shirt, and a chef's hat, entered the room. While three females in black and white rolled in carts with choices for salad, the chef related that the main course was fresh trout almadine and Cornish game hens. Several women servers asked each guest if his or her preference was fish or fowl. Side dishes were brought in so the guests could eat family-style. There were little green peas, sweet potato casserole, and tomato aspic. Soft classical music played in the background, ensuring there were no awkward silent moments.

Conversation was flowing, mostly about the fabulous food, and then Lydia asked Jason about his family. He told how his granddad had grown up in a house in Pine Valley, loved the area, and after he became successful in the newspaper business had built the big house on the mountain. Amy found it interesting that the more his family had succeeded, the more isolated from each other they had become.

On second thought, her family was scattered too. But they all came home for the holidays. Amy felt Jason would like to be closer to his relatives.

"Well, what did you all do over Christmas?" Lydia asked.

Buddy, a few seats down, heard the question and jumped in to answer. He opened presents with his parents and older sister, then went to a movie after dinner.

Lydia's husband had died years ago, leaving her to raise two daughters who were now grown and gone. They couldn't get home for Christmas, but as usual, Lydia had invited all the single parents to her house for Christmas dinner.

Amy said all the family was home as usual, which included two sisters, two brothers-in-law, their five children, one brother, a sister-in-law, their one child, her parents, and herself. "We eat and pass out presents to the children, open presents from our name-drawing, sing some carols, and talk over old times." She knew how blessed she was to have a loving family.

Janice related that her family had gone to a presentation of Handel's "Messiah" down in Greenland. "What did you do, Jason?" she asked.

Amy noticed the slight furrow of his brow before he smiled and said he'd gone to the retirement center on Christmas Eve night, had dinner with his granddad, and stayed for a musical program. He'd spent a quiet Christmas Day and did a lot of editing on a manuscript.

Amy wondered if the others were thinking what she thought. This man, who appeared to have everything, spent Christmas Day alone. Three weeks before Christmas, he'd stood out on the Interstate greeting travelers trying to get home to families, but then hadn't seen his own family. But she supposed that was his choice. He could have flown to be with his family. . .surely. Or friends in New York. She could imagine that he must have many business acquaintances and friends. She personally knew several females who thought him fabulous and would spend the day with him at the drop of a hat. Maybe he just liked himself and enjoyed his own company. But she thought he'd sounded a little lonely. Nobody should be alone on Christmas Day.

❧

After they returned to the great room, Lydia took the floor as cappuccinos were served. Jason turned his attention to

Lydia, who reminded them they should never feel obligated to talk about their resolutions. But some liked to report what they'd accomplished and it served as motivation for many.

"Mine was to lose at least ten pounds," said Janice. "And I did it."

They all applauded.

She grimaced. "Of course, thanks to Jason, tonight I gained it all back."

They all laughed and others told of their accomplishments. Buddy had brought his C up to a B and was on the dean's list. Peggy read the Old Testament through for the first time in her life. One of the older widows, Mrs. Bartlett, had donated two hours a week at a nursing home and felt it had been more of a blessing for her than for the patients.

Several made no report, and one of those was Amy. Jason wondered why not. She joined in all the activities and was an active Christian. Perhaps she had her life under control and didn't feel a need to make a resolution. Come to think of it, from what he'd seen, she was an exceptional young woman in every way.

"Okay, then," Lydia said. "I guess you all brought your resolutions with you. If not, I have some extra paper and pens. The envelopes this year are yellow. Make sure your name is on the outside of the envelope and on your resolution. And you all know this is strictly voluntary. Don't give it a second thought if you failed to keep your resolutions last year. I confess I failed mine by five pounds."

Maybe it was having the group in his home and feeling

so much a part of things that made Jason pick up a yellow piece of paper and write down a resolution. It was something he should have done years ago.

After everyone who wanted to do so had passed their envelopes to her, she said, "I'll just find me a spot somewhere and go through these."

Jason said she could use the living room if she liked.

He was glad they all seemed relaxed and conversed easily back and forth. He hadn't had this "down home" kind of feeling in many years. In New York, his life had centered on things like business or the theater. Here it was more about family and everyday living.

❧

Lydia returned, all smiles. "Oh, we have some good ones this year. As always, I'm tempted to tell, but I'm sworn to confidentiality." They laughed with her. Amy felt a little badly that she hadn't made some kind of resolution.

Lydia began reading off names of people who had made similar resolutions, leaving it up to each of them on how to proceed with getting together. About midway through calling off names, Lydia said, "Amy and Jason."

Amy grasped her cup more tightly, afraid she'd drop it. She quickly checked her surprise and took a sip of her cappuccino as Lydia continued to pair up the members with similar resolutions.

When Lydia began explaining that now the groups were responsible for organizing their own times of meeting together to work on their resolutions, Amy and Janice escaped to one of the many bathrooms.

"I thought you didn't make a resolution," Janice said.

"I didn't," Amy said. "Lydia must have paired us together because of Jason's resolution. I can't imagine what goal he might have that I could help him with."

"I could take your place," Janice offered, looking in the mirror to apply lip-gloss. "I mean, what's a friend for?"

Amy grinned. "Never mind. Just because I'm determined to write my book without asking for his help doesn't mean I'm not willing to help him. But I'm curious. What do I have to offer someone who has everything?"

Janice brightened. "He does not seem to have a girlfriend."

Amy shook her head, grinning. "He doesn't need to make a resolution to get one of those." She grew thoughtful. "Maybe he needs a secretary. But on second thought, he could hire one of those."

Janice shrugged. "Since you work at the college, maybe Lydia thought you could recommend a student who might want part-time work, typing or something."

❧

Janice said, "My boyfriend went to Germany and married a fraulein. I won a speech contest and sneezed three times when I was supposed to say, 'Thank you.' And I changed a flat tire on the side of the Interstate."

After much guessing, Janice was mortified. "Oh, no," she wailed. "I forgot to lie."

They all laughed. After Lydia had led them in a devotional period, emphasizing spiritual gifts, she'd suggested they play the game, "Two truths and a lie."

"Let me explain again," Lydia said. "Each person has to tell three things about himself or herself. Two of the statements should be true. One statement should be false. The group will guess which is the lie."

Lydia gave an example. "I was a volleyball champion in college, my late husband and I went to Barbados on our honeymoon, and last year I went bingy-jumping."

Everybody cracked up! If she didn't know the difference between "bingy" and "bungee," then it wasn't likely she'd done it. When the laughter died down, no one felt reluctant to reveal his or her truths and lies.

When Jason's turn came, he said, "I edited a book written by a maharaja. When I was a child I bicycled along the streets of Pine Valley delivering newspapers. And, um, I'd rather live on Pine Mountain than in New York."

He was delighted that almost all believed he preferred this area to New York. Most thought the newspaper boy was the lie. But he informed them he'd never edited a book written by a maharaja.

He was eager to learn more about Amy and listened closely as she made her statements. "I had a 4.0 average in college. I sponsor a child in Ecuador. And I won many events while on a college swimming team."

As the truth came out, he barely registered that she didn't have a 4.0 average. He was concentrating on the swimming remark. So that's why Lydia paired them together. He'd resolved to learn to swim, and Amy was an expert swimmer.

❧

Bringing in the new year was the last item on the agenda, and they watched that on TV at Times Square in New York City. Jason felt good that none of the guests left early but stayed long after midnight. They seemed reluctant to leave even after the closing prayer.

After all the guests had gone at last and the caterers had cleaned up and left, Jason looked around at the great room and smiled. It was kind of nice to see cushions awry, scuff marks on the tile, a cup on the floor beside a chair that the caterers had missed. The smile left when he realized that Stella and Slim would have to clean all that up in the morning.

He switched off the lights and basked for a moment in the cozy firelight and the colorful lamb/angel tree that had served as an excellent conversation piece. Yes, the party had been a success. He walked to a window. Soft snow was covering the landscape like a white carpet.

It reminded him of Amy, dressed in winter white, so becoming with her light hair. She hadn't thanked him for saying she looked like a snow bunny. Now that he thought about that, he realized his words didn't necessarily sound like a compliment. He, who worked with words every day, couldn't seem to find the right ones around lovely Amy.

Well, the evening had been fulfilling in all other ways. Everyone had received his hospitality graciously. He'd done his best to fit in with the group. He turned quickly and brushed against a tree limb, causing an angel to tip to the side.

With a wry grin he straightened the lovely blond in her flowing white dress and gossamer wings. *You are lovely, Miss Angel.*

He slumped into an easy chair and stared at the now-dying fire. Another year had ended. Another begun. He felt good about this one. He felt he knew his class members better and for the first time felt total acceptance.

Even Amy Treadwell had shaken his hand, smiled warmly, and thanked him for his hospitality. But how would she feel about being paired with him and his resolution?

Chapter 5

The Sunday after the party, Jason told the Sunday school class that he would be out of town for a couple of months or more. He would return to New York for a while, then had conventions and conferences to attend.

"Amy," he said after class, while she was gathering her coat and materials. "Could I speak with you for a moment?"

"Save me a place," Amy said to Janice, then turned toward Jason.

Jason could put words down on paper and was considered expert at taking other people's words and making them stronger. He could talk all day about business without a hitch. He could take a woman out to dinner and discuss literature, writing, the business world, or almost anything. But this woman had him so tongue-tied he was afraid to open his mouth for fear of putting his foot in it.

Perhaps he should start with a compliment. "I haven't had the chance to really express my admiration for the Interstate project. That is a wonderful idea. It's the kind of project that could work throughout the year if other churches joined in."

He saw her initial skepticism turn into surprise. "You

mean," she asked, "you think we should contact other churches and see if they're interested?"

"Indirectly." He tried to explain. "I was thinking in terms of an article about the project. That was such an exhilarating experience for me and apparently for others who go out there and greet travelers. I had unusual experiences. Nelson Howard has hundreds of stories."

She laughed lightly at that, meaning she was aware of Nelson's expertise at relating stories.

"Then there are the experiences of the travelers. Do you ever hear from any of them?"

"Oh, yes," she said excitedly. "Last year when we went out it started snowing. It was beautiful for us. Several days later the pastor got a phone call from two different drivers who said there was a bad wreck further up the mountain into North Carolina where visibility was about two feet in front of them. Had they not stopped earlier to accept our coffee and literature, they would have been right in the midst of the pileup."

"That's what I mean," he said. "What we could do is put a note on the tracts like, 'Let us know how this may change your or someone else's life.' Amy, you know God is working in this project. An article like that, making people realize the importance and joy of reaching out could make a major difference nationwide."

"You. . .want me to write about it?"

He saw the shock on her face. Much like he'd seen the first time he'd mentioned writing to her. Something in her seemed to have an aversion to talking about writing.

"Think about it," he said, dismissing the subject.

"Another thing I wanted to mention is the resolution. I resolved to improve my swimming. I assume that's why Lydia paired us together."

"That would be it," Amy said. "I was on the college swimming team. And since I work only part-time at the college during the summer, I teach a few swimming classes at the public pool."

"Then you probably wouldn't have time to give me lessons. I had planned to hire an instructor. I wouldn't want to impose upon you."

"Impose?" She smiled. "Believe me, getting into a pool like yours would be no imposition."

The church bells rang, signifying it was time for the worship service. Neither made a move to go.

"I didn't tell you everything, Amy." Jason knew he had to be honest with her. "My problem is not the swimming. It's the deep water. I have a fear of it." He cleared his throat nervously. "I would appreciate it if you'd keep that confidential."

He braced himself, but Amy didn't laugh. He was amazed that she was able to pretend that a grown man, afraid of water, was just another everyday event. In fact, this was the first time he'd detected a small glimmer of acceptance of him in her dark eyes.

"I'll be glad to teach you, Jason."

"Thanks. I'll call you when I get back from New York."

They walked out together and headed for the sanctuary. Jason knew the church bells had already rung, but strangely, he could hear them faintly in the back of his mind.

If this were a novel, it would have one of those surprising plot lines. *What's going to happen next?* he wondered. *How is this going to turn out?* In no way was Amy Treadwell predictable.

※

"Think about the Interstate project," Jason had said.

What irony!

Last semester, she'd tried to write a novel and ended up writing an article. Then, in mid-February she'd started the novel class and her big inspiration was working on the Interstate project article.

But she was still jotting down ideas about her book. Each week, Dr. Prince covered an element of storytelling, going into more detail than he had in the creative writing class. Each week, she added a little more to her story.

Spring rains and a cold spell prevented any thought of swimming lessons. The flowers were making their appearance when Jason called and asked if they could have their first lesson.

"I can be there by five," Amy said. She left work at four, drove home, and changed into her swimsuit, deciding that for lessons a conservative one-piece with its overlay skirt would be most appropriate. She wouldn't be swimming. She'd be instructing while standing in the water.

She called her dad's dental office; her mom, who worked as his receptionist, answered the phone. Amy told her she wouldn't be there when they came home shortly after five. Amy didn't like not giving details to her parents or to Janice, but she respected Jason's desire for confidentiality. "It has to do with Jason's resolution," she said, "but I can't tell you any more than that."

"At least we know where you're going," her mom said.

When she arrived he was sitting on the edge of the pool in a black swimsuit. A pair of goggles lay beside him. Yes, he was as impressive this way as he was fully clothed. But that was no surprise, she reminded herself. She shucked out of her beach robe and sandals.

When she neared him, he looked up skeptically. "Maybe we should have some lemonade and talk awhile first."

"No swimmin', no lemon," she said like a true teacher, then walked down the steps into the cool water, thinking how refreshing it would be to swim several laps. That was not her purpose here, however, so she told Jason to drop down into the water. Then she had him dip his goggles in before putting them on. That way he could see while swimming without having to deal with pool chemicals irritating his eyes.

She watched his expression carefully. The water here was only four feet deep and he didn't exhibit fear, just self-consciousness. When she showed him how to bob, he laughed. "I can do that kind of thing. It's not like I've never been in the water. It's when I get out there where it's up to my neck that I—" He shook his head and she saw that just the thought of it frightened him.

"With your fear of water, you need to learn more than just how to move your arms and legs," she said. "You have to know how to save yourself if you get in trouble, even if you're scared. Now, if I'm going to teach you, you'll have to do what I say, no matter how amateurish it may seem. Got it?"

"Yes, ma'am," he said, lifting his hand in a salute, sprinkling water on her.

She gave him a warning look. "Bob!" she said.

"Bob?" he jested. "I'm Jason."

Amy knew his joke was just a way to cover up his fear. She made a thumbs-down gesture at the water. "Jason, bob ten times."

It wasn't long before she could assess his ability in the water. He floated beautifully, on his back and his stomach. She taught him the correct way to bring his knees up to get himself in upright position from back floating. He had a strong stroke and could swim the width of the pool with ease, but he needed instruction on correct arm movement.

"I've swam the width many times in the shallow end," he said, "but apparently I didn't have the correct movement. Thanks for the help."

"A lot of it seems to come naturally for you."

"Not entirely," he said. "I did have instructions when I was quite young. I suppose part of that is still with me."

"You're doing well. Just bend that left arm a little more when it comes back out of the water. You tend to keep it too straight. You'll have a stronger and faster stroke if you do that."

After about forty-five minutes, Amy knew he had the stamina to swim the length of the pool numerous times—but not the confidence.

Chapter 6

Amy didn't even suggest the deep water until the fourth lesson, a week later. She'd had him bring life preservers and place them at the pool's edge. "Let's just walk out as far as you can." She stood in the shallow end of the pool and watched him carefully.

When the water reached to just below his shoulders, he glanced at her and made an uncertain sound. He took another step and it reached his shoulders. His breathing became unsteady. Another step and she saw the fear. He tried to step back, lost his balance, and reached out for her. "Sorry," he said, realizing he had a tight grip on her arm.

"It's all right. That's what I'm here for," she said. "Reach over and hold onto the side."

He did. The pool was clear enough that she could see he was standing on his toes although he was only in shoulder-deep water. This was going to be a tough one. She wouldn't dare get him out in deeper water. He'd drown them both.

"Okay. Just hold onto the side and get used to bringing your feet off the bottom while you go under. Then take your feet down and push yourself up. Hold onto the side until you think you can do it without holding on."

On the third try he let go of the side. When he came up she saw the exultation on his face. "I did it." His hands came out and lay on her shoulders, and his eyes reflected the late afternoon sky. "I was completely submerged without my feet touching the bottom or my hands holding onto the side." He was holding onto her shoulders while she was treading water, but she would have rather been totally immersed than dispel his jubilance.

"That's a major breakthrough." She hoped he thought the wetness in her eyes was pool water. "The first step is the hardest. There's hope for you."

"Thanks to you." Gratitude glinted in his brilliant eyes. He let go of her shoulders and reached to the side of the pool.

Amy paddled into the shallow water. "That's enough for today."

"Would you like to swim?" he asked. "You've been coming for two weeks teaching me and haven't been able to enjoy the pool."

"Oh, I'd love it," she said. "But you get out first. And if anything goes wrong, just throw me a life preserver."

She watched as he swam in the shallow water, reached the steps, and got out. Then she dove in and effortlessly stroked the water, as if she were moving through a cloud. It was relaxing and energizing at the same time. Thinking of nothing else but the joy of the water around her and the late afternoon sunshine over her, she crawl stroked for several laps, then backstroked, then swam underwater. She stood on her hands and wiggled her feet above the surface. Finally, feeling totally refreshed, she came up, pushed her hair away from her face, and got out of the pool.

"Incredible." Jason was now wearing his robe. "For a while there, I thought I'd have to throw in the life preserver. But you're a mermaid. Truly a beautiful mermaid."

Amy laughed self-consciously and rubbed herself with the towel. After such a lavish compliment, she might have stayed for dinner tonight had he asked. He didn't ask. Instead, he said, "How's your novel coming along?"

Amy hesitated. She could have told him she was still working on her Interstate article, but he hadn't asked about that. Her novel class had ended; she'd turned in a synopsis of sorts, but got a C on it. Dr. Prince said it wasn't fully developed. She didn't want to admit that to Jason.

"It's slow going," she said and slipped her arms into her robe. She flung her wet hair behind her shoulders, picked up her bag, said, " 'Til next time," and left.

⚜

Jason left again for two weeks, then returned in the middle of June. He was anxious to get back into the pool for two reasons.

First, he had conquered a small amount of his fear and wanted to continue. He could now go into the deep end and tread water. Amy stayed nearby in case that overwhelming sense of panic washed over him. She'd say, "Just float on your back and work your way toward the shallow," or "Reach out and begin swimming toward the shallow. You can do it." He had!

And second, the moment he and Amy stepped out of the pool, she became reserved. When he mentioned her writing, she turned distant. But in the pool, she was warm, kind, sweet, helpful, patient, and caring.

Amy came in the late afternoon for their lesson. The lesson consisted this time of his swimming in the deep end, always close enough to reach out and touch the side. Then Amy said it was time to swim across the length of the pool, from the shallow to the deep.

Jason thought he could. He tried. But when he got about midway, he felt the panic rise. A knot rose in his throat. The air became heavy and he had to open his mouth to breathe. He splashed furiously getting to the side.

"It's all right if you're not ready. Swim back to the shallow end."

Jason knew he should tell her what it was all about. If he didn't do it now, he would never do it. But he wasn't sure he could. He swam to the shallow end, walked up the steps, and sat in a chair. "I'll try to explain," he said.

Amy sat in the chair next to him. He grasped the arms and saw the scene in his mind while the sun faded, the blue sky turned gray, and he remembered the blackest day of his life.

"My seven-year-old brother drowned in this pool when I was nine," he said, for the first time in his life. The child psychiatrist had talked about it, had tried to make him believe it wasn't his fault. His family never blamed Jason. Granddad had tried to convince Jason of his innocence and even blamed himself, saying he should have been out there with him.

But it hadn't been anybody's fault. Or maybe it had been everybody's. The boys knew not to get into the pool without an adult. Many times they had waited impatiently for an adult to find time to go in with them. That particular day Jason's mom and dad were both going in with them. Granddad was doing something in the yard.

"Come on. Come on," little Phillip kept saying. He loved the water. He liked to jump into the shallow end and play around. He could turn flips in the water and come up laughing. They both could swim, but they were never allowed in without an adult. But that day, Phillip couldn't wait for an adult. He suddenly ran for the pool and jumped in.

Jason yelled, "No, Phillip! They won't let us swim if you jump in."

Jason ran to the edge. Phillip looked like he was swimming under water, acting crazy like he often did. Then he just hung there. Jason watched. "Phillip, quit it," he called, getting scared because that was a long time to be holding his breath. But Jason was afraid to jump in. He had strict orders never to do that.

"Granddad!" Jason yelled when Phillip turned and his mouth and eyes were open under the water. Jason jumped in and grabbed Phillip and started pulling him to the side. Phillip slipped from his grasp. Granddad got there and reached down for him. "Go call an ambulance." Granddad was immediately over Phillip, breathing into him.

Jason got out and ran, yelling, "Call an ambulance! Call an ambulance!"

"My childhood ended that day as surely as Phillip's did," Jason said. "His death couldn't be accounted for. 'A freak accident,' they ruled it. But my mom, dad, grand-parents, and myself all blamed ourselves. We should have done something differently. So you see, Amy," he said in a choked voice, "it's not the water so much that I'm afraid of. It's the memory of what happened that day in the water. I know it wasn't my fault, but a part of me says I should have been able to do something." He leaned forward and covered his face with his hands.

The next thing he knew, Amy was kneeling on the concrete in front of him. She moved his hands from his face. His own eyes dried while he looked at her wet ones. She reached up with her hands and with soft fingers wiped away the tears from his face.

She was so gentle, so sweet, so caring, he wondered if she forgot they were not still in the pool. Her gesture so touched him that he grasped her fingers and laid them against his lips and closed his eyes for a long moment.

Suddenly, he realized his grief had been replaced with the awareness of the beautiful woman in a swimsuit kneeling in front of him. She'd stroked his face. He was holding her fingers against his lips. Although the past would always be near him, his awareness now was in the present. What should he do when he opened his eyes? What would she do? Slowly, he moved her fingers and opened his eyes.

"I'm sorry I burdened you with this," he began.

"Don't be," she said softly. Then, as if aware of their closeness, she moved away from him and stood, reverting to her aloof on-land attitude.

While she readied herself to leave, he watched with a

trace of embarrassment. No, he didn't regret that he had told her the reason for his fear. He only regretted he hadn't told her while they were in the liquid pool of friendly camaraderie. The evening might have had a different ending.

❦

Amy returned to working full-time at the college in early August. The fall scheduling had been finalized last year, much of it a repeat of previous years. She helped with registration for a couple of days, then began typing into the computer the dean's notices that would go to all faculty members. Amy color-coded the various messages, made copies, and put them in the faculty information boxes.

By the time classes started in mid-August, she felt almost ready. There were always last-minute details to handle and unexpected needs of faculty members, in addition to the dean's correspondence. Amy loved her job, though, and she was excited when students flooded onto the campus. She liked the hubbub of voices, meeting new faculty members, returning friendly greetings, and answering the questions of freshmen who popped their heads in to ask directions.

Her swimming classes at the public pool had ceased. But Jason had invited her and Janice to use his pool while he was in New York.

"This is like the vacation I didn't have," Janice said as they stretched out in lounge chairs after several laps in Jason's pool one balmy September evening.

Amy agreed. "Why go to a crowded beach when we have our own private vacation spot?"

"Yeah," Janice said lazily, then sat up as Selma wheeled

out a cart of delicious goodies for them to eat.

When Amy had protested the first time she'd done it, Selma declared, "Jason left strict orders for me to do this if you came to swim." She smiled broadly. "And it's my pleasure. It's so nice having people around."

From then on, neither girl objected, realizing that Selma got satisfaction from bringing food to them and hearing their compliments.

After eating, they discussed Amy's book. Now that she was beginning to stir her story ingredients together, she felt the characters coming to life.

Janice read:

> *Lady Heather curtsied and Prince Rupert returned the gesture with a bow, an extended hand, and a smile on his elegant face. The sun shone brightly on the flowers and shrubs, where royal gardeners worked each day. "Let us take a turn in yon woods," Rupert suggested. "I do so long to be alone with you, away from prying eyes." Lady Heather's heart fluttered like a shaken tambourine. Was it because of Rupert's words—or was it the memory of those fearful words she'd overheard while hiding behind a tree?*

Amy always watched Janice's face closely for her reaction. Her friend looked out at the woods beyond the gardens, past where Slim was working in a flowerbed near them. "I can just visualize your story," Janice said. "It feels like I'm right there."

Amy jerked the paper from her. "If you're going to

make fun of me. . ."

Janice jerked it back and laughed. "It's really good, Amy. You said you're supposed to write what you know. You're doing that."

"Okay," Amy relented. "Now if you laugh at my knight, I'll never let you read another word."

She began to read:

> *The only way to get across the raging river was on the raft that someone had left on the bank. Lady Heather couldn't understand why Knight Xavier stood like a stone and didn't jump on immediately after pushing the raft into the water. He'd saved her from the barbarians, but she could hear their war cries and their bare feet beating the ground like a hundred drums as they raced through the trees, coming closer. Just as an arrow whizzed by her, catching the fabric of her gown and leaving a gaping hole, Xavier shoved off and jumped on. Midway, he fell into the water. Lady Heather could tell by the look in his eyes as he gasped and fought the river that he had an uncontrollable fear of water. Every instinct said she must save him. She jumped in. He grabbed her arm and she felt herself going under. They would both surely drown.*

Amy smiled as Janice expressed her delight at the way the book was progressing, but for a moment Amy's thoughts were elsewhere as she gazed out over the pool. Could she allow Xavier to express his love for Heather?

Or should Xavier, after overcoming his fear and gaining confidence, not need Heather any more? Had Heather already hopelessly lost her heart to a knight who couldn't return her feelings? Was she like a lady in distress, drifting on the river of life, on a raft all by herself?

Chapter 7

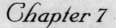

Little Piney Mountain was alive with the fall colors of red, yellow, gold, and orange when Jason returned. On a warm Indian summer Saturday morning, Jason called Amy to say he'd returned. Amy was eager to see him again, as excited as any teacher who wants to know how her student is progressing.

Before the lesson, they sat in the chairs, their robes shielding them against the evening breeze rustling the leaves on the trees.

"I know I haven't progressed as much as you'd like," Jason said, "and there won't be many more days like this. Our lessons will end."

Amy thought his words sounded regretful. She felt a stab of regret herself. She cherished these times with Jason.

"You've done so much for me, Amy," he said, facing her. "I wish there were some way I could thank you."

She knew he could help her. He'd done so already without knowing it, just by being an inspiration with her plot line. He'd caused her imagination to soar as she plotted *Knight of Dreams*. The only thing she could think to say was, "I don't want charity."

"Charity?" He stepped back, looking as if she'd struck

him. "Is that what you've given me?"

"No," she said with a lift of her chin. "I help people because Jesus commands us to, and I want to."

"That's certainly commendable. But it sounds to me that you're implying that I don't."

Oh, why did she always act like such a ninny around him? "No. I know you've done a lot for our class members and the church. You're hospitable with your home. Oh, I'm sure your position with your company is worthwhile. You edit books that will make a difference in the reader's life. You go to conferences and talk about writing. I know that helps." She was talking much too fast. She took a deep breath. "It's just that. . .after what I heard you say—"

"Heard me say?" he interrupted. "What? When?"

She stared at him, finding the air hard to breathe. "Okay, you want to know, I'll tell you. I think it was about a week after you first came to the class. I overheard you making fun of 'everybody and his brother' wanting to write a book, thinking they could sit down and type one out in a week or two. After hearing that, I felt too inhibited to even mention to you that I was writing a book."

She watched him look out over the pool, thoughtful, as if trying to remember. Finally, he not only turned back toward her, but he turned his chair as if to trap her in her seat. "Amy," he said, leaning toward her, "if you're going to eavesdrop, then you should stay long enough to hear the rest. Not base your opinion on part of a conversation."

Amy would have jumped up and run had he not been blocking her way.

"Now, I don't remember what you're talking about," he

said pointedly, "but I do know myself and how I feel. Yes, I've made statements like that, but I always say, and I mean it, that I'm always pleased when a beginning writer presents me with a manuscript that has promise. You see, I'm not obligated to go to writers' conferences. I do it to discover potential. I do it to encourage, to motivate, even to help."

Oh, at that moment she wished she were the one who couldn't swim. She'd just go take a dive into the deep end. That is, until he said, "So you've wasted almost a year holding a grudge against me, when that time could have been spent with the two of us discovering your talent, your potential, and whether your book is publishable."

Feeling totally reprimanded, miserable, like a dunce, and watery-eyed, she rose from the chair so quickly he had to grab the arms of his chair and hold on to keep from toppling over as she pushed against his legs to get by. She headed for her car.

"You leave and I'll swim out to the deep end," he warned.

Idle threat! He wasn't fully relaxed swimming in the shallow. She opened the car door and heard a splash. She turned. He'd jumped in. Usually, he walked down the steps, but he was swimming toward the deep end.

"No, Jason!" she yelled when she saw his even stroke turn to slapping at the water. She untied her robe and let it fall to the concrete. The life preservers weren't near her. She would jump in if she had to, but that could easily end in tragedy—for them both. Instinct sent her running along side the pool until she got to the other end.

She cupped her mouth with her hands. "Relax, Jason.

You can do it. Don't slap the water. Take even strokes. Float if you need to." If he panicked, all was lost. He'd never try again. "Come on, Jason. Just a couple more strokes and you've done it. Yes, that's right. Oh, good. Good."

She was shaking as he reached the edge, pulled himself up on the side, and stood. "I did it. Amy, I did it!" He opened his arms to her and she fell against his chest, shaking.

"You shouldn't have," she said. "It's too risky. If you're going to take lessons, you have to obey the teacher."

"You would have saved me, Amy. You have saved me. From that awful fear and feeling of guilt. Oh, Amy," he said against her hair. "I couldn't let you walk away from here." He held her away from himself and she saw the sincerity on his face, heard it in his voice; she was so glad for his victory, his ridiculous, chancy, stupid victory, that she couldn't find any words. She didn't want to argue, and she was just too weak with relief to pull away. She leaned back her head and lifted her face toward him.

Before she knew it, his head came close; her smile faded when she felt his firm lips against hers. The kiss was fleeting and he moved back, looking a little surprised and more scared. She was too surprised to do anything. "I need you, Amy," he said. "Don't you know that?"

"Well, yes," she said, moving away as he dropped his hands from her arms. "The first time is a breakthrough. It's a beginning, not the end." *What about the kiss? Was that a beginning? Wasn't that just an impulsive reaction to the fact that neither of us drowned today?*

"Okay," she said, forcing her eyes away from him.

"We might as well get started. Jump in and swim to the shallow end."

Jason tried to hide his disappointment as they finished the swimming lesson. Did she really think he had been talking about swimming? Didn't she know what he had been trying to tell her?

As they climbed out of the pool, he stopped her with a hand on her arm. "Amy, let's talk some more. Tell me more about your writing. What are you working on?"

He saw her take a deep breath. "I'm writing an historical romance novel."

He didn't think he moved a muscle. He tried to hold still for so long he felt like a tree in a petrified forest. His reluctance to speak, for fear of alienating her again, apparently froze her, too. Her glow faded, her smile vanished, her eyes darkened. Her stare was like dark chocolate.

He should have known better than to think this would be so easy. Selma came out with two plates laden with barbecued pork sandwiches, coleslaw, corn chips, lemonade, and a few brownies.

"Thank you, Selma." Seeing Amy stare at the food, he wondered if she was going to ask for a doggie bag or if she would bolt. "Let's say the blessing." He reached for her hands.

He felt her reluctance and hoped God would forgive him for saying words primarily for Amy's benefit. "Thank You for the food, Lord," he said. "And most of all thank You for Amy's helpfulness to me. Guide me as I try to be helpful to her. May this be a wonderful afternoon of

Christian companionship and fellowship. Amen."

He watched her face. It looked determined, but even if she couldn't stand him, she couldn't resist Selma's lunch. But the tension between them was thick enough to obscure the trees of Little Piney.

"Come to think of it," he said. "I'd say you look like a romance writer. I mean, long shiny blond hair, dark chocolate eyes, a lovely face." He dared say no more.

He didn't think she was taking that as a compliment. She nodded. "And I'm sure all editors look exactly like you."

He got the point. He'd goofed again. "Look. I'm sorry I didn't respond the way you wanted me to. I'm just not into romances. I edit some fiction, but mostly nonfiction."

She chewed her salad very fast, finally swallowed, washed it down with lemonade, coughed, then said, "Most people I know are concerned about romance and who will be their life's mate. Most people I've heard of fall in love. In fact, haven't you heard that the Bible is a love story? What will change people more than the love of God?"

Are you concerned about love and your life's mate, Amy? Why are you not out seeking him? Would you rather spend your days and evenings with me? He'd like to ask those questions out loud, but considering her touchy alarm button, he wouldn't dare. "I understand about God's love. That's the primary theme of the work I do. And it's not just a job. It's my mission."

She was eating fast. "Oh," she said, "then it's romance you don't understand."

She was trying to hit him where it hurt. She was right. He knew all about relationships, going out to dinner, kisses, emotional involvement. But romance? That would depend upon the definition, he supposed. He wasn't experienced along that line. "Maybe you could teach me what romance is."

"That was not part of our deal, Jason Barlow. I doubt your definition is the same as mine. And I don't believe you can help me with my book." She stuffed a corn chip into her mouth, crunching loudly as she spoke. "You don't take seriously something like falling in love, or two people gazing into each other's eyes, or the heart beating wildly."

"Yes I do," he rebutted. "But I thought that was caused by a fear of water."

She wiped her mouth and tossed down her napkin. "That's what I thought all along. You wouldn't take my writing seriously at all." She stood. Then she picked up the sandwich and took another bite.

She glared at him while chewing. He tried not to laugh. "Amy, you're afraid."

"Afraid? Of you?"

"Afraid of rejection. Afraid your book isn't any good. Look, it doesn't matter if I know anything about a romance book or not. I can still recognize talent. I know a good story when I read it. I can let you know if you have potential." Seeing her stare, he said kindly. "That frightens you too, as much as the water frightens me. Let me help you."

She grabbed the remainder of her sandwich and headed for her car.

He turned. "Where are you going?"

She looked over her shoulder and spoke with her mouth full. "To work on my book. Maybe I'll give it to you before you go back to New York. We'll just see how much you know about romance."

Romance? he was thinking. *Not much.* But he did know that a fiercely independent young woman had huffed and puffed her way into his life, threatening to blow away that fragile shell he'd carefully built around his heart.

And he knew something about the feel of her soft shoulders beneath his hands, the touch of her lips against his, and his fear that she would know the depth of his feelings for her.

Jason thought it was a breakthrough that Amy brought her articles for him to read, although she hadn't yet brought the novel. While there were still a few warm days in September, he had his lessons, then read and commented on her writing.

"I agree with Dr. Prince's giving you an A on this one," he said.

"A–," Amy corrected. "I sent it away but I got a rejection."

"Did they say why?"

"No. Just said it didn't meet their publishing plans."

"Where did you send it?"

"Life on Campus."

Jason thoughtfully stared at the first page. "It could be the editors thought it had too limited an appeal. It's an interesting, inspiring story, but not something that a lot of readers identify with in the sense that they can imitate what this girl has done. Not only does a story need to hold interest, it needs to have a motivating quality for the general audience."

Amy felt better about the rejection then. She smiled, nodding.

"They might feel differently about the international exchange student. Most colleges do have exchange programs and there are classes that travel abroad as part of their studies." He handed her the articles, but held onto the Interstate one.

"Now this one," he said, "has real possibilities. How did you come up with the idea, Amy?"

Amy felt sad, remembering. "I knew a couple of college students who were killed by a speeding driver. This is sort of my own private memorial to them."

"I'm so sorry," he said. "But, Amy. That's what you need at the beginning of this. You have to touch the emotions of the reader. Give them a reason to slow down on the Interstate." He began to read again and make notations on the pages.

Watching him thoughtfully, Amy realized how important his words were. She'd wanted to protect the memory of those students. But the best thing to do was reveal it for the benefit of others. That's what they would have wanted. She realized too that she needed to put that kind of emotion in her novel. Lady Heather had gone too long wondering whom she loved. Even Amy realized Lady Heather was undeniably in love with Knight Xavier.

❧

Jason took Amy's synopsis and three chapters of her novel with him on the plane, along with her revised Interstate project article. As soon as the plane leveled off high above Little Piney he began to read. The Interstate article had real merit.

Knowing her novel was closest to her heart, he felt reluctant to read it. He knew if it were no good he'd have to be honest about it. Recently, he had read several best-selling inspirational historical romances, so he could have an idea of the books being published. He would know better how Amy's story rated against those.

The title was good: *Knight of Dreams*. He smiled when he read about Lady Heather standing in the fog, looking across the wide river to find her true love, Knight Xavier. That reminded him of the morning he'd stood gazing across the foggy Interstate, wondering what was happening on the other side.

His smile faded when the castle on the hill, the court-yard, and the surrounding gardens had a striking resemblance to his own place. He couldn't believe it when Xavier fell into the water and nearly drowned because of his fear of water.

Jason knew that writers drew from people and situations around them, and he shouldn't make too much of this. It was just a story, not real life. However, he was disappointed that Amy had neglected to put into the synopsis just how the novel ended. Was her true love Knight Xavier or Prince Rupert? He read it again and had to be content with the fact that Lady Heather had a particular warm spot in her heart for Knight Xavier, in spite of his character flaw. Actually, that flaw seemed to endear the knight to the lady.

❧

Jason called Amy from New York that evening.

"I wanted to let you know that I won't be returning for a while. My publisher has sped up the publication date on a major novel, and I'm having to rush to meet his deadline. I'll be working nonstop, but as soon as I return we'll get to work on your novel."

Amy couldn't tell if he were pleased with her novel or not. She dared not ask.

"I doubt that I'll return in time for the Interstate project. But I really like your revisions on your article. Do you think you can get more material?"

"I think so. I plan to pass out a note, asking travelers to let us know how they felt about our being out there for them. I know we're going to get a great response. And I have more stories from the volunteers."

"Wonderful," he said. "Send those to me here in New York."

It seemed pretty obvious to her which project Jason liked best!

Chapter 8

J ason wanted the evening to be perfect. However, it not only rained, it poured. He'd missed Amy more than he had expected during the almost three months he'd been away. However, she'd never been far from his thoughts.

He pulled into the carport and knocked on the kitchen door. Amy's parents warmly welcomed him into the cozy-looking country kitchen. He lost his line of thought when Amy walked into the room, wearing a lovely black dress and carrying her coat. Her hair was done up at the back of her head in an elegant, fancy style. He took her coat and placed it around her shoulders, bid her parents good night, and held the door open for her.

"You look wonderful, Amy," he said, after they were in the Bentley.

"So do you," she replied, smiling.

"Your hair's different," he said, turning the key in the ignition.

She gave him a mischievous look. "I don't always go around looking like a stereotypical romance writer."

He laughed. "Oh, Amy, it is so good being back, seeing you. This is our first real date, isn't it?"

"I believe it is," she returned, smiling at him as if she

hadn't thought of that. When he'd called, however, and asked if she'd like to have dinner with him, she'd immediately said she'd love to go. He returned her smile, looked out at the downpour, started to complain about it, but, he remembered, he should be grateful for the rain. He and Amy always had related well in water.

The best restaurant in Pine Valley, where he'd made reservations, was only a ten-minute drive from her home. There was hardly time to talk about anything but the weather and the fact that his trip had gone well.

After parking, Jason took his briefcase from the backseat, then the two of them hurried inside. The maitre d' led them to a corner booth, as Jason had requested, where they might have a little privacy while talking about her book.

When they had eaten and were sipping cappuccinos, Jason took her manuscript from his briefcase, then came over and slid onto the seat next to her.

❧

Amy's heart raced. He'd said such complimentary things. And he'd called this a date, implying it was not just to talk about her manuscript, but like it was a special evening for them to be out together.

Then her heart almost stopped when she looked at the marked-up papers. It was awful! She just knew it.

She wasn't sure she heard him correctly when he said, "Your book has merit." She became lost in his blue eyes shining in the candlelight. He gave her a favorable estimation of her work. He talked as if she were a real writer. He explained her strengths and weaknesses, saying she should expand on the strengths and work harder with the part of writing that didn't come so naturally.

Before she knew it, over an hour had passed. He'd gone through chapter one, page by page, word by word, telling her what was wrong and what was right. Amy realized what a dedicated, knowledgeable editor he was and how valuable his constructive criticism was.

"I've learned more in an hour," she said, "than in all the writing classes and books I've read for years."

He smiled. "That's why publishing companies have editors. We can all help each other. But I have to agree, it can be an asset, having one's own personal editor." He pushed the manuscript toward her. "Now it's all yours. There's much work to be done. But I think you can revise by looking at my notes. My company doesn't publish romances, but I hope I have encouraged you to rewrite and submit it to a romance company." He paused. "I am now highly in favor of romance."

Looking into his eyes, she had to ask, "Just in books, Jason? Have you had serious relationships in the past?"

After a thoughtful moment, Jason replied. "Over the past years one of the editors and I became close. We went to parties together, theater, that sort of thing. I thought I must be in the first stages of settling down. However, this past summer, when I was taking swimming lessons, she went to her high school class reunion, met an old boy-friend now a widower, and they took up where they left off years ago."

"How did you feel about that?" Amy asked.

"Relieved." He smiled and looked into Amy's eyes for a long time. "What about you?"

"I've thought I was in love a couple of times. The last

one borrowed my savings to help get himself through medical school. Oh, he paid it back. With interest. But he found another love. Apparently it wasn't meant to be or I'd be more heartbroken."

"Same here." Jason stacked the papers to return to the folder. "And I don't know how this works, Amy. But I think my fear of water caused me to fear life and held me back from allowing myself to fall in love. Overcoming that fear has seemed to free me in other ways too."

She ceased to breathe when he turned toward her again, reached up, and gently touched her cheek, as his eyes searched hers. "I'm not sure how romantic I might be," he said, "but I could easily fall in love, Amy, without even trying."

"I know the feeling," she said softly, allowing him to look into her eyes and know what lay deep in her heart.

❧

Late into the night, lying in bed, but not wanting to sleep, Amy wrote the ending to *Knight of Dreams:*

> *With Lady Heather's encouragement, Knight Xavier conquered his fear. His incredible physical strength enabled him to reach the safety of the raft for himself and the wonderful woman he loved. Heather allowed him to see the love light shining in her eyes. They expressed their undying love, agreed to wed, sealed their pledge with a kiss, then sat on the raft while they drifted toward the shore. Heather breathed a prayer of thanks to God for delivering them and for giving her the knight of her dreams.*

"I can end the story however I want," Amy said aloud to herself. "After all, it is fiction."

Could it be? Could it possibly happen that way for me?

Jason returned to New York for Christmas, and it was a couple of days before New Year's when Amy got a phone call from him.

"Amy. I can't get a flight out until New Year's Eve," he said. "I won't be at the resolutions party, but I wonder if you might stop by my house after the party. I would like to spend a portion of New Year's with you."

"Yes, I'd love to do that," she agreed quickly.

Amy went to the resolutions party, held at Lydia's. By ten o'clock, she couldn't keep her mind on any of the festivities. Naturally, Janice noticed and agreed that Amy should leave early and drive up to see Jason.

A light snow had begun to fall and lay in soft white layers on the trees as she drove up Little Piney to the lighted mansion. Jason was at the back door by the time she reached it. He took the big package she was carrying and set it on the floor, then helped her take her coat off. Neither said anything about her coming before the party had ended, but Amy thought he looked as pleased as she felt.

Selma greeted her warmly and brought in cappuccinos, then disappeared into the kitchen. Jason led Amy over to the couch, in front of a blazing fire. His decorations were like the year before, including the lamb tree.

"That present is yours," she told him.

He went over and got it, then smiled as he unwrapped the box.

He began to laugh, turning the box to make sure he was seeing right. On every side was a picture of a brightly colored inflated plastic raft, with a little boy on it, floating in a swimming pool.

"Is that what's really in here?"

"Yep," she said.

"Well, on the first warm day we'll try it out and see if it's strong enough to hold the two of us."

"Now there's an intriguing thought," Amy quipped, as if the thought had never occurred to her.

"Now," he said. "A little something from me. As I told you, my company doesn't publish romances, but I had one of our artists do this."

Amy unwrapped the long, thin box and removed the tissue paper. There, in a gold frame was the most beautiful picture she'd ever seen. Her name was printed in gold letters. AMY TREADWELL, below the title in fancy cursive letters: *Knight of Dreams*. In the center, against a deep blue background, was a handsome knight, holding the hands of a beautiful woman with long golden hair. They gazed at each other with love light shining in their eyes.

"To commemorate your first book," he said, "that has real possibilities."

Her voice was choked. "This is so wonderful. Thank you so much." Her face was wet with her tears.

He took the gift from her and laid it on the table, then took her hands in his. His loving expression took her breath away. "Amy, I made a resolution again this year. To be the kind of man who could deserve a wonderful woman who has helped me overcome fear, taught me to swim, and wants to publish a book about the greatest ingredient in life—love."

"Oh, Jason," was all she could say. She didn't look away; she let him see the love light in her eyes, what she had been so afraid to reveal, so afraid he might reject.

"I love you, Amy," he said softly. "Can you love me?"

"Yes, Jason, I love you." She swiped at the tears of joy and relief that flooded her eyes. "I'm sorry. I shouldn't cry."

"Oh, please do," he said. "We relate better around water, remember?"

She laughed through her tears. "You've already fulfilled your resolution and the new year hasn't yet begun. But I don't know about myself. Last year I vowed never to make another resolution."

"Never say never," he said. "Make one more vow. To spend the rest of your life with me."

"Yes," she said, just before his lips began to finish what he'd started long ago that day at the pool.

Soon, she settled next to him, with his arm around her shoulders as they watched with anticipation the ringing in of the New Year.

Amy looked over at the book cover he'd had made up for her. She loved it. Maybe her dream of getting it published would never materialize. But that was all right. God had given her something even better. She had her own personal knight, better than any book or any dream.

YVONNE LEHMAN

As an award-winning novelist from Black Mountain, North Carolina, in the heart of North Carolina's Smoky Mountains, Yvonne Lehman has written several novels for Barbour Publishing's Heartsong Presents line. Her titles include *Southern Gentleman, Mountain Man,* which won a National Reader's Choice Award sponsored by a chapter of Romance Writers of America, *After the Storm, and Call of the Mountain.* Yvonne has published more than two dozen novels, including books in the Bethany House "White Dove" series for young adults and *Coffee Rings* by Barbour Publishing. In addition to being an inspirational romance writer, she is also the founder of the Blue Ridge Christian Writers' Conference and enjoys being a grandmother.

Letters to Timothy

by Pamela Kaye Tracy

People often ask where I get my ideas. *Letters to Timothy* was born in the hearts, smiles, and hugs of the 1998–1999 third-graders at Southwest Christian School. "Okay, class, get your pencils out, put those folders up, and remember: always write your name on your papers."

The Third-Graders:	*The Pen Pals:*
Savannah Brady	Donelle Ryen
Steven Garcia	Lee Marik
Tiffany Kutnick	Florence Potter
Kalynda Powell	Edna Adrian
Erin Ray	Thelma Smith
Ashleigh Rayburn	Ethelmae Kauffman
Justin Shelton	Reida Whisler
Kyle Simpson	Marguerite Moore
Zach Swift	Curt Sanders
Josh Terry	Jo Nell Cross
Jesse Wagoner	Elizabeth Whatley
Katie Westerholm	Elsie Burman

"Let the little children come to me, and do not hinder them, for the kingdom of God belongs to such as these."

MARK 10:14

Chapter 1

"O kay, take your first resolution and tie it to your coat hanger." Rita Sanderson held up her completed mobile. Her New Year's goals—four of them—hung neatly in a row. Goal one, get in shape, was on a pink square. Goal two, read the Bible everyday, was on a white circle. Goal three had to do with finances and the fourth was a private one: Find a nice guy with whom to form a relationship. In previous years, she hadn't experienced much success with any of her goals, especially money and men, but she didn't need to share *that* with her class. Maybe this time she'd meet the goals she had set every January since graduating college.

Small hands struggled to tie ragged shapes of paper onto coat hangers. A few hands waved in the air. The third graders attached to those hands wanted help. Their strings of yarn lay tangled on their desks. But in the class of sixteen, one child stared at his coat hanger instead of working.

Assigning helpers to the hand-wavers, Rita knelt beside Timothy Carter. "Have you thought of any resolutions, yet?"

"Taking care of my dog?"

Rita picked up a piece of clumsily cut, blue construction

paper. A misspelled word had been half-erased and then scribbled out. "Your grandmother says you do a great job caring for Terminator. Let's think of something you've been meaning to do but haven't done. What about working harder on your spelling?"

Timothy's brown hair fell forward as he bowed his head. Spelling was a nightmare as far as the skinny ten-year-old was concerned.

"Okay, how about this? We get that letter written to your pen pal each week with at least nine sentences."

Timothy bit his lip. "Five."

"Seven, and that's my final offer." Rita stood, holding her hand out for Timothy to shake. Slowly, he took it.

The warning bell rang as Rita hung the last mobile. Stepping off the bottom rung of her stepstool, she watched her students shove textbooks and paper in their backpacks. Glancing at her desk, she smiled. For the first time this school year, sixteen pen pal letters were in the turn-in box. Timothy was keeping his resolution.

Rita clapped her hands. "I'm counting to ten. When I'm done, I expect your desks to be clean and the floor picked up."

With winter holiday right around the corner, the students were unwilling to chance getting their names on the board. Soon every desktop was clean and the floors almost spotless.

"Timothy."

"I'm hurrying, Miss Sanderson." A few pencils and a fistful of paper scraps later, Timothy went to the end of the line.

Rita led her students outside and waited until every small charge was either picked up by a parent or safely stashed in daycare. Then she headed for the fourth grade classroom for a faculty meeting. After closing the door, she sat in the first desk, banging her knees against the bottom, and waited for the meeting to begin.

Mrs. Womack, the principal, entered the meeting with paper and pen in hand. "Harriet, did you check the sound system?"

"Everything's fine."

Connie Womack drew a check on her list and asked, "Rita, how about refreshments?"

"I have everything taken care of." The winter program was tomorrow night, and Rita had recruited brownie bakers over a month ago. Mints and hot cocoa were on the menu, too.

"Good." Mrs. Womack took a breath and leaned against the teacher's desk. "Any prayer requests today?"

"I have a blessing to share." Rita turned to face the teachers behind her. "Timothy finished his pen pal letter."

Every teacher at Boundaries Christian School knew Timothy Carter. His past teachers attributed their gray hair to him. His future teachers discussed retirement. Rita couldn't say she'd looked forward to having him in class, but truthfully, his reputation exceeded his problems. Sometimes Rita even believed Timothy might overcome his learning disabilities.

"What did you do?" Tina Lidell asked. The second-grade teacher had arranged for Timothy's speech therapy.

"It wasn't me. All I did was make a spur-of-the-moment deal. Something I never do. And it worked."

Tina led the prayer. Rita bowed her head, but she had a hard time focusing. Timothy was a true lost sheep, and looking after him took more energy than she spent on the rest of her flock. His letter today to Clint Reeves was a milestone. To date, the elderly man had received one drawing. The other pen pals, all residents of a nearby retirement center, received some type of correspondence each week. So far, though, Timothy was the only third grader who hadn't received a reply from his pen pal.

Rita hoped Clint Reeves responded this time. Of all her third graders, Timothy needed attention the most.

❧

David Reeves did not like the Greater Hope Retirement Home. Every time he passed through the lobby on his way to Grandpa's second-floor apartment, there was a new three-by-five index card stuck on the downstairs bulletin board with the name of a newly departed tenant. Today was no exception.

"What do you have in the Crock-pot?" Clint opened his door and sniffed the air.

"Philadelphia Pepper Pot Soup," David answered while heading for the kitchen. "We served it last night. I want you to tell me what you think. I've also brought stuffed capons with cranberry-poached pears. I don't think I've mastered them yet. You tell me and don't make a face. These fancy fixings earn me a good living."

David crumbled crackers into the soup and grabbed a spoon from the drawer. While Grandpa started eating,

David cut the capon into small pieces. Clint Reeve's arthritis made handling utensils awkward. If it weren't for the crippling disease, Grandpa would still live in his previous apartment, the one a few blocks from David's restaurant.

"Did you bring soda?" Clint looked hopefully at the half-full Styrofoam cup David placed in front of him.

"Milk is better for you."

"At my age, nothing is better for me."

David winced.

"David, you have to accept I'm going to die one of these days. Now, you'll remember I have some money hidden under the dresser. Pull up the carpet and—"

"I know, Grandpa." David repositioned the TV tray and handed over the remote control. Clint was the only family David had. As a small boy he'd been placed in his grandparents' care after an accident claimed the lives of his parents. His grandmother died while David was still in junior high. Then two years ago, after David decided not to re-enlist in the air force, his girlfriend had decided the adventurer turned restaurateur was not exciting enough for her. At twenty-six, David figured he had already lost more than his share. He wasn't ready to lose his grandfather.

Clint's hand shook as he took a folded piece of paper off the coffee table. "Hey, look what I got in the mail today."

The paper was smudged with enough pencil lead to leave a smear on David's fingers. The letters were oversized and slanted so they seemed to fall on each other. "What is this?"

"It's a letter from my pen pal."

David choked back a chuckle. "When did you get a pen pal?"

"I've had him since September, but this is the first letter he's written."

"I can see why. Is this some kind of code?"

"You want to talk about your grade-school handwriting?" Clint chided.

"It wasn't this bad."

"You have a short memory. I cannot make hide nor hair of this. Maybe I need stronger glasses?"

"I don't think that's it. Here goes."

Dear Mr. Reeves

  how are you my techer says yer old she says you prably never git to leve yer hows is that tru do you want to her a joke What's black and white and red all over? did you gess Ok A sunburned penguin writ back Ill write you agin after winter brake

                              Timothy Carter

Chapter 2

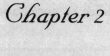

N o! No more pepper!" Susan Marcos set down the tub of mayonnaise on the counter and made a face. David held the shaker aloft and grinned. "It's flavoring."

"You need to forget some of the seasoning techniques your grandpa taught you. His stint as an army cook had some drawbacks." Snatching the pepper from his hand, Susan stuffed it in her apron pocket.

The gray-haired waitress had worked at Our Place since its opening. She was manager material, and the only thing keeping David from promoting her was his fear that if he had more time, he wouldn't know what to do with it. "I like pepper." David snagged his spare shaker and added a pinch more.

"What are you making now?"

"It's Chunky Lamb and Bean Soup."

"And that called for more pepper?" Susan seized the second pepper shaker before returning to the front of the restaurant.

David didn't dare add more, although that's what Clint would have done. Susan was right. Grandpa's wartime culinary habits consisted not only of the natural ability to slice and dice to perfection, but a tendency to overdo pepper.

He covered the vat of soup as the timer on the bread machine went off. Our Place opened in ten minutes. The business was breaking even; their reputation was growing; and as long as David could keep guesstimating how much food to prepare on a given night, they'd keep afloat long enough to become established.

Susan handed him a glass of water. She was a find, no doubt about that. David brushed butter on the fragrant rolls and wondered what his grandpa was doing. Clint must be going nuts sitting in that lonely apartment. Could it really be that just five months ago Clint had the mobility to walk to the restaurant and pitch in with the last-minute details? His grandfather's favorite table was by the front door, and he had eaten there almost every night.

"At least I knew he was getting a good meal."

"Are you muttering again?" Susan handed him the first order.

David scanned it and wondered who was lonelier: he or his grandfather.

❧

Genesis 4 had to do with Eve giving birth to Cain and Abel.

Rita placed her bookmark in her Bible and tried not to think about how old Eve had been at the birth of her first child, if age mattered back then.

After turning off the light, Rita huddled under the covers. Reading the Bible was easy and gratifying. The getting-back-in-shape resolution wasn't as easy. Rita squeezed her eyes shut, willed sleep to come, and tried to forget she was hungry.

The alarm sounded. Was it minutes or hours later? Rita didn't know. Now she was sleepy. The gray skies outside her window matched her mood. January in Flagstaff, Arizona, meant extra blankets and a whole lot of snow.

Although the diet she followed specified the amount of cereal she should eat, Rita knew two spoonfuls wouldn't carry her through until lunch. Not with morning recess duty and certainly not with the national spelling bee to plan. Rita needed to send out reminders about the date. Plus, she needed to round up three judges and find some daring soul willing to be the pronouncer.

She mentally narrowed down the list of potential pronouncers during the drive to school. As she walked into the building, Cameron Jones—one of her students—held the front door open. Watching him scamper down the hall, Rita figured he'd forgotten his homework.

"Morning, Grumpy, how's the diet?" Darla Yates, the school secretary, was entirely too happy in Rita's opinion, but then Darla could exist on chocolate and never gain an ounce.

"May a giant pop tart fall on your head and knock you unconscious," Rita retorted.

Darla giggled and popped a piece of candy in her mouth. "You're the only one obsessing about your weight. You look fine. Oh, and guess what? Timothy got a letter!"

Like a curtain had been flung open, Rita's dark mood lifted. "You're kidding."

"Nope. It came while we were on winter break."

Rita almost skipped down the hall. Timothy had better not be absent. Her classroom door was open, and Rita peeked in. Yes! Timothy's backpack was on his desk. The small boy was outside, but Rita wouldn't bother him there. She would set aside some time this morning for letter writing. Timothy would moan. He'd groan. He would make a neat, structural design with his pencils and erasers. Then, she'd casually lay the letter on his desk.

She started her morning with history. While the students made tall, black hats, Rita took the Lincoln family out of Illinois and moved them to the White House. Cameron's hat fell over his ears. Without missing a beat, Rita adjusted the brim and stapled it smaller and told the class about twelve-year-old Grace Bedell, the little girl who wrote to Lincoln, recommending that he grow a beard. Grace didn't exactly rate as a historic pen pal, but she knew how to write a letter and who to write to.

"But wouldn't it be rude to write the President and tell him to grow whiskers?" Lindsey Shoop wanted to know.

"She wasn't trying to be rude," Rita said. "Facial hair was popular back then. Grace's father probably had whiskers."

Cameron pushed at his hat. It fell on the floor, and he left it there while he studied the copy of the letter in his history book. "There are lotsa misspellings in this letter."

"Many children didn't get to attend school, like you do today. And back then, they only had the *Blue-backed Speller*. It wasn't very big. Where would Grace go to find out a correct spelling?"

"Her father?" Lindsey said, forgetting to raise her hand.

"Are we sure he knew how to spell?" Rita said. "You know, we sure are lucky to have dictionaries. Why don't you take them out, and let's write letters to our pen pals."

Perfect timing. Fifteen students suddenly thought their dictionary a worthwhile endeavor.

Timothy put his head down, ignoring his dictionary. His history book fell to the ground, crushing Cameron's hat.

"Timothy, pick up your book and hand Cameron his hat."

Slowly, Timothy obeyed.

Amy Tucker's hand went into the air. "Miss Sanderson, how do you spell—"

"Did you open your dictionary, Amy?"

"Oh, I forgot."

Rita made one more sweep around the room. In that time, Timothy managed to scrawl, *dear Mr. Reeves.*

"What did you do last night, Timothy?"

"I played with Terminator."

"Why don't you write and tell Mr. Reeves about that."

Timothy raised one eyebrow. There was trauma involved in trying to spell Terminator.

Squatting down next to his desk, Rita urged, "Okay, what are you doing tonight?"

"Nothing."

"What about this weekend?"

"Nothing."

"Hmm, Cameron, what are you writing to your pen pal about?"

At the beginning of the year, Cameron had sported a

smile destined to be on toothpaste commercials. Now, with the front two tucked away somewhere with the tooth fairy, Cameron constantly had his tongue working on his next contribution for the envelope that went under his pillow. "I'm telling Mr. Burnes about my new baby sister and my loose tooth. Oh, an' in his last letter he asked me if I liked math, and I'm telling him no."

Timothy didn't wait for her to begin prodding. "I don't have any brothers or sisters to write about."

"So, what you need is a letter from Mr. Reeves?"

"Weellll, that would help."

The letter landed on the corner of Timothy's desk. Two crayons rolled and joined a pyramid of circular pencil shavings by the boy's tennis shoes.

Knowing Timothy would act like it wasn't important if she stayed there, Rita went to her desk and started grading papers. One eye kept track of double-digit addition; the other eye watched as Timothy mouthed the words one at a time.

If Clint Reeves had been handy, Rita would have kissed him.

Then Timothy's hand went in the air. "Mrs. Sanderson?"

"*Miss* Sanderson."

"Oh, yeah, what does dictate mean?"

"Did you look it up?"

Lindsey found the word first and brought her dictionary over to Timothy's desk. "It means: to speak or read aloud for another to transcribe or record."

Timothy moaned, "Do I have to look up transcribble now?"

"Transcribble. I think I like that word." Rita laughed. "No, I'll tell you. It means Mr. Reeves had someone write the letter for him. He told the other person what to write."

"Oh, cool!" Timothy's grin stretched across freckled cheeks. "Can I do that?"

Dere Mr. Reeves

I got yer letter I thenk its coole that you had yer granson rite it I ask my techer if she wood rite for me but she sed no I thenk Ive eten at yer res resttt restorant You dint hav penut buter an jelee You no you shood com visit me at church O! Why did the ruler where a shoe? Because it was a foot. rite back

Timothy Carter

Chapter 3

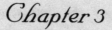

Four weeks in a row, Rita almost danced toward her mailbox. Timothy had made writing to Clint Reeves a special part of his week. And the way the child looked forward to getting the return letters! Rita had to hand it to Clint's grandson, the letters were getting longer and longer. Often they included news articles highlighting the Arizona Diamondbacks. Last week a box arrived with a baseball cap. Timothy took pains to write his letters more neatly now, claiming Clint wore glasses.

Rita took out the *Weekly Readers* from her teacher's box and grabbed some pink construction paper. It was time to prepare for Valentine's Day. Checking her watch, she wondered if this day could get any better. Wednesdays were a close fit to get everything done, but she might even manage to get an hour's workout in before church this evening.

"Rita, phone!"

A few minutes later, she hung up the phone, amazed. Her time on the phone was short; it consisted of Mr. Reeves shouting his name three times and then telling her he wanted to attend church, tonight. Timothy had invited him. Timothy had promised to pick the man up at seven.

Trust Timothy to get the time wrong, Rita thought. Church started at seven. Timothy had left no room for travel time, but that made sense: Timothy and his grandmother were usually late to services.

"Well?" Darla asked, "Was that who I think it was?"

"Yes, it was Mr. Reeves. Timothy invited him to church, and the man wants to come."

"I think that's great!"

"Yes, great, but I'm elected to pick Mr. Reeves up. I don't know where—"

Darla held up the pen pal letter. "Here's the address."

"This man's an invalid. His grandson writes the letters. What if I can't get him to the car? How do we even know he's able to travel?"

Darla pulled a phone book out of her bottom desk drawer. A few minutes later, Rita was on first-name terms with the director of Clint's retirement home. According to the woman, the only problems Clint Reeves had were crippling arthritis and an over-protective grandson.

Rita checked out her car in the school's parking lot. Suddenly the Chevette looked too small. "Maybe I should ask the grandson for permission to take Clint for an outing. Do we have his name?"

"Timothy probably knows." Darla dialed Timothy's number and hummed "Jesus Loves Me" while waiting. After a few moments, she hung up. "You think it's on Timothy's return letter?"

"We can't open the letter, not once it's sealed. I told the students their letters were private. I did a whole lesson on rules and etiquette according to the US Postal Service."

"Well, go pick up Mr. Reeves. One evening out for the old man probably won't hurt."

Clint Reeves turned out to be a gentle bear of a man, with John Wayne looks and Jimmy Stewart manners. He used a cane with an eagle carved on the handle, its beak curved in a polished downward hook. With swollen fingers grasping the cane, he followed her out his apartment door, waving away her offer to help.

The trip through the Greater Hope Retirement Home's lobby was a study in popularity. It took about ten minutes for Clint to explain to about a dozen elderly people—all using the lobby for a social outing—that Rita was his friend, not David's girlfriend.

He told each and every person she was a schoolteacher, and he made sure to mention they were on their way to church. That they were late to church obviously never entered his mind, although in his apartment she had mentioned the need to hurry.

She forgot her annoyance later, as she sat by him in a pew toward the back of the church. Although they were only privy to the sermon's closing remarks, one song, and a short prayer, Clint was obviously thrilled to attend church, glorying in all the handshakes and after-service visiting. For Rita, church wound up being a lesson in how services looked to someone who hadn't sat in the same pew since birth. The singing was better, the lesson refreshing, and the smiles more real. After the closing prayer, when Mrs. Tucker invited Clint to the Senior Saints luncheon on Sunday, Rita arranged to pick up Clint again.

As she drove Clint home, Rita let out a sigh of relief. Her Wednesday had been one of the best she remembered. She'd missed her workout, but that was no real hardship. She'd lost three pounds since January 1. Killer aerobics was responsible for the decreased poundage, but she didn't look forward to sweating to the oldies.

All in all, Rita was feeling pretty good about the evening. That is until they arrived back at the Greater Hope Retirement Home and came face-to-face with Clint's very tall, very good-looking, very angry grandson.

❧

When his grandfather didn't answer his phone, David left the restaurant and drove to the retirement center. He knew there were pull cords in all the rooms, but what if Clint had fallen and couldn't get to one?

When he reached the retirement center, he found out from the people in the lobby that his grandfather had gone to church with a young woman. He let himself into his grandfather's apartment and put supper on the stove, but he kept an eye on the front window, watching for his grandfather's return. At last he saw a Chevette pull up in front of the retirement center. The woman he saw helping Clint out of the car didn't look big enough to handle his grandfather's two hundred pounds. David ran to the elevator and then through the lobby.

"Let me." He tried not to let his words sound curt, but he knew they did. "And you are?"

"I'm Rita. Rita Sanderson."

He knew that name. From where? The restaurant?

"Timothy's teacher," Clint supplied.

"Oh, so what was tonight, some sort of school event?"

"I took Mr. Reeves to church."

"I told you to call me Clint."

"Church! It was supposed to snow. The sidewalks could have gotten slippery." David took ahold of Clint's elbow and with practice ease propelled him toward the front door. Rita Sanderson was not as he pictured. His own third-grade teacher had been gray-haired and over-bearing and smelled like paste. This woman smelled like vanilla, one of David's favorite flavors. She barely came to his shoulders and had hair as black as midnight. Right now her hair was blowing in the wind, and he found himself wanting to reach out a hand, to touch the blow-ing mass, to still it. Her chin had a stubborn tilt; it made him suspect that, should he touch her hair, she might bite his hand.

Her chin went up a full inch as she insisted, "Every-thing was fine. Timothy invited Clint to church. When Clint called to say he wanted to attend, I volunteered to take him."

"It never occurred to you to call me?"

"I didn't know your name."

"I'm David! I've been writing all those pen pal letters. I bought the Diamondbacks cap."

"Gerrumph," Clint interrupted. "I tried to get you to take money. Timothy is my pen pal."

Rita tried to explain. "Timothy's very guarded with his letters. He reads me sections, but not everything. I didn't know your name, and Timothy wasn't home when I tried to call."

David hit the button on the elevator. "You know my grandfather's sick."

"But not dead!" Clint gave David a look that clearly stated who was in charge.

"Grandpa—"

"Don't Grandpa me. I keep telling you, arthritis may be crippling, but it will only stop me if I let it. I'm attending church again on Sunday. You can either worry or come with me."

The elevator opened. Clint freed his arm from David's grasp and entered. When Rita followed, David knew he had no choice but to do the same.

※

Rita watched as David opened the door for his grandfather and stepped back. She could see the grandson's tension by the way his shoulders stiffened. Maybe infringing on their time wasn't the smartest choice, but to leave now seemed cowardly.

The smell of noodle soup had dominated the room when she'd picked Clint up. Now, something else permeated the air. Something mouth-watering, something rich, something heavenly.

Clint noticed her sniffing. "David's a chef."

"I'm impressed." Rita followed her nose into Clint's tiny kitchen, where a covered pot was on the stove. Lifting the lid, Rita's knees almost went weak. Whatever was warming on the stove was scads better than the tiny piece of grilled chicken with vegetables she had had for supper.

The lid slipped from her fingers, and without thinking she grabbed the edge. "OUCH!"

Behind her, she heard David say, "It's Pennsylvania Dutch Chicken and Corn Casserole, and it's hot." He opened a drawer and took out a tube of Neosporin, then he pulled her fingers from her mouth and dried them with a clean dishtowel. Before she could protest, he had smeared ointment on her fingers.

David was standing too close, but then in a kitchen this small there wasn't much choice. Funny, it was almost worth the burn to feel his gentle fingers—*Oh, no, no.* What stood in front of her was a skinny, young man with long hair. Her father had always distrusted men with long hair. Plus, chefs were supposed to be chubby from sampling their own wares. This guy didn't have an ounce of fat on him. It was unfair. This gorgeous—no, not gorgeous—this awkward, unappealing member of the opposite sex could probably eat three helpings of this casserole, even though it was after eight, and not gain an ounce. Rita disentangled her fingers from his grasp. "So, you managed to whip this up while Clint and I were at church?"

"No, I started about ten this morning. Most people use frozen whole-kernel corn. I use fresh. Then, I keep it on a slow simmer for hours and add dumplings before serving."

"Huh?"

For a moment, Rita thought he might crack a smile. Apparently, he was as passionate about cooking as she was about teaching.

Gently, he took her by the shoulders and pushed her aside. Taking a potholder from the counter, he removed the lid and tested the consistency with a fork. "Ummm, perfect." He took three plates from the cupboard.

Without his cane, Clint came to stand in the doorway to the kitchen. He managed to look even more bent. His smile was a perfect curve, though. "I taught him how to cook, and he turns it into an art form. He even studied while he was stationed in Paris. Me, I learned in the army. We had some great songs. Want to hear one?" He didn't wait for an answer but began, "Oh, the biscuits in the army, they say they're mighty fine, but one fell off the table and killed a buddy of mine."

"Grandpa, you might want to think before singing that next verse." David dished casserole onto the plates.

Clint trailed off. "You've got a point, Boy."

"We usually eat in the living room. I set Grandpa up with a TV tray. I eat on the coffee table."

"Oh, no, I couldn't possible eat this late."

David's eyebrow raised. "You're not hungry? You certainly acted interested in food a few moments ago.

"Well. . ." Rita hesitated.

When he held the plate under her nose, Rita knew she'd lost. But only this one time.

Chapter 4

Pink hearts were taped to the windows of Boundaries Christian School. David wondered which class belonged to Rita. He'd managed to drive by the school twice since last Wednesday. For some reason he couldn't get the teacher out of his mind. He kept envisioning the way she helped his grandpa out of her car, the way she stoically followed them into the retirement center, as if she'd been invited. But most of all, he remembered the color of her eyes as she looked at him while he administered first aid to her fingers.

The classroom at the end of the building had the best Valentine's Day decorations. That teacher had added legs and arms to a giant heart. A host of little hearts—all with arms and legs, a few with cowboy boots, one with ballet slippers—pranced merrily on each window. Each heart clutched something in its grasp. He drove into the almost-deserted parking lot. Yep, that had to be her room. And the giant heart had to belong to her. One Valentine-colored hand clutched a Bible. The other hand held a candy bar.

He wondered what Rita was doing at this moment. He didn't see her car in the parking lot. School had been out an hour by now. She was probably at home eating yogurt and peaches. He had heard her mutter about being on a diet last Wednesday, but he wouldn't change a thing about her—except maybe that obstinate streak she'd already demonstrated.

She was one stubborn teacher. She'd taken Grandpa to church again! The woman didn't understand the hours of therapy Clint had undergone. The man had virtually curled right in front of David's eyes, and it had taken months of aggressive treatment to keep Clint free from constant pain. Now, a wheelchair looked as if it might be a necessity in the near future. But Rita couldn't know all that. All she saw was a man who needed to get out more, who needed a bit more personal attention, who was lonely. Yes, Clint was all that, but even more he was an elderly gentleman who might never walk again if he fell.

Putting his car into gear, David carefully pulled into traffic. The restaurant opened again in an hour, and he still had a few odds and ends to prepare. As he drove into the restaurant parking lot, he wondered how he'd gotten so lucky as to realize his dream. If not for Grandpa, David might be just another cook making minimum wage in a restaurant chain.

Our Place was in the historic part of Flagstaff. It had been a falling-down mess of debris when Clint had co-signed the loan for David to purchase it. With its fake front, its general store motif, and down-home yet exotic food, it catered to a mixture of townies and tourists.

Right now a supply truck was at the back door

unloading boxes of potatoes. David nodded at the driver and headed for his office.

Susan stopped him. "There's a lady waiting up front."

"Why didn't you give her an application?"

"I don't think she's here about a job." The twinkle in Susan's eyes should have warned him.

Rita Sanderson was seated at one of the booths sipping iced tea. She stood immediately. His smile faded when he saw sparks of anger in her green eyes.

"What were you thinking?" she demanded.

He didn't need to ask. She held a piece of paper in her hands, and he recognized it as the side note he'd slipped in Timothy's letter this week. He'd folded it, stapled it, and wrote her name on it.

"I was thinking I must not have made myself clear last Wednesday." The fact that he was completely in the right somehow didn't make his words more convincing. Why didn't she look more like his old third-grade teacher? Mrs. Abraham never would have assigned elderly pen pals and then escorted one to church. Mrs. Abraham never would have showed up in his restaurant wearing emerald green pants and a silky flowered top. The green in her shirt was the same shade as her eyes.

"Your grandfather told you he intended to go to church on Sunday. He said you could either shut up or go with him! And, I'm not really talking about that. I'm talking about the fact that you wrote in Timothy's letter that you didn't want your grandfather going to church again."

"I wrote your name on it."

"You thought that would keep Timothy from reading it?"

"Well, sure."

"It didn't. Timothy had a conniption this morning. He didn't attend church last Wednesday because of homework, and Sunday he was sick, so he didn't get to meet Clint. Now he's convinced he'll never get to meet him. He has his grandmother so upset, she's threatening to not allow him to participate in our pen pal activities."

"I didn't realize—"

"No, I can see that. You're too busy controlling Clint's life. Your grandfather had a wonderful time Sunday. He stayed for the Senior Saints luncheon and met another gentleman who had been in World War II. You should have heard his stories."

"I've heard all those stories. Look, have a seat, let me take care of a few things, and then I'll tell you why I'm so against you cruising all around town with Grandpa."

She opened her mouth, obviously intending to protest, but then she sighed and sat down. She gripped her glass of tea as though it were a weapon she wanted to throw at him.

David excused himself and found Susan hovering in the server's alley. "Who is that?" she asked.

"A teacher I know. She's here purely to cause stress."

Timers were buzzing, telling him that tonight's main entrèe had finished baking. He put his mitts on, opened the oven, and took out a pan of meatloaf. He set it on the counter and went back to the walk-in freezer to get the next pan. He stuck that one in the oven and then took the main dish up to Tom, his head cook.

Stirring the gravy, David asked, "Are the mashed potatoes ready?"

Without answering, Tom ladled helpings onto two plates, dished up generous servings of meatloaf, and covered each meal with brown gravy.

Susan met him at the exit to the dining room. "I refilled her tea and got you a Coke. You have fifteen minutes before we open."

Rita's eyes narrowed as he walked toward the table. "I hope that's not for me."

"You don't like meatloaf?" He set the plate down.

She pushed it toward him. "Don't you have a nice salad?"

"Sure, I can get you a side salad. What kind of dressing?"

She had a great face. Right now one side of her mouth was turned down as if he'd just served her the equivalent of baked skunk with mustard and anchovy gravy. The other side of her mouth was twitching, as if she were fighting off a smile. He wondered what that would look like. This was only their second meeting, and he had yet to see her smile.

She put her hand on the table, inched it toward the plate, and then one finger carefully drew the whole thing in front of her. "Skip the salad. I'll eat this. But stop feeding me. I didn't come here for a meal. I came here to talk about your grandfather. He's enjoying church. I don't mind taking him. I don't understand what all the fuss is about."

He watched her take a bite. Her smirk disappeared, replaced by appreciation.

"How much do you know about arthritis?" he asked.

"I know it hinders movement. I can see Clint's swollen fingers. We move really slow. I can handle that."

"Grandpa not only has osteoarthritis—which means he's lost so much cartilage some of bones are rubbing together—but he also has a touch of rheumatoid arthritis. That's why his fingers are so swollen."

"But surely," Rita interrupted, "he needs to get around and move so his joints don't stiffen."

"You're right, but Grandpa is one of the few sufferers who wound up needing joint replacements. He's not as strong as he looks. Up until six months ago, I took care of him. Can you believe it? Just six months ago I would have shouted for joy if you took him to church. Then he had surgery. For some reason, he hasn't bounced back. He's lost weight. Worse, the pain has increased. His doctor recommended the retirement center. Now he has occupational therapists supervise his exercise. I go three times a week, and we walk."

"Why are you so worried about a fall? I mean, more people are hurt in their own homes than anywhere else. I watch him closely. He's sitting down most of the time he's at church."

David took a bite of his meatloaf. "He's coming down from a flare. This last month all his symptoms have increased. Except, last week. . ."

Taking a sip of his soda, David reconsidered. Clint had cheered up a bit after Timothy started writing. And this last week, he'd almost been his old self. Could church, Rita, and Timothy do all that? "Maybe I'm being unreasonable." After all, if Clint's doctors were against his leaving the center, they would have put it in writing.

"Why don't you come to church with us?" Rita burst out.

David almost spewed his soda.

"It's not that funny." Rita scolded.

"Okay, listen, I'll talk to his doctors. If they have no problem with him going to church on Sunday morning only, I'll back off. That is, if you'll go to the movies with me?"

Before Rita could answer, the waitress came back. "Brandy called in sick."

David clutched his fork so tightly his knuckles went white. He had done that last week, Rita remembered, when he'd helped Clint from her car.

"You'll have to do double duty." The words were barely out of David's mouth when the front door opened. A family walked in, and Susan led them to a table by the windows. "We'll talk more later." He looked Rita full in the face, daring her to object. "Seems I'm shorthanded tonight."

Gone was the man who seemed so agreeable. Back was the man who didn't have time to listen. It was hard to believe this guy who could change from hot to cold in a matter of minutes was related to Clint. He walked away before Rita could respond.

"Can I get you anything else, honey?" Susan was back.

"Who's Brandy?"

"She's our hostess."

"What does a hostess do?"

"Oh, it's simple. When people come in, you ask them how many. Then you either lead them to my station or Carol's. Plus, you hand them menus."

"I can do that."

"You're just what he needs." Susan nodded. As the waitress headed away, Rita had the strangest feeling the gray-haired waitress knew something Rita didn't.

Five hours later, Rita realized she'd discovered a better way to lose weight. Her feet felt like she'd climbed a mountain. Worse, she was hungry again, and David was headed her way with what looked like a hot fudge sundae.

Susan stopped wiping off tables. A devious chuckle started low in her throat as she accused, "You've never hand-delivered me dessert before."

David looked taken aback. "Do you want one?"

"No, and I'm pretty sure I have something to do in the kitchen." Susan picked up her wet rag and scurried out of sight.

David shrugged and kept coming. He set the dessert down. "I can't believe you stuck around. I had to cook tonight, but usually I manage to make a few rounds up front. Susan says you were a big help. You interested in a part-time job?"

His words were in jest, but his eyes were serious.

Rita laughed. "I don't think I could keep up the pace. My feet are killing me. That ice cream is not for me, right?"

"No, it is for you. I figured if you put in an evening's work at such last-minute notice, the least I can do is feed you."

"You already fed me once."

He leaned against the hostess stand and stirred the chocolate before taking a big bite.

She nodded at the sundae dish. "That equates to three days on a Stair Master."

David rolled his eyes. "What are you dieting for? You're not fat."

Since the compliment came from a man who obviously spent much of his time cutting slabs of meat, Rita wasn't sure she felt flattered. Then she couldn't decide whether she was pleased or annoyed as David downed the last bite of her ice cream. "You said you'd let Clint go again Sunday if I went out with you. Don't you have to work most weekends?"

"No, I can leave Tom in charge."

"Can't we exchange my working tonight for you allowing Clint to attend church Sunday?"

"No."

"Don't you need to ask your boss about getting time off?"

"My boss?" David laughed. "Rita, I am the boss. I own this place."

Rita gulped. He didn't look like a restaurant owner. He looked like a renegade. His hair was too long, his smile too young, and his manner too offhand—except when his knuckles turned white or when his back stiffened.

No, the offhanded manner was an act. This man

calculated every move and pretty much wanted to control everything and everyone around him. He didn't fit any mold with which she was comfortable.

Chapter 5

David hadn't taken a weekend night off in months. Rita had mentioned going to a game night at her church, instead of a movie, but he'd reminded her he was giving in to her by letting Clint go to church on Sundays. And this dieting business was for the birds. He wanted to wine and dine her. Of course she didn't drink, so there went the wining, and she watched her calories too closely for him to have much luck with the dining part. What did that leave?

He thought back to his last few dates, all with waitresses. Those had been casual happenings at after-work parties. Since he worked Tuesday through Sunday, dating after work was convenient—too convenient. He'd never agonized over what to do or what clothes to wear.

It had been easier during his eight years in the military. Then the uniform did a lot of the work, and there were always women hanging around the base. Single women who thought traveling to foreign lands was exciting. Single women like his ex-girlfriend Lydia.

Sometimes the military had been exciting, but other times it was monotonous. Greenland had been a lesson in never having anything to do. Clint had been a lifesaver, mailing videos and board games weekly. But David never wanted to play Monopoly again. Turkey had made him never want to leave America again. Lydia had made him never want to trust again.

The memory of Rita dressed in emerald green had him stopping off at the mall to buy new clothes. He didn't own a single stitch of clothes that hadn't been worn to work. The new tie looked funny. No doubt about it, David was a jeans and T-shirt kind of guy.

Forget the diet. He was taking her to a nice restaurant. If she wanted to spend twenty dollars on a simple salad, he wouldn't say a word. Then he'd be magnanimous and let her pick what they did next.

The khaki pants felt stiff, but he had to admit they looked sharp. He'd have to force himself to not wear the new golf shirt to work. Once he got Rita out of his system, maybe he'd start dating again. Nothing serious, which was why he needed to get Rita out of his system. Now there was a woman who oozed serious. For the life of him, he couldn't figure out why she was still single, unless the men in this town, and at that church, were blind.

Rita lived on a street in the older side of town. Her apartment was the upstairs of a brick fourplex, built probably more than sixty years ago when closets were small, ceilings were high, and woodwork spectacular. He could identify her place from the street. Hers was the apartment on the left. He knew because Rita's apartment had Precious Moments window stickers— complete with four leaf clovers—displayed in front of blue gingham curtains. His grandmother had had those same curtains.

The window slid up. Rita poked her head out. Her breath evaporated white in the winter air. "You gonna stay out there staring at my window or are you going to come up?"

He should have brought her flowers. Anyone with that much sass in her personality deserved a dozen of the best.

The stairway up to her place smelled like cinnamon. She stood at the door of her apartment. No making a guy wait, he liked that. Tonight she wore an orange pair of pants, a white turtleneck, and a flowing orange jacket. A white headband restrained her shiny hair.

Giving in to temptation, he brushed her lips with his and entered the room. Glancing behind him, he was glad to see her standing shocked and still at the doorway.

She shook her head, not in denial but as if clearing her mind. "Where are we going?"

"Maxy's first. We'll decide later what to do next."

Her eyes lit up. "Maxy's?"

David watched her emotions war. Maxy's was by far the most expensive restaurant in Flagstaff. To go there and order only a salad was simply not done. She stood, her coat in her hand. He waited a moment, to see what she had in mind, then realized she was waiting for him.

She was different: self-reliant, bossy, opinionated, and then willing to act like some chick from the sixties and let him help her on with her coat. She kept up the scenario once they were downstairs, and he held the door of his car open while she settled inside. Yeah, buying new clothes had been a good idea. Asking Rita Sanderson out had been a better one, even if he'd had to resort to blackmail to arrange it.

✌

She might have known he'd drive a Camaro. It was fire-engine red and still smelled new. Her first impression, that he was skinny, was way off. He was slender maybe, but not skinny. When he got behind the wheel of his car, the true magnitude of his size—no, not size but power—hit her. No wonder Clint's kitchen had seemed so crowded. Suddenly the Camaro felt like a telephone booth, a small telephone booth. And he'd kissed her! It was so quick a gesture. She fought the urge to touch her lips.

"Have you ever eaten at Maxy's?" David asked.

"My parents used to take me there."

"Where are your parents now?"

"They retired to Sun City. What about your parents?"

He was quiet, and for a moment she didn't think he intended to answer. "They died, when I was seven years old. They dropped me off at my grandparents' house and went hiking. Grandpa says they were caught in a flash flood. They were both experienced hikers. Grandpa had guided them all over the Grand Canyon. They'd kept up with the weather and everything. It was a freak of nature. If only I'd have. . ."

Rita watched his shoulders tense again. For the first time she saw the Native American ancestry on which he blamed Clint's arthritis. His profile was sad and strong and proud, and was that a hint of vulnerability? "You'd have what?"

302

"Nothing."

His shoulder felt as tight as it looked. Rita had a momentary twinge of *What am I doing?* Still, she couldn't keep her fingers from touching, from massaging, his shoulder. When David took his eyes off the road to look at her, she knew what she was doing and why. Yes, there was a lot of Clint in his grandson.

It was too quiet in the car. Rita reached down and turned on the radio. She should have figured it would be a rock station. At least David had the taste to listen to seventies music. Journey blasted out something about the lights in the city. Rita folded her hands in her lap. Funny, she'd dated plenty, kissed her share, hugged more than most, but she had never felt a touch that lingered after the contact was broken.

Maxy's was a low ranch-style monstrosity. The servers dressed in cowboy duds and live entertainment was on the menu. Every hour, for about ten minutes, all the servers ran to the stage and performed comedy songs and slapstick jokes.

David sat across from her and scrutinized his culinary competition. He'd eaten every bit of his steak and put away enough French fries to make Rita's stomach bloat. She'd let him do the ordering, impressed with the details he'd thought to specify. He'd ordered a side of cottage cheese. Once she'd tried the cottage cheese in place of butter—on her baked potato—she knew she'd found another decent meal to help her succeed with her New Year's resolution. Hmmm, there were some benefits to dating a chef; now if she could just convince him to stop feeding her every time they met.

He'd kept conversation neutral. Every time she tried to draw it to Clint, he steered the topic to books, movies, and politics. For an hour they agreed, argued, and discovered new avenues of compatibility.

Afterward, he let her pick the movie. He didn't even make a face when she picked a romantic comedy. His smile was indulgent, as if he were bestowing a gift. As if he'd been doing it for years, he slid out of the driver's side and walked around to her door. Helping her out, he put a hand to her back; she could barely feel it through her coat, but she liked that he wanted some sort of connection with her. His hand was gentle on her elbow as he walked her to the ticket booth. This was unlike any date she'd ever had. In many ways, David was a stranger, but a stranger shouldn't make her so nervous. Maybe her discomfort came from the fact that he wasn't a Christian.

Two of her students were in the theater. She heard whispers of, "There's Miss Sanderson! Oh, who's she with?" At the concession stand, a boy and girl she'd taught years ago, when they were in fifth grade, were holding hands and staring at her holding hands with David. When had he taken her hand? Why did it feel so natural that she didn't even notice until someone else had?

Separating her hand from his, she took the soda he purchased for her and followed him into the theater. He paused halfway down and waited for her to pick the seats. He held her soda while she took off her coat. Sitting down, he balanced the popcorn on his knee, raised the armrest so they could be closer, and grinned at her while taking a sip of his soda. What was with this guy? It was like he thought nothing could go wrong with this date. No way; all first dates are destined to have bad moments. Rita checked the front of her shirt to make sure she hadn't dripped any ketchup or something on it.

He set the popcorn and his soda on the floor and took off his black leather jacket. When he settled back in the seat, brushing her shoulder, Rita wished he'd kept it on. If she thought they were connected before, she had been wrong; now it was electric.

She never caught the plot of the movie. She missed all the jokes. And she had to use the rest room two times simply because of nerves. When the evening ended and David walked her to her door, she finally began to breathe normally. That is, until he pulled her to him.

The kiss surprised her into acquiescence, but when his fingers brushed aside her coat and started a little tap-dance on her side, she came to her senses.

"David, no."

"What do you mean?"

She pushed him away. "I mean no. I had a nice evening. Thanks. It's time for you to go."

"I don't understand." He reached for her, his fingers heading back toward skin. "We had a great time. We got along."

"It's time for you to go. Our date is over."

His eyes darkened. "It doesn't have to be."

"Yes, it does."

"I want to know you better," he insisted.

"You're going about it all wrong then."

"Yes, but—"

"What you're thinking isn't even a remote possibility."

"But—"

"Good night, David. Thanks for dinner and the movie."

He backed away. She had her key out and the door open and closed in seconds. Her apartment had never felt so empty, as if something, someone, was missing.

Later, lying in bed and starting her evening Bible reading, she decided to stray from Exodus and go to Proverbs. She started at chapter 31, verse 10. It talked about wives of noble character. What about single women of noble character? For the first time, striving to be more valuable than rubies came with a high price tag.

The cost: staying away from David Reeves.

Chapter 6

Figuring out David's schedule was easy. David came over to Clint's on Monday evenings, the day the restaurant was closed, and Saturday afternoons. He was easy enough to avoid.

Timothy's grandmother, Ellen, finally started driving Clint back and forth to church on Sundays. Timothy guarded the cane as if it were made out of gold. Rita took charge of Wednesdays, usually coming over well before church time.

"Now, I'm not the cook David is," she told Clint one Wednesday before prayer meeting, "but I guarantee you'll like my sloppy joes."

"As long as you don't make me drink milk, I'm happy."

"I'm not giving you soda, either. What do you want instead?"

"Sprite?"

"That's no caffeine. Okay." Rita slipped out the front door and went down to the retirement center's laundry room. An overpriced soda machine gladly took her money.

It had been three weeks since her date with David. Either he hadn't told Clint about the evening, or David had sworn the old gentleman to silence. Setting up the

TV tray, she cut the sloppy joe in half, added a few fat-free potato chips to the plate, and stuck a napkin on the side. Taking her own plate, she sat down on the floor and used the coffee table for her plate.

She looked intently at the leftovers from Clint's refrigerator, something Clint had given her. "What is this again?"

Clint paused from chewing. He swallowed and said, "Zucchini Vegetable Casserole. David's been on this kick lately and cooking some strange combinations. He's added a new special to his menu everyday, always some sort of diet dish. If I didn't know any better, I'd think he was out to impress you. Is he?"

"Nope," Rita said. "Our only contact is arguing about you." She didn't mention the job application that had arrived two weeks ago in Timothy's letter with a side note instructing her to fill it in for tax purposes. Nor did she mention the check for thirty-two dollars, for five hours of work, which came last week. Today, Timothy's letter had been a bit bulky. Inside was an employee nametag with Rita's name on it.

Clint slowly took his first bite, chewed for a moment, then said, "I think David's calmed down. He hasn't made a snide remark about me attending church in a week. He's a worrier, that boy. Has been ever since his folks died. It got worse after his grandma died. He likes Timothy's grandmother. That Ellen's a sweet lady. We all ate at his restaurant Sunday."

"Timothy told me. I hear David made him drink milk."

"That boy and his milk. One of my doctors made a

remark about calcium strengthening the bones. I think David would inject me with milk if he thought I'd let him."

They ate in silence. Rita wondered if ketchup would help the flavor of the casserole but decided against all the sugar. Instead, she spread a few spoonfuls of cottage cheese on top. Cottage cheese was the one good thing that had come of the date—the one good thing she didn't feel guilty remembering.

Clint ate every bite. Rita washed the dishes and waited while Clint put on his jacket, stuck a fresh handkerchief in his pocket, and took his cane.

He set off slowly. "This stupid left foot. It's like a rubber band is wrapped around the ankle, cutting off circulation. Half the time it's like someone's poking me with pins, and the other half it's numb. Plus I've got this pesky sore that won't go away."

They reached the lobby. Clint waved, reintroduced Rita, and invited anyone who would listen to church. No one took him up on his offer, but a few looked interested.

As they settled in her car, Clint said, "Did you happen to see that letter Timothy wrote me Monday? It came today."

"I don't read the students' letters. They're private."

Clint chuckled and took a piece of paper out of his shirt pocket. "You should take a look at this one."

Rita read it at the next red light.

Dear Mr. Reeves.
Were lerning molteplikshun. Its hard. I dont lik
it. Miss Sanderson keeps forgeting things an looking

owt the windo. Shes a OK techer. I thenk yer son
liks her. He keeps sendng her thengs. Well be glad to
come to yer birthday party in a few weeks. Do you
want to here a joke. What does a ghost wear to
school in the rain? Ghouloshes.

Timothy Carter.

"This is pretty good." Rita handed it back.

"I told him he needed to put periods because I was too old to figure out where his sentences stopped unless he told me."

"You think that will work with spelling?"

"Hey, he spelled that joke pretty good!"

"That's because he copied it out of his favorite joke book." Rita waited while Clint put the letter back in his pocket. She pulled up to the church's front door and let him out.

When she joined him again, she asked, "What's this about a birthday party?"

"Oh, Timothy's already planning my birthday party. It's more than a month away." Clint laughed. "As if I want more birthdays. You will come?"

"I don't think—"

"It's my seventy-first."

"Wow."

"So if the only contact you have with David is about me, then what things are you receiving in my letters?"

"Nothing important."

After church ended, she helped Clint into the passenger side of her car and considered her "nothing important" response. David's letters were taking up too much of her time. Written on behalf of Clint, the letters were always addressed to Timothy, but for three weeks straight, there had been folded squares of papers addressed to Rita. Timothy thought it the coolest thing to get up out of his seat and personally deliver her section of the pen pal letter. It was getting so when a letter for Timothy arrived, Rita's stomach began butterflying.

She dreaded the week when she wasn't mentioned in the letter.

※

"Sloppy joes? Tell me you're not eating these." David held the refrigerator door open.

"They're good," Clint said. "You ought to add them to your menu."

David squatted and moved a pickle jar. "Hah, that would make me the only restaurant in Flagstaff with sloppy joes on the menu. Next you'll want me to add peanut butter and jelly."

"Timothy would like that."

"Did Ellen make the sloppy joes?"

"No."

"Grandpa, you did?"

"No."

Well, then, who. . . ? David knew. Rita. She'd been involved in their life a little more than three months and already her exquisite stamp was demonstrated everywhere. There was an undertone of perfume accenting the air. Clint was the only resident in the retirement center to have April flower window stickers displayed. A new, pastel crocheted afghan was on his bed. Also, David knew it wasn't the biweekly housekeeper who actually lifted the ancient knickknacks and dusted under them. David wanted to think Ellen was making all the subtle changes, but he knew it was combination of both, and mostly Rita.

"Don't tell me, Grandpa, but was it Rita who made the macaroni and cheese last Wednesday? So Ellen's taking you to church on Sundays, and Rita's your chauffeur on Wednesdays."

"Right." Clint rubbed his hands together. "What are you cooking?"

Leaning on the open refrigerator door, David peered at Clint. It never failed, wherever Grandpa was, friends happened. The regulars at the restaurant still asked about him. Clint had made just as many friends at the retirement center. Already he was involved in a Tuesday night dominos club, and on Thursdays he played checkers. Lately his partners managed to mosey over right at mealtime. David wondered if Rita experienced the same thing, though with such entrees as sloppy joes and macaroni with cheese, he doubted Walt—who beat David at checkers—was marking Wednesday on the calendar for a let's-eat-at-Clint's rendezvous.

"I said, what are we having for supper?" Clint called.

"Halibut Creole."

"What are you looking for?"

"Salt."

"You're looking for salt in the fridge?" There was a chuckle in the old man's voice.

David closed the door to the fridge. "No, Grandpa, don't get up. I'll find it."

The salt was right where it should be, in the cupboard above the sink. David couldn't believe he hadn't seen it. But then, someone had taken all of Clint's staples out of the cupboards and laid contact paper, sky blue with tiny white flowers. Things were in their legitimate places but moved a bit. Rita's fault, he was sure of it. Now that he looked closer, he could see more than a hint of change in Clint's kitchen. A new, floral-scented hand soap was by the faucet. Butterfly magnets—the same colors as the contact paper—were on the freezer door.

To be honest, David knew Rita was here a lot. Clint certainly wasn't eating the low-fat meals David brought over, and cottage cheese was disappearing at an alarming rate.

David added the salt, then poured Creole sauce over the fish. Heading for the living room, he said, "I brought a movie."

Clint squinted at the label. "Seen it."

"When?" David burned his thumb on some of the butter dripping off the edge of his plate.

"Ellen and I watched it Friday night."

"Grandpa, is there something I should know?"

Clint laughed. "I'm not telling you anything until you start confiding in me."

"What do you mean?"

"I mean, what's going on with you and Rita? I invited her to my birthday party, and she turned me down flat. I got the impression it's because of you. What did you do to her?"

"Do to her? Me? Nothing. I took her to dinner and a movie. I thought we had a great time, but then she didn't. . ."

"Oh, David, don't tell me you treated her like an Army Annie?"

"What? No. I treated her fine. She got uptigh—" David stopped. Uptight wasn't the word for it, but this wasn't the usual type of conversation he had with Clint. Sure, along about junior high Clint had sat across from him at the kitchen table and did a short narration about the birds and bees. Only with Rita, the bees stung and the birds flew quickly out of sight.

Clint finished eating, wiped his mouth with a napkin, and took a thick leather book from the table. "Your answer is here."

"What?"

"I was amiss not to tell you before. Truthfully, my own mother used to drag me to church. When I went into the army I stopped attending. Didn't miss it until Timothy kept bringing it up in his letters. Four times in a row that boy invited me to church, got me to wondering what I was missing. Your Rita—"

"She's not my Rita!"

"Well, Rita's been raised in the church. She believes in baseball, hot dogs, apple pie, Chevrolet, and God. Not necessarily in that order. She's probably only gone out with nice boys from the church or that Christian college she attended."

"There aren't that many nice boys, Grandpa. If you're

Chapter 7

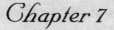

R ita had never been to an auto show before. Following David, she tried to figure out the attraction to old Model T Fords. Well, she did like the fact that at one time manufacturers had installed a place specifically for a picnic basket.

David knew many of the exhibitors by name. He tossed out comments like, "Where'd you get this flivver, Tim? Rex, I thought you were getting rid of the Ford landaulet? Justin, nice side pipes."

During one interval, when David was discussing radial tires with an elderly man who looked a lot like Clint, Rita took the time to sit down and sip on a soda. This had to rate as the strangest date she'd ever gone on. She wondered if David was putting her through some kind of test, and whether or not she was passing, or if she even wanted to pass. In the pit of her stomach, she worried maybe she'd been so eager to say yes to coming with him because of the disconcerted feeling she'd had last week when Timothy's letter was to Timothy alone.

This was the Saturday afternoon David usually spent with Clint. But Clint was more excited about David making alternative plans than she was. A sports auto show?

Greg, one of her college boyfriends, had been heavily into weight lifting. He'd dragged her all through Abilene, Texas, looking at bench presses and such. But she'd been dating him for over a year before she became his weight partner of choice, and then Rita had known she'd crossed over some invisible line that changed her from girl who was a friend, to girlfriend. What was David's rationale?

His phone call had roused her from a sound sleep. That had to be the reason she'd agreed to go with him. After their first date, she'd decided that dating David was not what God wanted. Yet at eight this morning, two hours before she wanted to get up, the phone rang and his voice had her wide awake and coherent. She'd said yes into the telephone and no to the mirror five minutes later. And she still wasn't sure what God wanted.

He looked good. So far she'd seen him in his work clothes—torn jeans and white T-shirt—and his dress clothes. She had the feeling she was looking at the Real McCoy today. The jeans weren't torn: They were black and formfitting. He still wore a white T-shirt, but it was nicely tucked in. His black, leather jacket swayed when he walked. Rita fought the urge to link her fingers through his back belt loop.

"You ready?" He grinned down at her. His black hair shone like ebony. "I take it you've never explored the classics of the automobile world."

She grabbed her coat off the back of the chair. "No, somehow I've managed to miss the adventure."

"There's one more aisle, then I need to take you home so I can get to work." His eyes scrutinized her. "You look about ready to go anyway."

"I am having a good time," she insisted. And she was. What she didn't tell him was that the good time had everything to do with him and nothing to do with cars.

The final aisle was devoted to dragsters. The customized cars, built solely for racing, came in every color imaginable. Rita's father had owned one, well before Rita's time. He had the picture—complete with his own black, leather jacket—displayed in the living room. Her mother claimed Rita inherited the lead foot from his side of the family.

"Rita Sanderson! What are you doing here?" J.J. Grimes, a member of Rita's church, left the folding stool he was sitting on and came to the aisle.

"Hi." Rita's fingers went to David's belt loop. She secured a finger and tugged. Now would be a good time to move faster.

"I didn't know you knew David." J.J. shook David's hand. "Come take a look at the booster I added last month."

Maybe Rita would have succeeded in tugging David out of J.J.'s space if not for the booster.

"Isn't she a honey?" J.J. said, taking a white towel and polishing an already sparkling hood. "She can do 0 to 80 in about four seconds. Much like your girlfriend."

"What?" Rita felt David focus more of his attention on her than on the cars.

"Yep," J.J. continued. "Your little lady gets on the Interstate and thinks it's powder puff. Eighty miles an hour. Can you believe it?"

There should be a law against cops telling tales, thought Rita.

David wagged his eyebrows. "My little Rita's had a speeding ticket?"

It wasn't the peace sign J.J. displayed.

Great, the first time David used an endearment and it was in response to finding out Rita had trouble obeying traffic signs. She tried to regain control of the conversation. "Both times it was after midnight; I was late; I didn't realize how fast—"

"You can get that Chevette up to eighty?" David looked doubtful.

"New car?" J.J. asked her. He turned back to David. "When I dated her she had a Camaro."

"I got rid of the Camaro after you gave me the second speeding ticket. I couldn't take the defensive driving class, so my insurance went up."

"Low blow, J.J." David stuck up for her. This time his finger went to her belt loop, and he did the tugging. In a soft voice, he muttered, "You traded a Camaro for a Chevette?"

It didn't amuse her to listen to David chuckle. She started to turn to tell him but realized his finger was still in her belt loop, his arm almost around her, and she didn't want to risk separating him from her. Then, on the tail of that thought, she went still. He was looking at her; she felt as though all the spectators at the auto show had suddenly disappeared, and it was the two of them.

His finger went to her forehead and brushed aside a strand of hair. "What are we doing?" he whispered.

"Getting to know each other," she encouraged.

He let go of her belt loop. "That's probably not wise."

"Why not?"

"Come on, Rita. You're from *Leave It to Beaver* land, and I'm from. . .well, think Spock from *Star Trek*. I don't need anybody. Even more, I don't want anybody."

"You called me," she reminded him.

"You're right. I did. Call it madness. Call it a fluke. Call it whatever you want, but don't read too much into it."

His cell phone rang. Looking relieved, he flipped it out and turned his back to her. Rita stepped away and stood next to a life-size cardboard cutout of a stockcar driver. The stiff lines of the figure looked hauntingly like David right now. Hot to cold, the man had the method down to an art.

"That was Susan. I need to get to work. Tom, my head cook, is going to be late. Brandy called in sick again."

"What's wrong with Brandy? She's sick a lot."

"She's sixteen years old and pregnant."

He moved toward the doors, held them open, and looked at her expectantly. An idea was forming in her head, but she needed a moment. What was it about this guy that made her want to try harder, go farther—

It was resolution number four! Find a nice guy with whom to form a relationship. Why hadn't she realized it sooner? Everything else was falling into place. It was April, and she was down twelve pounds. In her nightly Bible reading, she was more than halfway through Leviticus. Her checkbook, while not precisely balanced, was within five or ten, okay, twenty dollars, and that was an improvement.

Was she trying so hard with David because subconsciously he fit nicely into that number four goal?

No, please.

If it were New Year's, she'd add one more resolution: Introduce David Reeves to Christ, because without Christ he couldn't be the answer to goal number four. And she very much wanted him to be.

She felt like they were in slow motion. David's eyes narrowed as she stepped up to him. Cool air seeped in from outside. The background blasted the blaring of horns and the song "Wipe-Out." The smell of oil tinged the room. Rita took both ends of David's jacket and slowly zipped it. He watched, with a detached look, but the change in his breathing showed he was human and interested.

"You know," Rita said, "you do have a hostess who happens to have the night free."

"No, I can get by."

"Of course you can. David Reeves can always get by. But think of how much smoother the night will go if I'm there. Last time I worked for you, you paid me with money and allowed me to take Clint to church. Remember?"

He took her hands and gently guided them away from his jacket. "What are you thinking?"

"Oh, this is easy. I'll work for you tonight, and then tomorrow come to church with Clint and me."

"No."

"Why not?"

"I don't do church."

She'd invited people to church before, but never like this. "You know, sometimes I find it's not so much the place where you are, but who you are with. I can honestly say the reason I've never attended an auto show is because staring at cars doesn't interest me. I, however, became interested when I imagined you in the scenario." Rita changed from jabbing David in the chest with her finger to biting her lip. This was not the usual method, but according to statistics, more new Christians were brought to the faith through friends than by any other means. If she could get David in the door, God would surely do the rest.

David took her finger off his chest. He covered her hand with his. "Rita, I'm not going to church with you tomorrow."

"All right. I'll work tonight anyway. Clint's birthday's coming up. I can use the money."

❧

David fixed Clint a bowl of grapes in lemon-cheese gel and wondered when Grandpa had rearranged the inside of the refrigerator. On the heels of that thought came the answer: Rita. And now she was working at Our Place. He could have, should have said no. For the life of him, he had no idea why he hadn't. But the customers were warming up to her, especially when they found out she was a friend of Clint's.

He hadn't asked her out again. She didn't act like she cared. He hadn't attended church, either. And again, she didn't act like she cared.

Susan had all but adopted the girl and was suddenly asking for Sundays off so she could attend church. In some ways it felt like David's once-so-organized puzzle was now in pieces because of Rita's tampering. Of course, thanks to Rita, the puzzle was more pleasing to the eye. But the difficulty of the puzzle had increased also. Ellen started bringing Clint in to eat on Saturday nights. It was agonizing to watch Timothy hold the door for Clint. Then, from the back, David could see Rita hovering at Clint's side. They all acted like the arthritis was no big deal. Just wait until one of their loved ones became crippled. No, that was unfair. It was clear they already loved Clint. Because they loved Clint, they tolerated David.

David shook his head and poured Grandpa a glass of milk. He needed to stop thinking about Rita, especially during the few hours he managed to spend with Clint. Checking his watch, he realized he had only a few minutes left to visit. Sitting down, David picked up the pen and said, "What do you want me to write this week?"

"Tell Timothy I liked his joke, but to stop making them so funny because it hurts when I laugh. Oh, and tell him you've decided to add peanut butter and jelly to the menu."

"That's not true."

"Can't blame a guy for trying. Remind him my birthday party is this Saturday at noon."

"As if the kid could forget. He's told me three times what he got you."

Clint laughed. "Yeah, well he told me at least four. Just what I need, another watch."

David signed Clint's name, stuck the note in the envelope, slipped in Rita's paycheck, and sealed it. There had been a few weeks when David had excluded Rita from the correspondence, and for some reason he felt like a Santa who had purposely left a stocking empty. He no longer bothered with a stamp; instead, he dropped it off at the school.

The secretary, Darla, looked forward to his visits. If he had to harbor a guess as to why, David would blame desserts. Two weeks ago, the first time he'd personally dropped off the letter, he'd brought in a piece of Cocoa Sour Cream Cake for Rita. The following week, Darla had complimented him on the cake; Rita had given it to her. Now, David always brought in two pieces of cake, one for Darla and one for Rita. This way Darla would tell him what Rita was doing with the desserts and maybe other tidbits of information. . .like her favorite color, flower, perfume. . .

So far, Darla reported that Rita had given away all the desserts, except for one bite from the Picnic Caramel Cake. Her weakness to caramel discovered, David concentrated his baking exploits in that direction, although he didn't know why. It was like he was wooing Rita, while at the same time pushing her away with both hands. She knew it, too. Even at the restaurant she only came around him if she absolutely had to. And she only came to Clint's when she knew David wouldn't be there. Maybe at the birthday party there would be a chance to clear the air and make some "strictly friendship" boundaries.

David tossed Timothy's envelope on the passenger

seat and drove home. Home was a minuscule apartment with a hide-a-bed and a kitchen table. He owned a television but was no longer sure it worked.

Used to be, after he left Clint's, David would stop at one of the local joints to play pool, sit back, and relax. The last few times he had gone, the conversation had been dull, the people phony, and the smiles fake. That was Rita's fault, too.

David was coming dangerously close to opening that Bible Clint had given him.

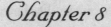

Chapter 8

The Saturday of Clint's birthday dawned one of the clearer days of April. David went to work early. He needed to start the Braised Sirloin-tip Roasts and get the soup going. The delivery truck was due at ten; Grandpa's party was at noon. Things should go smoothly.

Of course, *should* was the operative word, David realized a few hours later as he checked his watch. It was almost noon. The truck was two hours late.

"David, go ahead," Tom told him. "I'll see everything is unloaded and stocked. I'll get the busboy to help. The waitresses will have to handle the front on their own for a little while." Tom scooped mashed potatoes onto the plate for one of their regulars.

Leaving went against David's better judgment. Only to an owner did the exact number of mayonnaise jugs or heads of lettuce matter. Every dollar counted. Still, it was Clint's seventy-first birthday. David took the cake out of the walk-in freezer.

This would actually be one of Clint's better birthdays, he thought as he drove away. Last year, he'd spent his seventieth birthday in the hospital, with David as the only visitor. This year Ellen and Timothy were stopping by, as was

Rita, and that crazy secretary Darla was bringing her kids. It would be a menagerie.

No, he decided twenty minutes later, *it is a zoo.* The noise hit him after he exited the elevator on the second floor. The door was halfway open, and the first thing David saw was children. David tightened his grip on the cake. Someone had pushed their kids' "go" buttons and forgotten where the "stop" was.

Ellen stood at the sink, washing dishes. Timothy dried. There were shards of broken glass in the trash can. David made a mental note not to hire Timothy as a busboy. In the living room, Darla sat next to Clint—*Why is Grandpa wearing a Lincoln hat?*—looking at a photo album. David winced, imagining what page they might be on. *At least it is Darla, and not—*

No, Rita was on the other side. Her black hair fell forward as she studied the Kodak moment in front of her.

"Grandpa, which album is that?" David's voice made the three people on the couch stop talking.

Clint's eyes sparkled. "You can guess."

David's fingers itched to take the album out of Clint's hand. Why do parents think naked babies on bearskin rugs are so cute? Of course, he wasn't sprawled on a bearskin rug. No, instead he was posed on a piece of shag carpeting cut in the shape of a foot, complete with toes.

"And I thought you'd always had long hair," Rita teased.

David set the cake and his present on the coffee table, amidst a slew of other gifts. "Do you like Clint's hat?" A child crawled from under the coffee table. Offering his hand like an adult while he whistled through missing teeth, the boy stated, "I'm Cameron Jones. I wanted to meet Timothy's pen pal, so he said I could come."

David took the offered hand, noting the smears of frosting, and wondered who else had brought a cake.

"That's David with my late wife." Clint turned the page and pointed. David sat down on the arm of the couch, close to Rita.

She looked up at him. Her impish expression told him she was thinking about babies and bearskin rugs. Then she stopped smiling and stood up. "You can sit here."

"No, that's—"

But she was already heading for the kitchen, her gentle voice reminding Timothy to keep his shoes on until she picked up the rest of the glass.

Darla and Clint frowned at him in unison.

David held his hands up in surrender. "What?"

"Is there more cake now, Mama?" A redheaded imp stuck a finger in David's cake. Before Darla could stop him, the finger went in his mouth and the child sighed. "This is better'n the one you bought at the store."

"David's a chef," Clint said.

"I know, he brings desserts to the school," Darla said.

Clint sat a little straighter. "Really, now, and why do you do that, David?"

"They're extra, and I drop off your letters in person."

Timothy carried plates into the room. "Time for more cake."

Soon all that remained of David's cake was the platter it arrived on. Darla collected her offspring and left. Ellen needed to get Timothy to a soccer game. Clint announced his foot hurt, and he was going to take a nap."

"I'll clean up," Rita offered. "You need to get to work, David."

"I can help."

"I'd rather do it alone."

"Why?"

The look she shot him resembled the one his old third-grade teacher had often used.

"Rita, we need to get past this. For Clint's sake, we can be friends."

"We are friends."

"Every time I come near you, you run."

"Well, Mr. Spock, you said it so eloquently." She looked at her watch. "It's time for me to return to Beaverland. You can clean up by yourself."

Not one word came to his head. His fists clenched. He deserved her ire.

He heard the sound of the front door softly closing. She was serious about keeping her distance, and it made him want her all the more. He picked up the platter his cake had been on. Stuck to the bottom was a torn letter, from Timothy.

Dear Mr. Reeves.

    I'm realy loking forword to yer party. I'm not sposed to tell you abowt the watch I got you. I'm eeting a cold hot dog for lunch. What is a snake's favorite thing to study at school? Hissssstory. I wish I had a cane. Tell David to come to church?

                    Timothy Carter.

David put the letter on top of the television where his grandpa would be sure to see it. Yep, Clint had really found a wonderful group of friends.

Picking up errant piles of gift wrap, David figured it was time to face the fact he'd fallen in love with Rita Sanderson: baseball, hot dogs, apple pie, Chevrolet, God, and all.

※

Ellen Carter paced the classroom. "Timothy's doing better. I see improvement." Her short, straight gray hair was so starched it didn't move.

Rita sat on top of Timothy's desk. Stacks of work were arranged for Ellen to see. For once, Rita had not encouraged Timothy to clean up before he left; she wanted Ellen to see Timothy's work area. School ended in two weeks, but for Timothy, summer could not be three long months of relaxation.

"You're right," Rita said gently. "I see the improvement, too. But what I also see is how his work is lagging compared to the other third graders. In multiplication, he's up to his twos. Most of the class are up to tens. That's a big difference. Especially when he still relies on his fingers for what he does know."

"Well, that's your fault." Ellen's voice had changed from concerned to angry. "You're the teacher. Obviously you're not giving him enough attention."

Rita tried not to wince. She'd heard that claim before, many times. "Ellen, Timothy is using his dictionary for the first time. He's trying hard at spelling, and his handwriting has never been better. I'm seeing some advances in reading, too. I still urge you to have him read aloud fifteen minutes each evening. It's math I'm worried about, and his organization."

"There are plenty of disorganized adults. I don't want to hear about that. What are you trying to say about math? You're not thinking about flunking him! Are you?"

"No—"

"Because I'll not have it. He didn't start kindergarten until he was seven. You know that. He's already more than a year older than the other kids. He got a late start. . . ." With that, Ellen started crying and left the room.

Rita stayed on the desk. She knew Ellen would be back as soon as she dried her eyes. Ellen's only crime was caring too much. Rita sometimes thought it would be easier teaching at a school where she didn't also attend church. She'd known Ellen since childhood, and Ellen's daughter Mitzi had been a good friend.

Ellen came back, her head held high and her eyes clear. "We're not talking retention, right?"

"No, not at all." Rita assured her. "I'm really talking only about math. I recommend summer school."

A frown creased Ellen's brow. "I can't afford that. It's all I can do to keep him in the private school."

Rita knew. For tuition aid, Ellen came in every Saturday morning to clean.

Ellen sat on Cameron's desk and picked up one of his papers. It was multiplication. There was a circled 100% at the top.

"Do you have any other suggestions? How about tutoring?"

It was a no-win situation. Rita knew a few people who did private tutoring, but they all charged more than what summer school cost. Rita could recommend a high school student, but that was a hit-or-miss option. There were very few high school students who knew how to deal with youngsters who needed more than one-on-one attention.

"Let me make a few phone calls," Rita said. "I'll see if I can find someone reasonable."

"I can work with him more," Ellen muttered. "It's just by the time we get home from soccer practice, work on homework, and then read for fifteen minutes, our whole evening is gone."

Ellen was Rita's last conference. After Ellen left, Rita tidied up the classroom, thinking about Timothy. At just past seven, she slipped on a light jacket and headed outside.

"Rita!" Tina Lidell, the second-grade teacher, waved frantically and scurried across the parking lot. "We're going for dinner. Want to come?"

Rita's first mistake was not asking where they were going. Her second mistake was jumping in Tina's car. When they pulled up in front of Our Place she had no choice but to go in. This didn't bode well for her plan to avoid David.

The restaurant was busy. A pregnant, slow-moving Brandy sat them in Susan's station.

"What made you choose this restaurant?" Rita whispered.

"Darla says they have great desserts. Oh, there she is!" Tina waved.

Rita crossed her legs and looked around. Maybe David would stay in the back and never know she was there.

Darla sat down, and they ordered. Rita chose Herb-baked Cod. It had David's new Healthy Choice symbol next to it.

"When did you start eating salads with salsa dressing?" Tina asked after listening to Rita rearrange the meal so it was fat proof.

"New Year's."

"Oh."

Instead of salad, Susan delivered French Onion Soup. Rita started to complain, but the smell of onions always made her mouth water. She decided not to point out Susan's error.

When the London Broil, carved in very thin slices, appeared in front of her, Rita knew she'd been had. Darla's case of the giggles could not be blamed on an overindulgence of iced tea. Tina was just as bad. The way her neck was craning, Rita wondered how long it would be before Tina fell out of her chair.

"Okay, guys," Rita ground out. "What are you up to?"

"Moi?" Tina said innocently.

"Um, your steak smells wonderful." Darla's words were muffled, but then it was hard to talk, giggle, and cover your mouth with a hand all at the same time.

"Yeah," Tina said. "You'd think the chef made that especially for you."

Rita pushed the plate away. Well, she relented, maybe a bite of the Quick Dill Potatoes. . . The conversation turned to the national spelling bee winner, Mrs.

Womack's upcoming retirement, and the broken arm Amy Tucker suffered during yesterday's morning recess.

"One minute she was dangling from the monkey bars; the next minute her arm was dangling. I didn't even see it happen," Tina said.

"Not your fault." Darla shook her fork at Tina. "Mrs. Tucker came in tonight. They think Amy broke it Tuesday night at roller-skating. Really, yesterday just irritated it and got them to X-ray. Amy's mom says she's not surprised. Amy loves to skate and would do anything to stay at the rink longer."

"What a relief," Tina sighed. "Today I didn't let the kids play on the monkey bars. I was so afraid one of them might fall."

"Your food must have been good," Darla observed, focusing on Rita. "You've eaten every bite."

"It's a conspiracy," Rita accused. "You know I'm dieting, yet you bring me here. If David has his way, I'll be wearing tent dresses soon."

"And you'll look lovely in them," David said from behind her. He filled their iced tea glasses, his gaze never leaving Rita.

Rita fought the urge to scratch her cheek. Lately, every time this man came near, she got itchy.

He winked. "Just wait."

What he should have said, Rita thought, was *just weight*. The entire evening had focused on food. Her pants pinched. If someone rubbed her stomach, she'd purr and go to sleep.

A hush settled over the restaurant, and Rita glanced

around. All eyes were on their table. David was making his way through the tables carrying a tray of desserts. But it wasn't the Baked Coffee Custard that had caught the customers' interest. It was the dozen caramel-colored roses balanced in the center of the tastefully arranged display.

He served Rita last and if she hadn't slapped his hand, he would have fed her the first bite.

"What are we doing?" he had asked.

"Getting to know each other," she had encouraged.

"That's not a good idea," he had said.

So what on earth was he thinking now?

"Oh, look at the time!" Tina jumped up. "My babysitter has to be home by nine. I gotta run."

"I'll tell Susan we need the bill." Rita started to stand.

"I'll take care of everything." Darla snapped her purse shut. "Don't worry, Rita, I'll see you get back to your car."

Tina sailed out of the restaurant. Darla patted her lips with a napkin and mumbled something about the rest room. When Darla exited the restaurant instead, Rita knew she'd been had for the second time.

"You ready?" David gently pulled out her chair. His black leather jacket was already zipped.

"As I'll ever be." Rita took the hand he offered.

Twenty minutes later, after David had taken her to her car, followed her home, and walked her to the door, Rita wasn't sure what to think. She had been escorted home by a perfect gentleman. One who kissed the back of her hand as his good night.

Chapter 9

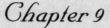

Although the school was housed inside the church, David had not seen the sanctuary half of the building before. His hands were moist with sweat as he pulled open the door. Services started at ten, and it was straight up ten now. A few latecomers hurried from the parking lot, shook the usher's hand, and took a folded piece of paper before disappearing through another set of doors.

"Welcome. Are you a visitor?" The usher was all smiles.

"I'm Clint Reeve's grandson."

"Oh, let me point out where he sits." The usher stuck a blue bulletin in David's hand and headed for the auditorium. David saw his grandpa first, sitting tall and singing loud. The group was toward the back, a whole row of them. Clint was at the end, with Timothy and Ellen close by. Rita came next, with Darla and her two kids in the middle. Susan, his one-time Sunday morning waitress, was last.

David took a breath. This wasn't so bad. He could sit by Susan, no pressure there. Except, when Susan saw him, she stood up so he could scoot by. Darla's two kids actually stood up on the pew, their mission obvious. He was to pass by them, also. Darla looked up, her mouth forming an O, and then she shifted closer to her kids.

Rita didn't notice him until he sat down. Then her purse tumbled from her lap and hit the carpeting. David picked it up. He watched as Rita scanned the pew, then shrugged as she held a songbook for him to share. He liked to sing, but he didn't read music, nor had he ever heard this song before. It sure wasn't from the seventies. By the time two more songs passed, he knew none of the songs were familiar.

The songbook trembled in her grasp. David wanted to put his hand on hers, to stop the shaking, but he figured right now any physical contact would send the songbook flying. Clint stopped singing; he had such a goofy grin on his face David almost laughed.

So this was church. David followed Rita's lead: He stood when she did; sat when she did; prayed when she did; listened when she did. He also watched her.

She did a lot of listening. Since she obviously didn't intend to carry on a whispered conversation, David started listening, too.

Forgiveness, that was the message. It didn't make much sense to David. There were some things you couldn't forgive, like mass murderers, crooked politicians. . .flash floods.

After the final prayer, David followed Rita into the aisle. Clint was involved in some sort of handshaking chain.

"Well, what did you think?" Rita asked.

"I'm not sure."

"Did you like the message?"

Like? How can I like something I don't believe? "It was okay."

"The preacher is wonderful, isn't he?"

David nodded.

Rita linked her arm in his. "Are you coming tonight?"

David opened his mouth to answer, but a sharp popping sound came from a few feet ahead. One moment, his grandpa's head was bobbing above the crowd; the next, Clint was on the floor. The cane had snapped in half. The eagle landed at Timothy's feet. The rest lay uselessly against Clint's trembling fingers.

❧

Everything in the hospital moved in slow motion. David stayed with Clint in the emergency room cubicle for hours. He knew Rita and everyone else were in the waiting room, hoping for news. He knew they wanted to join him, or at least for him to keep them posted, but he didn't feel like talking.

From the emergency room, Clint went to a hospital room. From the hospital room, Clint went through every kind of test imaginable. For two days the doctors whisked Clint through X-rays, blood work, MRI scans, and more. David stared out the window of his grandpa's hospital room and waited. Across the street, a family did the ordinary task of entering a convenience store and coming out a few minutes later carrying a bag of potato chips and a gallon of milk. Would that be Grandpa and him next week? Grandpa, with the gallon of milk balanced between his knees while he sat in a wheelchair.

"Where is he?" Rita stood in the doorway, her hair pulled back in a loose ponytail. She took a step closer to David but stopped when he didn't move to meet her.

"They're doing some more blood work."

"Does he have feeling in his leg yet?"

"No."

"How long has he been gone?"

"Two hours."

"That's a lot of blood work."

Silent, David stayed by the window.

"Do you need anything?" Rita sat in the brown, padded chair by the bed. She crossed her jean-clad legs and her foot waved in slow, nervous jerks.

"No."

"Who's taking care of the restaurant? I noticed you didn't schedule me for the weekend."

"Tom's doing it. We're okay for now. Brandy had her baby."

"David, I—"

"Don't. Now is not the time."

She left, swiftly, without tears, her ponytail streaming behind her like a fleeing colt's tail.

"David Reeves?" The doctor standing in the doorway consulted a chart.

"Yes."

David followed the man to a consultation room. There were X-ray photos clipped on a long, glowing panel, and the smell of antiseptic stung David's nose. The doctor sat behind a desk, took off his glasses, and rubbed the tight area at the apex of his nose. "Has your grandfather

Chapter 10

Grandpa was still somewhere off in the labyrinth of the hospital, having yet another test. David stared out the window, willing back the vision of his grandfather in a wheelchair balancing milk and potato chips with two feet.

"May I come in?" The voice was familiar. It belonged to the minister who had preached forgiveness.

"I read part of your book, you know." David didn't look away from the window, but the man took the words as an invitation.

"My book?"

David glanced at the man, taking in his black suit, shiny shoes, tie, and look of compassion. "The one you have in your hand."

The minister stroked the cover of the Bible fondly. "My book? In many ways it is. It was written for me. Of course, it was written for you, too. I don't think we actually met on Sunday. I'm Derrick Jerrod. How is Clint?"

"He's not enjoying much of that healing the New Testament talks about. Do you suppose we can arrange for some of that?"

"What kind of healing did you want?" the minister asked softly.

"They're going to amputate his foot. Do you suppose you can, ah, stop that?"

"Do you want to pray, son?"

"If I pray, will Grandpa keep his foot?"

"I don't know," Rev. Jerrod said honestly. "But God answers all prayers. Sometimes yes; sometimes with a no."

David made a face. "I've never prayed before. Do you think He'd say no the first time?" The words sounded harsh. David didn't believe them himself. If prayer was so wonderful, why didn't someone pray before his parents were killed in the freak flash flood? Before Grandma fell over with a heart attack for David to find when he came home from school?

"It's too late to pray." David decided. "Thank you for stopping by. I'll tell Clint you were here."

"I'd be glad to stick around, tell him myself, keep you company."

"No."

"Son, if only you'd—"

"No."

"I can—"

"No."

❧

David went to work early in the morning. He prepped for the day, scheduled his employees, answered their questions, and then returned to the hospital. He spent two more days watching Grandpa lie restlessly in the hospital bed. David avoided mentioning amputation. When

Grandpa tried to bring it up, David went to the window and stared at the convenience store across the street. When Grandpa pressed him, David left the room and went to the cafeteria.

One thing for sure, the hospital's cafeteria could use a little culinary assistance. David took a bite of mashed potatoes that gummed to his fork like paste. Shoving the plate away, David returned upstairs. Hopefully, Clint would be asleep.

He wasn't. A nurse had just finished taping a clumsily drawn mural on the wall.

"Rita's third graders," Clint informed him.

It looked like half the church had sent cards. Clint had a pile inches thick on his stomach. "Can you read this one to me?"

David took it, recognizing the thick, pressured pencil marks. The envelope was sealed haphazardly, as bent and wrinkled as Clint's fingers.

Dear Grandpa Reeves,

I glewed your cane back together. It didn't stick. Mom's going to by me some spechail glew. She says I can't come vizit becuz I'm to yung. I don't thenk that's fair. I love you no matter how old I am. She says they are going to saw one of your legs off. Who needs two feet? You can hop. A rooler only has one foot, rember? Please hurry home. It's lonely at church without you. Tell David. Want to here a joke? How do cows greet one onother? With a milkshake.

Timothy Carter.

"You remember he invited you to church?" Clint asked.

Sure, David remembered. The one time he attended had been the time Clint fell.

"You should have seen Timothy glow when you sat down next to his teacher."

David had been glowing himself, but this was not the time to talk about that.

"The minister came by while you were at lunch."

"Really, and did you pray?" David went to the window, opened the curtain, and perched on the sill.

"We did."

"For healing?"

"We did."

"Do you feel any better?"

"I do, but I should tell you. We didn't pray for me; we prayed for you."

A little girl came out of the store, sucking on a Popsicle or something. Before she could climb on her bike, she lost the Popsicle. It fell to the ground at her feet. She picked it up and stuck it back in her mouth, nothing lost. David stepped away from the window. "You prayed for me?"

"For healing."

"Grandpa, you're the one who needs healing."

"No." Clint shook his head and touched his heart. "The best healing is here. I don't care if they take my foot—"

"But, Grandpa, you—"

"I've lived a great life, and it's not over. Sure I'm a little scared, but something tells me the next few years will be more blessed than I can imagine."

"Now you'll be stuck in that home forever."

"Nope. I'm probably moving out come June or July."

"What? How?"

"I'm marrying Ellen."

David couldn't help it; cynical laughter bubbled over. It must be the drugs they had Clint on. David had read each and every label, and hallucinations hadn't been mentioned, but certainly that didn't mean they couldn't be used.

"Yup." Clint grinned. "She's taking classes to get certified in home health care. For a while, my hospital bed will be right in the living room."

"But—"

"And according to Rita, Timothy's in desperate need of a math tutor. So I need to get the operation over with quickly so I can help out."

"This is ridiculous, Grandpa. If I couldn't take care of you by myself, then—"

"Ellen won't be alone. There will be visiting nurses. She lives two blocks from Greater Home. I can continue my therapy. As far as I'm concerned, I'm healed. God answered my prayer. His answer was yes, only where He healed me, you can't see."

David almost choked, but he stopped. Clearing his throat, he stumbled from the room. "Okay, guess I'd better see about renting a tux or something," he said over his shoulder. "Gotta go."

In the hospital's stairwell David Reeves finally sank to his knees. What was going on? Clint should be screaming. He was about to lose a foot! A whole foot! And he didn't care. How could he not care? What did Clint know that David didn't? What was it? What did all the people who sent the cards, the students who drew the mural, Rita. . . What did they know?

David wept.

And then he went to find that minister.

※

On the next to the last day of school, Cameron Jones gathered all the history books and stacked them in a pile, then counted them. Lindsey Shoop carefully washed the chalkboard so the room would be spick-and-span. Tomorrow they were going to the park, and no one wanted to spend any of that time cleaning. Most of the students were in the process of transferring personal belongings from their cubbies into paper sacks. Timothy grumpily scrubbed the inside of his desk. His insistence that the hardened, spilled glue must be from last year only got him a raised eyebrow from his teacher.

Darla stuck her head in the door. "I thought I'd deliver the mail."

"Hello, Mrs. Yates!" All the children except for Lindsey —she liked cleaning chalkboards—stopped what they were doing.

Rita smiled and let Darla hand out the letters, but there was just one.

Timothy rocked back and forth on his tiptoes, anxious. Darla looked around, as if she couldn't see who she was looking for.

"I'm right here." Amy Tucker jumped on her chair

until Rita pursed her lips.

Darla tried to look confused. "Oh, there he is. Timothy."

"Ohhhh." A collective groan came from the class, but disappointment was put aside as the students edged closer to watch him open his mail.

He was not one who liked to be crowded, however. He held the fat envelope behind his back and walked back to his desk.

A few minutes later, Rita glanced over to see him scratching his head, studying a small box that was in his hand. "Mrs. Sanderson. David says I'm not s'pose to open this, but I want to."

"Is it for you?"

"No, it's to you. An' he wrote if I didn't open it, an' if I gave it to you right away, he would take me to a Diamondback game and buy me a hot dog."

"Well," Rita asked, "what are you going to do?"

"It's pretty small. Can't be much. You open it."

Turning the awkwardly-wrapped offering in her hand, Rita wondered if per chance it was her final paycheck. It would be just like David to fold it into a paper football. The students kept cleaning but watched to see what their teacher was doing.

Rita sat at her desk and slowly tore at the paper.

A diamond ring fell on her desk.

"Oh," said Timothy. "And now that you opened it, I'm s'pose to read this to the class." Like a soldier barking out orders, Timothy read, "There is ice cream and cookies in the school cafeteria. Mrs. Yates will take you."

Her hands trembled, and so did her heart. Rita picked up the ring and looked at the classroom door. Darla almost fell into the room, and Tina Lidell stood on her tiptoes trying to see in. Mrs. Womack was alternating between her stern principal look and her nurturing, mentor look. Actually, checking the hallway, Rita was pretty sure every teacher was out in the hall, along with most of the students.

"We have plenty of ice cream and cookies," Mrs. Womack said calmly. "Class, line up."

"Cool!" Cameron knocked over the history books in his hurry to leave the room first.

After the class relocated, and the teachers dispersed, David stepped forward. His hair was brushed back from his face, and his golf shirt—from their first date—was tucked into Dockers. He looked a bit shy and freshly scrubbed. "Do you have time to talk to a stubborn man?" he asked.

Rita twirled the ring in her fingers. It was so small, so perfect. And it contained such a big request.

David's head almost brushed the top of the door as he stepped in. The room seemed to grow brighter. "You asked me last Monday if I needed anything."

She set the ring on her desk, swallowing so hard it hurt. *So this is how love feels? He loves me.*

He stopped by her desk, looking down, and the expression in his eyes was as calm as she'd ever seen. "I said no, but that wasn't true. I need you. I need your God. I need whatever it is that you, these kids, and my grandpa have. You want to help me find that peace?"

"Okay," she whispered.

"What do you say, if after we take care of finding that peace part. . .because I happen to, ah, be in love with you. . .so why don't. . . ," he dropped to one knee, ". . .we get married."

She smiled down at him. *Wow,* she thought, *so this is what I was waiting for!* At last, with God's help, she had finally kept all her New Year's promises.

※

Dear Grandpa Reeves,

Did you know David came to my school? He made me give my teacher a ring. It wasn't from me. It was from him. Then he gave the whole school ice cream and cookies. I got a stomack ak, but everthing tasted good. I shooldn't tell you this, but I saw them kissing. Now they ar getting married. Just like you. Maybe I'm glad. Grandma says I have to be the ring bearer. Just like for you. I don't know why I have to do it twice, but that's OK. Do you want to here a joke? How does a skunk call home? With a smell-a-phone.

Timothy Carter.

PAMELA KAYE TRACY

Pamela is a popular writer and teacher in Scottsdale, Arizona, where she lives with a newly acquired husband and two cats. She was raised in Omaha, Nebraska, and started writing while earning a BA in Journalism at Texas Tech University in Lubbock, Texas.

Her first novel *It Only Takes a Spark* was published in 1999. Since then she's published seven more writings in both romantic comedy and Christian inspiration romance. *Promises and Prayers for Teachers*, an August release, is her first nonfiction book.

Pamela is an English professor at Paradise Valley Community College. Besides writing, teaching, and taking care of her family, she is often asked to speak at various writers' organizations in the Phoenix area. She belongs to Romance Writers of America, The Society of Southwestern Writers, and The Arizona Authors' Association. Her biggest dream of the moment is to change her status of newlywed to newlymom. In February, that dream should come true.